THE STALKER

An addictive psychological thriller full of twists

BECKI WILLIS

Originally published as *He Kills Me, He Kills Me Not*

Revised edition 2023
Joffe Books, London
www.joffebooks.com

First published in 2017 as *He Kills Me, He Kills Me Not*

This paperback edition was first published
in Great Britain in 2023

Cover art by Nick Castle

ISBN: 978-1-83526-192-7

Dedicated to my husband Roger.
Thank you for supporting my dream!

CHAPTER ONE

"These all-night stakeouts are going to be the death of me yet," Lange Sterling groaned, shoulder-opening the door to his downtown Richmond office and staggering inside. Muttering a reminder to himself about getting the door jamb fixed, he threw his crumpled jacket near the vicinity of the coat rack and started for the sofa.

A persistent red light flashed from his answering machine, determined to catch his attention before he crashed for an early morning nap. Lange knew it was old-school, but he still liked his landline and answering machine. He hit the playback button as he plunked himself down on the sofa, marveling at how soft the worn leather felt after a night spent in his pickup truck. At thirty-one, his body was beginning to protest the erratic lifestyle he had led over the past five years.

Hell, who was he kidding? He had been existing with psychotic sleeping patterns for half his life. As a half-wild teenager, sleep was something done primarily in class. After graduation and that fateful summer he turned nineteen, his life changed forever, but not his sleeping habits. Lack of sleep was all a part of his newfound career with the sheriff department. And now, as an ex-cop turned private investigator, the hours were even worse. There was no one to relieve him when his shift was over, no one to wake him when the bell rang. Everything was left up to him, and he had so few hours in a day to do it all.

Lost in self-pity, he almost missed the first message on the machine. It was Diane, reminding him of their dinner arrangements with one of her clients. Lange winced as he belatedly remembered to call off their date. The second message was from her, as well, as *she* realized he had forgotten to cancel their date. She told him what she thought of him in no uncertain terms, bringing a sigh of resignation from the prone body sprawled across the couch. She had some painful suggestions about what he could do with the cell phone he refused to answer while on a stakeout. Eyes drooping in fatigue, he listened to the next message, a pre-recorded message assuring him there was nothing wrong with his credit now, but by enrolling in their latest program . . .

Diane called a third time, apparently after returning from her dinner and having cooled off. She regretted her earlier outburst and wanted to make it up to him. Known for her mercurial mood swings, the auburn-haired attorney obviously had some bipolar issues. Lange snuggled down deeper into the cushions, thankful to have missed the brute force of her latest swing.

The final message was from the same woman who had called earlier in the week, the one with the soft, breathless voice. With his eyes shut, it was easy to conjure up an image in his mind — iconic screen legend Marilyn Monroe, perhaps, or his grandmother's all-time favorite, Doris Day — batting her big blue eyes and appealing to him, a lowly flesh-and-blood male, for help. How many times had he watched a scene like that from the big screen? He grew up watching those old classics. However, neither of his favorite stars from the silver era of films had ever spoken with a quiver of fear in her voice, as this woman did.

"Mr. Sterling, I-I need your help. I've called before but seem to keep missing you. I prefer to speak with you in person, so I'll come by your office in the morning, about a quarter till nine. I hope you'll be there; this matter is urgent. Thank you."

Lange moaned in protest and opened his eyes just wide enough to consult his wristwatch. She would be here in thirty minutes. He fished his cell phone from his pocket and set the alarm, hoping to see the tiny numbers correctly through his sleep-depraved eyes. Then he settled back to claim twenty glorious minutes of sleep before the mysterious woman arrived.

* * *

He was dreaming of daisies. Doris Day ran through a field of them, warning him not to eat the daisies. He could hear her soft, gentle voice; he could even feel the petals of a flower brushing against his face. They tickled.

He awoke with a start, realizing he wasn't alone. A woman stood over him, her face bent close as she peered hesitantly at his inert form. Her white-blonde hair fell forward, tickling his cheek, and he felt the warmth of a summer breeze flood his senses. It was something in her scent, something in her sky-blue eyes. Something in the brilliant smile that spread across her gorgeous face.

"Oh, good, you're awake," she said.

It was her, all right — Doris.

"Uh . . . yeah," Lange muttered. Was he awake, or was this a dream? His brain was still foggy. He reached out a hand and touched her. She pulled away from his touch with a small gasp, her big blue eyes widening.

Lange didn't know which hit him first — the realization he wasn't dreaming, or the feel of her skin. He couldn't dream up something that soft. Somewhere in his befuddled mind, he knew he should be fully alert and moving, but he was mesmerized. All he could do was lie there and stare.

"Are-are you sure you're all right?" the woman asked in genuine concern.

Snapping out of his trance, Lange swung up from the couch in one easy, fluid motion. As he pulled himself to his full six feet, three inches, the woman straightened with him, until she had to tilt her head backwards to peer into his face. Lange stared down at her, fascinated by her strawberry-red lips, still wondering if she was anything more than a figment of his imagination. Before he reached for her a second time, he controlled the impulse to touch her by running his hands through his hair.

"I came at a bad time," she said with sudden realization.

"No, no, you're fine," Lange insisted, smoothing his dark hair down. "All-night stakeout," he said by way of explanation, stretching away some of the fatigue. Remembering his manners and, most importantly, his career, he extended his hand and made a formal introduction. "Excuse my manners; Lange Sterling."

She placed her small hand into his and met his gaze as she smiled and said, "Ashli Wilson."

A thought vaguely registered on his mind, how he never knew until now that sunshine had a given name. Her hand was small and soft and smooth; his was big and rough and callused. Somehow, the feel of her crept up his arm, across the general area of his heart, and down to regions known only to man.

All this from a handshake? Hell, he was more exhausted than he thought.

"What can I do for you, Ms. Wilson?"

"I'm in need of your services."

"I gathered. Exactly what did you need?"

Ashli glanced around the room and spied the desk and chairs behind him. "Could we sit down, please, to discuss it?"

"Certainly." He waved toward the chair absently, his hand still warm from holding hers. When she simply stood beside the seat, waiting, he realized she expected him to get the chair. Masking his irritation, Lange pulled the chair out for her while murmuring an apology about his lack of manners.

Shoving papers aside to prop one lean hip on the edge of the desk, Lange returned to business. "What is it I can do for you, Ms. Wilson?"

"It's Miss," she corrected him in that whisper-soft voice. "And I need to hire you to protect me."

"Protect you?" He went on full alert. "Are you in some sort of danger?"

"I don't know. I hope not. I don't intend to be, if you'll help me."

Trying to digest her three answers to his one question, he came up with another. "Who do you want me to protect you from?"

"That's just it, I don't know."

For all her beauty, she seemed to be a bit shy on brains. Slowly, as if speaking to a dim-witted child, he asked, "Then why do you need my protection?"

She reached up to push an errant lock of hair from her forehead. "I think someone is watching me," she replied.

His eyes — and his mind — tangled in the blonde strands she pushed away. Damn right someone was watching her; every red-blooded male in Richmond, including himself.

Seeing her tiny frown, he wondered if he had voiced his thoughts aloud. "What makes you think that, Miss Wilson?"

"Well, it's more a feeling than anything else," she admitted.

"A feeling." *Oh, great, she is worse than I thought!* "You know that funny little feeling you get when someone is watching you? The hair stands up on the back of your neck, and you can just *feel* their gaze on you." She used her hands to illustrate her words. "Well, someone is definitely watching me."

Lange stared at her for a moment in silence. The woman wanted him to protect her because the hairs were standing up on the back of her neck. He interrupted his nap for this?

Trying to control his growing irritation, and overlooking the fact she answered simple questions in the most unusual way, he took a steadying breath before speaking again. "Miss Wilson, have you ever considered the fact most men like to look at beautiful young women? What you're describing is just a part of human nature."

"Mr. Sterling, I'm hardly a model. Men don't look at me like that." She sounded completely sincere as she discredited her own beauty. "But even if they did — which they don't — I'm not talking about normal oh-there's-a-pretty-girl kind of watching. Someone is stalking me."

"There's a big difference in someone watching you and someone stalking you, Miss Wilson."

"And I hate to use the word, because it sounds so sinister. But I don't know how else to describe it. There've been a dozen little odd instances. For one, someone went into my office, scattered the mail across my desk, and changed the stereo to an oldies station."

"A prank by a co-worker."

She continued as if he hadn't spoken. "Someone gifted me a lifetime membership to the ASPCA and a magazine subscription for dog lovers, even though I don't have a pet."

"Hardly a crime."

"Someone was watching me at the grocery store, even though I never saw them. When I went to check out, an employee brought over a bottle of wine. Someone purchased it and left it for me."

In spite of himself, interest flared in his eyes. "Maybe a little odd," he admitted. "An admirer, probably. Did you get a description?"

"The employee was an older woman, one of those retirees that works as a greeter. She described him as a 'delightful young man in a yellow shirt'."

"I don't suppose you remember seeing anyone in a yellow shirt?"

Blonde tendrils danced across the tops of her shoulders as she shook her head. "A few days later, someone followed me through the mall. At the beauty supply store, someone gifted me a bottle of my favorite shampoo. Because of my light hair color, some products give it an odd greenish tint, so I have to use a specific brand." She twirled a lock of purest blonde around her finger. No green now, just rays of sunshine.

"Could have been someone with a background in beauty products," he mused aloud. "Did the clerk give you a description?"

"The teenager at the register described him as an 'old dude in a yellow shirt'. I was a little rattled, so I stopped at one of the restaurants in the mall and treated myself to dinner. My tab was picked up anonymously."

"Let me guess, a man in a yellow shirt?"

"I don't know. It was a shift change, and the cashier who took the money was already off duty."

Lange processed the various bits of information. "Okay, so someone leaves you random gifts in public places and buys you dinner. Witnesses say the man is either young or old. It could be a difference in perspective, or it could be two different men, both who happen to own a yellow shirt." He released a heavy sigh. "I need more than that, Miss Wilson. Do you know what kind of car he drives? Has he directly contacted you in any way? Have you had any harassing phone calls, any emails, anything of that nature?"

"You sound as if you don't believe me." She frowned, on the defensive with all his questions.

"I didn't say that. I simply must know the facts if I'm to help you. You can't very well go to the police and ask them to arrest someone just because the hairs stand up on the back of your neck."

"I've already been to the police, thank you very much. They practically laughed in my face," Ashli Wilson said with an indignant sniff. Their casual handling of her complaints still smarted.

"Surely you told them more than you've told me, or I can understand why they would be laughing."

"I hardly find a Peeping Tom a laughing matter, Mr. Sterling. The police felt it was a waste of the taxpayers' money to help me. I came to you because I'm willing to pay for the help they denied me."

"Hold on, here. What Peeping Tom? Why didn't you mention that to begin with?"

"I told you, someone is watching me." Now it was her turn to speak as if to a dim-witted child.

"But you've never actually seen this person?"

"Not exactly. But I know he's there."

"Do you have a former husband or boyfriend who's harassing you?"

"No, I've never been married."

"Any old boyfriends that may be jealous over a current relationship?"

"No, none."

"No jealous ex-boyfriends or no current relationship?" he clarified.

"Neither."

Lange rose and walked around to the other side of the desk. He refused to acknowledge the little flash of relief he felt when she admitted she wasn't currently in a relationship. He had more important things to worry about. For instance, if she was as batty as she seemed, or if she truly had someone stalking her.

He realized she was waiting for him to speak again. "Tell me about the Peeping Tom incident," he finally said.

"It's happened several times. I'll get the strangest sensation that someone is watching me. Once, I saw a flash of white when I glanced up from my desk at work. Another time, I heard a noise on the balcony and found an overturned plant. I reported it to the police, but they dismissed it as a stray cat."

"Isn't it possible it was a cat?"

She met his gaze without hesitation and answered in that soft, breathless voice uniquely hers . . . and a screen legend's. "Yes, of course it's possible. But cats don't wear white shirts. I know someone is there, Mr. Sterling. Especially after last night."

"What happened last night?" He was almost afraid to ask. She came in complaining of being watched, then revealed someone stalking her. Almost as an afterthought, she mentioned the Peeping Tom. *What next?* he wondered.

"I received this note," she said, reaching into her purse and withdrawing a sheet of paper. "I went out to dinner with a friend, and when I got home, this was taped to my door."

Lange inspected the note thoughtfully, studying the careful lines of each letter. It almost appeared as if a child had written the note . . . Or an adult trying to disguise their writing as a child's . . . Or a demented mind not capable of anything but childish scribble. It was the last thought that sent a chill of foreboding racing down his spine as he read the words: *I'm watching you.*

"Who's handled this note?" he asked.

"Myself, of course. And my next-door neighbor. And maybe a friend of mine, I'm not sure."

He rolled his eyes skyward and sighed. "Did it ever occur to you that you were destroying whatever hope we had of lifting a set of fingerprints off here?"

"No."

He released another weary breath and pulled the note closer, trying to gain some clue from it. "Did you call the police?"

"No, I called you."

"Who was the friend you were with? Did he or she pick you up or drop you off? Is it possible they could have seen whoever left this, or did a neighbor, perhaps?"

"No, I've already asked everyone. I drove myself to and from dinner, where I met a friend named Mitch Greenway. I asked my neighbors, but no one knew anything about a note."

"This Mitch Greenway . . . you're not involved with him?"

"Just friends. We work together, actually."

Again, feeling that same rush of relief, he asked another question. "Ms. Wilson—"

"Miss," she interrupted. When she flashed him a smile, he remembered why he had been smitten in the first place. Her smile was like the sunshine, warming him all the way to his toes.

"Miss Wilson, can you think of anyone this person might be?"

"No one."

"Is there anyone who has been making unwanted passes at you, anyone who seems to be obsessed with you?"

To his surprise, she laughed. "Obsessed? I hardly think so, Mr. Sterling."

Lange swept his gaze over her. She was small, he had to admit. Barely five-foot-four, at best. Her bright yellow dress was a loose, flowing creation that somehow managed to hug her body in all the right places. She wore sensible flat-soled shoes and carried a purse big enough to double as a briefcase, making a fashion statement of duty, not beauty. A full head of white-blonde hair fell from a center part and billowed into soft curls just past her shoulders. There was nothing glamorous in her light dusting of makeup, but the effect was fresh and unique. To Lange, she looked like sunshine itself.

In a moment of pure honesty, the hardened ex-cop spoke to her softly. "You, Miss Ashli Wilson, are a beautiful woman. Yes, I can see where a man might be obsessed with you. I will ask you again, is there anyone you can think of that might be obsessed with you, or that might wish you harm?"

"Harm?" The thought seemed to startle her, more than his words embarrassed her. "Do you think I'm in danger, Mr. Sterling?"

"The question is, do *you* think you are in danger?"

"I-I don't know." She shuddered at the very thought. She raised her big, blue eyes up to his. "Mr. Sterling, the police won't help me, not until this person makes a move against me. By then, I'm afraid it might be too late. That's why I came to you. Will you help me? Will you protect me?"

Even though the case's validity was questionable at best, and even though he was already stretched thin on time and resources, there was no way he could possibly refuse a plea such as hers. Even though an inner voice warned him to think it over, Lange Sterling heard his own voice answering as he stood and extended his hand.

"Yes, Miss Wilson. I will take your case. I will protect you."

CHAPTER TWO

Less than eight hours later, Lange regretted his hasty decision. What was he thinking, taking on another case? He barely had time to eat and sleep, let alone devote the time and surveillance a case such as this required. And yet, here he was, rearranging his entire schedule to take on a questionable case, and he was breaking one of his cardinal rules to do it. He was going in completely unprepared.

Lange was a stickler about prepping for a case. Normally, he would go in with a case file already established. It was his policy to know as much as possible about each case he worked on. To that end, he always did a complete background check after taking on a new client. There would be notes, photos, sometimes even preliminary legwork, all tucked inside a file he carried to this initial meeting. He prided himself on being well informed and well prepared; surprises could be disastrous in his business.

But today, there was no time for prep work. After Ashli Wilson left his office, he spent the remainder of the morning handling paperwork and phone calls. He spent the afternoon with clients and realigning priorities. He wrapped up one investigation, delayed another, and lost the business of a third client not willing to share his attention. Without a decent meal or any additional sleep, he was now running on fumes.

And as if going in unprepared wasn't enough, he was also going in late.

Turning onto the street given as Ashli Wilson's address, Lange scanned the neighborhood to get a feel of the demographics. Typical for an old city such as Richmond, there was a mix of old and new in the neighborhood. On the right side of the street, a huge antebellum mansion, complete with six white columns, sprawled across half the block; its counterpart stood on the left, a newly constructed complex of upscale condominiums. The neighborhood was nice, just shy of affluent. The other residences were neatly kept but more modest — a handful of Craftsmen-style homes, a couple of ranches, a new construction of stone and cedar, and another with a more modern feel.

As he swung into the condo complex, he belatedly punched her name into the search engine on his phone, thinking any information was better than none. When it only brought up some television personality, he tossed the phone onto the seat in frustration. He compared the house number on the paper to the house numbers on the units, but the sequencing wasn't making any sense. Circling the building, he cursed himself again for going in unprepared.

"I'm on the wrong side of the street," he muttered aloud, realizing his mistake. She lived in the antebellum mansion. Which meant she either came from money or wasn't as ditzy as she seemed. "If I'd done my research, I'd know these things."

He continued to berate himself as he pulled his truck into the circular driveway gracing the front of the mansion.

Lange grabbed his phone and tucked a small notebook into his shirt pocket. As he walked up the steps of the mansion, he looked around in appreciation. The lawn was neatly trimmed, the flowerbeds were blooming with color, and the porch boasted a fresh coat of slate-blue paint. A set of yellow wicker furniture beckoned from one end of the long veranda, while a half-dozen rocking chairs, painted yellow with blue cushions, welcomed from the other. The house itself was three stories tall, painted white with slate-blue shutters and doors, and, despite its advanced age, was obviously well cared for.

The double doors were a work of art, with thick stained-glass panels that depicted a beautiful bouquet of daisies. Above the doors was a plaque proclaiming: *The Daisy House, circa 1853, Register of Historical Places.* A modern intercom system and electronic keypad were tastefully hidden behind an intricate metal panel beside the doors.

Finding her number on the panel, he pressed the intercom button. After a slight delay, he heard her breathless reply float out onto the porch. "Yes?"

"It's Lange Sterling. I'm here for our appointment."

"Is it that late already?" She sounded truly surprised. "I just got home."

As he rolled his eyes in exasperation, he hoped there was no video cam. Trying to keep the irritation out of his voice, he asked, "May I come in, Miss Wilson?"

"Oh, yes, yes, of course. I'll buzz you in. I'm at the top of the stairs and to the right. Apartment 5." A pleasant melody sounded, granting him access behind the heavy doors.

Stepping into the foyer was like stepping into another era; houses just weren't made like this anymore. A wide hallway divided the home in half and ran from the front stained-glass doors all the way to a set of identical ones in the back. There was marble beneath his feet, but the floor down the corridor was a gleaming hand-hewn wood, darkened with age. The walls were papered in dark-blue damask, with enough white trim molding, all elaborately carved, to keep the color from feeling heavy. The few pieces of furniture in the foyer were all antiques, from the massive hall-tree beside the door to the small settee and side chair tucked into a corner. But the real beauty of the room was the stairway, a curved creation that swept from the right of the foyer, up and over the hallway, to float into the second floor of the grand old home with style and grace.

Lange ran an appreciative hand over the banister, admiring the fine workmanship of a century past. The wood was warm beneath his touch, worn smooth from years of handling and polishing and perhaps, he imagined, a dozen children sliding down its curved path. If he ever took the plunge into home ownership, this was exactly the kind of house he would want.

He ascended the magnificent stairway, his steps practically silent on the heavy wool runner of muted gold, cream, and blue. The second floor opened into another wide corridor, this one flanked by paned windows in the front, double French doors at the back, and two apartments on either side. Lange turned right, toward the doorway marked with a scrolled wrought iron *5*.

Just as he rapped on the door, he heard a shriek from inside the apartment. He reached for his weapon. "Miss Wilson! Are you all right? Open up, it's Lange Sterling!"

The door swung open, and the woman inside launched herself at him. The force of her hurled body into his unsuspecting arms was enough to make him stagger backwards. He quickly regained his footing, his arms instinctively closing around her for security.

"What is it? What happened? Is there someone in your apartment?"

"N-no," she managed to say.

Easily lifting her feet off the ground, Lange stepped forward into the apartment, kicking the door shut after he carried her through the threshold. She was obviously terrified, so he slowly eased her away.

"Are you all right? You're not hurt, are you?"

"No, just-just frightened."

"Why? What happened? Did you hear from him?"

"I-I'm not sure." Untangling herself from his arms, she moved forward into the living room on unsteady legs. "Sorry. I know I over-reacted," she murmured. Her tone was still dazed as she elaborated, "I got a letter. An envelope. When I opened it, something cold and wet fell out."

"What was it?"

"I don't know. I was opening it just as you knocked, and between the sudden noise and the feel of something wet . . . I-I sort of panicked. I flung it across the room." She indicated the scattered mail strewn about on the floor. Bending down, she searched for the mysterious object. Soon, she was on all fours, looking in earnest.

Trying his best to be a gentleman and not stare at the delightful view she presented as she crawled around the floor in a dress, he diverted his attention by asking what she thought it might have been.

"Whatever it was, it was wet and wiggly."

With a little groan, Lange decided the only thing to do was to help her. Dropping down onto one knee, he ran his hand over the carpet. His fingers touched something beneath the chair, something wet, and his wayward thoughts snapped to attention. "I think I found it," he announced.

"What is it?" She scooted closer to him as he turned his palm upward and offered the object for inspection.

Having expected something much more sinister, she cried in relief, "A goldfish!" Then, as confusion set in, she repeated, "A goldfish?"

"A goldfish. A practically dead goldfish."

"What does it mean?" she asked in utter vulnerability.

He thought of several things a dead goldfish could mean: a stupid prank; an ill-chosen joke; a subtle warning from a sick and twisted mind. He reminded himself not to overreact as the last thought sent a chill of fear to his heart.

"I don't know what it means," he told her, getting to his feet. "But I need to dispose of it. Where's your bathroom?"

"Corner, beside the stairs."

As Lange went into the small powder room and disposed of the goldfish, Ashli continued to crawl around on the floor, collecting her scattered mail. She was unaware that her dress had inched its way up as she moved, until he came out of the bathroom and stopped with a sudden intake of breath.

He saw two flashes of pink, one in the form of silky nylon, the other in her cheeks. Ashli hurried to her feet, painfully aware that the man had just seen her underwear. Covering her embarrassment with a sudden flare of indignation, she whirled on him and demanded, "*Now* do you believe that someone is watching me?"

"I wouldn't be here now if I hadn't already believed you," he told her.

"Why on earth would someone send me a half-dead goldfish?"

"Maybe it was supposed to be a completely dead goldfish. Are you earlier than usual getting home?"

"No, a little later, actually."

"Is that the envelope it was in?" He nodded to the one she held in her hand. When she offered it to him, he inspected its blank front and empty contents, finding nothing whatsoever to even suggest a clue. "Was it on your door?"

"No, it was in my mailbox."

He shrugged his broad shoulders, dismissing the goldfish for the time being. He was more interested in the balcony, where the Peeping Tom had been. A wall of French doors opened onto the outdoor space, offering plenty of light and extended living space, and, perhaps, very little privacy. Typical for homes of its day, the veranda was long and wide, projecting out at least fifteen feet.

"The balcony runs the length of the house?" he asked.

"Yes."

"It's all connected, giving anyone access?"

"We each have our own space. Mine runs the length of my apartment and is accessible from these doors only. Same for the other back unit. The two front units each have a smaller space in the center, accessible from the French doors in the hall, which are electronically coded. Each space is divided with a lattice panel." She nodded, indicating the white lattice wall. Hers was covered in potted plants, strategically placed decorative tin panels, and clinging vines. Though not completely covered, the arrangement offered adequate privacy from her neighbors.

"Anyone with a sense of adventure could swing out around the panel, or shimmy up a rope from the ground floor," he surmised.

"Basically. Assuming they had access to the other balconies or to the grounds."

"Privacy fence?" he asked, jotting notes into his little notebook.

"No," she admitted.

"Where's your bedroom?"

"Upstairs."

Not bothering to ask for permission to see it, Lange started for the stairs. Ashli followed behind, reluctant to let a stranger see the core of her privacy without being there to somehow defend it.

Twisting and turning its way to the third floor of the grand old mansion, the staircase opened directly into her bedroom. The oversized room was spacious and light, but as she tried to look at it through someone else's eyes, it seemed such a lonely room. Only one body slept in the bed meant for two, only one nightstand stood by its side. The room's soft colors of pink and green were intended to make it appear cool and refreshing, but suddenly to Ashli, it just felt cold.

Lange walked past her bed, headed for the set of doors leading outside. This balcony was much smaller, by both length and width, and was exclusive to her apartment. With no center balcony, just its twin on the far end of the house, there was no need for a privacy panel up here. A wrought-iron chair and side table nestled into one corner of the balcony; a cushioned chaise lounge stretched out in the other. He noted the singular chair, meaning she probably didn't make a habit of bringing men to her bedroom.

"Do you keep these windows covered?" he asked.

"Only if I'm up here during the day. At night, I pull the curtains shut."

From where he stood, he surveyed the room, all visible from the balcony. Opposite the wall with the bed, a comfortable reading chair and cluttered side table created a cozy scene around the fireplace. One corner housed an entertainment center filled with a flat screen television and a collection of digital movies; the other held a bookshelf, overflowing with books and magazines and assorted trinkets. Ashli was glad he didn't survey the titles too closely; he would know her weakness for romance novels. She rather doubted Lange Sterling would appreciate a tender love story.

Lange glanced through the opened bathroom door, spying a lacy bra on the granite counter. "Keep those curtains drawn at all times," was all he said as he turned and left the room.

The stairway, just to the right of the front door, emptied into what was a sitting room in its former life. It now served as the entry/dining room and was occupied by a small antique oak dining set. Sectioned off by wide pocket doors, the sitting room flowed into the bedroom turned living room, which boasted an elaborate old fireplace at its far end. Built-in bookcases surrounded it, housing everything from a television and photographs to dried flowers and a stack of patchwork quilts. The floors were hardwood, covered by a large red and cream wool carpet in an intricate pattern. The room was uncrowded but somehow cozy, inhabited only by an antique sofa, wingback chair, an odd table with a lamp, and an old trunk that served as a coffee table. Against buttery yellow walls, all the woodwork was painted white, including the louvered wooden blinds over the French doors.

Lange roamed about freely, concluding his tour in the kitchen. Seeing the space, he let out a surprised whistle.

In more accusation than statement, he said, "There's not a kitchen like this in any apartment I've ever seen."

CHAPTER THREE

"It's a condo, actually," Ashli corrected him. "I was fortunate enough to have it all custom-done."

Although she loved her entire home, the kitchen was Ashli's pride and joy. What the room lacked in size was compensated by design. The long wall was filled with custom cabinets, double wall ovens, and a state-of-the-art cooktop. A corner pantry offered ample storage space, as did the commercial refrigerator. The four-foot granite island was bi-level, sporting a sink on one side, stools for eating on the other.

"Very nice," he murmured. For the umpteenth time, Lange regretted not having done his customary background check. Kitchens like this didn't come cheap. Nor did owning a chunk of the stately old mansion. He glanced around the kitchen again, appreciating the eye for detail in the glass-fronted cabinets and the white-painted millwork. When he noticed the yellow bakery boxes on the counter, he asked, "Are you expecting company?"

"What? Oh no, that's just left from lunch."

"You must have a huge appetite," he murmured, raising one dark brow skeptically as he looked from the boxes to her slim figure.

Ashli laughed, and the light, twinkling sound was so magical, Lange felt a crazy spinning in his head. "No, not *my* lunch," she amended. "It's from the Tea Party."

"You had a tea party today?"

The incredulous look on his face generated another laugh, but a niggling doubt wedged its way into her mind. Lange Sterling came highly recommended as a private detective. Why did he seem so surprised by key elements of her life? Despite his reputation, she was beginning to think the man might be more beauty than brains.

Okay, so beauty might not be the word. Gorgeous was more like it. Handsome. *Hot.* The man was tall and lean, with ridiculously long legs stretching out a denim-clad mile. His body toned and fit, his muscles were well defined. He could use a haircut and shave, but the shaggy edges lent him the fashionable air of a rogue. More hazel than brown, his eyes were brooding and mysterious. He would make the perfect PI on television, she decided.

Pulling herself from the depths of his soulful eyes, Ashli forced herself to focus. What was the question? Oh yes, now she remembered.

"No," she told him, "that's the name of my restaurant, Ashli's Tea Party."

"You have your own restaurant?" The woman was full of surprises.

Lange hated surprises.

"It's more of a coffee shop. Choice of the day, since I do all the cooking."

"*You* do all the cooking?" he asked in amazement.

"Can't trust my secret family recipes to just anyone." Her eyes twinkled as she opened a box to reveal an array of scrumptious desserts.

Dazzled by her smile and twinkling blue eyes, Lange murmured distractedly, "Surely you weren't planning on eating all this yourself."

"Of course not. I take it around to my neighbors and share with them. I hate waste, don't you?"

He mumbled a reply, thinking what a waste it was for her to have such a kissable mouth and him not using it justly so. Dragging his eyes away from her lips, he forced himself to study the food as she opened more containers. "What's that?" he asked.

"Chicken Puffs. Have one."

"No, thanks."

"Have you already eaten?"

"No," he admitted.

"Then sit down over there and let me fix you something."

"No." His protest became weaker as he thought of her serving him a meal she cooked herself.

Southern hospitality demanded she feed him. Hostess mode kicking in, Ashli automatically reached into a cupboard for plates. "I insist. And I won't take no for an answer."

Watching her graceful movements in the kitchen, he was struck with the memory of his grandmother, and the way she, too, had loved to cook for company. Feeling an unexpected flutter in the region of his heart, he tried once again to protest.

"Really, I didn't come here to eat. I came to discuss the case."

"No reason you can't do both." She paused in her task of searching an overhead cabinet as something occurred to her. "Oh, I'm sorry, I didn't think. Is your wife expecting you for supper?"

She looked so contrite, so sincere, so damned innocent, standing there with her shapely body stretched out to reach a top shelf, and her beautiful face flushed from the effort. Most of all, she looked so at home in the kitchen; exactly like Grams, so unlike Lauren. Unlike Diane, for that matter. Feeling as if he might choke on the words, he managed to squeeze them out. "I'm not married."

A brilliant smile appeared on her face. "Then there's no reason for you not to eat, is there?"

For the life of him, Lange couldn't think of a single one. Not even the thought of a furious redhead was reason enough to pass up the opportunity before him.

"Here, let me," he offered, stepping closer so he could retrieve the platter she reached for. In the process, he brushed against her, and he could have sworn he saw sparks fly.

Sidestepping the sizzle, Ashli moved quickly away. "Dinner will be ready in a jiffy, if you want to clean up."

"Sure. And I need to make a phone call, if you don't mind." Hopefully, there was enough distance between the kitchen and the powder room so she wouldn't hear the story he fabricated for Diane's benefit.

When he returned from making the call — his ears still smarting from the heated words Diane flung at him — Ashli breezed back and forth in the kitchen, humming some tune. She was like a butterfly in her sunny yellow dress, lighting here to pick something up, touching down there to leave her special mark, gliding gracefully to the next task. She had a veritable feast laid out on the bar, and there was even a centerpiece. A small cluster of white daisies graced a slim glass vase he suspected had once been a jar.

"What would you like to drink?" she asked, looking up and seeing him there.

"Beer?"

"Sorry, the closest I can do is wine."

"That's fine."

She began to hum again, a tune that sounded vaguely familiar to him. Unable to recall the words, he gave up trying as he simply enjoyed watching her move about the kitchen. Watching her was like watching an old memory, grown warm and fuzzy with age. Watching her felt so good, it almost hurt.

"I hope you don't mind sitting at the bar," she said, setting a bottle of wine between the plates. She carried the glasses as she came around the bar. "Shall we eat?"

Lange took the stool she indicated, belatedly realizing why she simply stood beside her own. Damn, he'd done it again. He started up, but she shooed him away.

"No, no, don't bother," she sighed. She pulled the stool out with her foot, then boosted herself onto it.

"Please keep in mind that I specialize in lunch," Ashli warned, passing him the first platter. It was piled with flaky chicken puffs, individual bacon and jalapeno soufflés, and chunky ham salad. The second platter was filled with assorted rolls and breads, the third with carrot sticks, radish roses, and wedges of lettuce drizzled with poppy seed dressing. A fourth tray stood waiting, filled with desserts.

"Lord, woman, you must have thought I was starving!" he said, yet he filled his plate with generous portions of almost everything she offered.

"You're working, right? You need nourishment." She smiled.

"Come to think of it, I didn't eat any lunch."

"Then by all means, fill up. Have anything you want. Except the daisies," she added with a twinkle in her eyes. "Please don't eat the daisies."

He merely stared at her, wondering if she had any idea how much she sounded like his grandmother's favorite movie star. His, too, if he were honest.

"What?" she asked, laughing at his dumbfounded expression. "I'm only joking!"

"That-that was the song you were humming earlier. The song 'Please, Don't Eat the Daisies', from the old Doris Day movie with the same name."

"It's a catchy little tune that kind of sticks with me," she confessed with a shrug. "I think of it almost every time I see a daisy. Which, living here in Daisy House, is often."

"Has anyone ever told you that you sound like Doris Day?"

She laughed again, as much in delight as in amusement. "A few people, including my landlord. And especially my dad. My parents have all the old Doris Day movies, so I grew up watching them. I take it as a compliment, by the way."

"Absolutely."

"Here, have another chicken puff."

"They are good. What's in them?" he asked, helping himself to two more.

"A chicken, watercress, and wild rice mixture, stuffed inside a croissant."

"Delicious," he said with wholehearted approval.

A foolishly delighted smile came to her face. People had complimented her food before; why did his praise make her feel so pleased? Hoping to hide her ridiculous reaction, she reached for the wine bottle and opener, but he took them from her, saying, "Let me."

As he worked on easing out the cork, he realized this wasn't the first time he had seen the trademark yellow boxes gracing her counter. "Where did you say your restaurant was?"

"In one of those wonderful old pre-Civil War buildings down on tenth. We're right in the heart of the city, near the statehouse and Court's End and the Medical College. It's one of those tall, narrow buildings, originally built as a bachelor's residence. It's just the perfect size for a coffee shop on the first floor, a dining room on the second, and space for private parties on the third."

"I've never been inside, but I've eaten your food," he said, pouring the wine. "Several clients have brought me lunch from there, and for Christmas, I got some sort of wicked brownie with cashews. And I've had the tomato basil soup several times." Diane often brought it to him, as it was one of his favorites.

They ate in silence for a few minutes, until she said, "Tell me, what's it like being a private investigator?"

"It's like being paid for being nosey."

"Hmm, I guess I never thought of it that way. What made you become one? Just naturally nosey?"

Her teasing smile made it easier to answer the question, the very question he so often avoided. Still, his voice was flat, merely offering the basic information. "I was a detective with the Prince George County Sheriff Department. Becoming a private eye seemed a natural extension of that job."

"I imagine it must be dangerous at times," she said.

He merely shrugged his broad shoulders and said, "At times."

"You work alone?"

"For the most part. Occasionally, I find someone to help on paperwork, maybe a little research."

"Why did you open your business in Richmond?"

"What, are you applying for a job with me?" he asked, growing irritated with all her questions.

"Are you saying I'm being nosey?" she asked, a smile twitching at her lips as she sipped her wine.

It was impossible to stay angry with her. In spite of the scowl he tried to maintain, a smile broke on his lips. "Yeah, maybe I am," he admitted, but he no longer looked mad. He looked so rakishly handsome, Ashli's breath caught in her throat.

"Have another roll," she said, shoving the platter at him.

"I don't think I could eat another bite," he protested, pushing away the plate he had filled at least three times.

"But we haven't had dessert yet. I was going to make coffee." She was off the stool, already clearing away the dishes. Picking up her own empty plate, she realized she had eaten a full meal for the first time in days.

As she busied herself in the kitchen once again, Lange stretched his long body and moaned in exaggeration at the amount he had eaten. Taking his wine glass with him, he wandered into the living room, where he inspected the photographs along her built-in shelves.

"Careful, you might disturb my dust," she called in warning. "Cooking, I love. Housework, not so much."

"I notice this one guy is in a lot of your pictures, the one you went to prom with. Old flame?"

"High school sweetheart," she confirmed from the kitchen.

"Still see him?"

"No, he went away to college and met a girl from Alabama. They moved there after they married, and now have a second child on the way."

Was that a touch of heartache he heard in her voice? Was that regret he listened with? Why did he even care? Her love life was of no interest to him. These questions were strictly on a professional level, he assured himself.

"And this other guy, the one with blond hair?"

"That's Mitch. Mitch Greenway, the one I was out with last night." She came into the living room, carrying a tray of coffee and dessert.

"I thought you said he wasn't your boyfriend." God, why did his voice come out sounding so accusing?

"He's not, he's just a friend. And like I told you, we work together." Suddenly understanding the line of questioning, she looked appropriately shocked. "Wait a minute, if you think any of my friends are behind this, you're dead wrong."

"Well, someone is stalking you, and my guess is that it's someone you know. Most cases like this turn out to be spurned lovers or ex-boyfriends."

"I can assure you, that's not the case this time."

"How can you be so certain?" he challenged her.

"Not that it's a very long list, but none of them would do something like this. Besides, what's the point?"

He shrugged as he came around and joined her on the sofa. Taking the coffee mug she offered, he explained his reasoning as he set aside the wine glass. "Sometimes it's jealousy. They see you with a new lover and can't handle it, so they attempt to make your life miserable. Sometimes it's their way of getting you back. The new lover walks out, the old one walks back in. Sometimes it's just pure vindictiveness, pure malice. Sometimes . . ."

"Yes?" she prodded, when he hesitated.

"Sometimes it's something deeper, something more sinister. Sometimes they try to harm you, thinking if they can't have you, nobody can."

"Well, like I said, none of those apply in this case."

"You can't be certain of that."

"Yes, I can. I'm not seeing anyone right now, so it can't be jealousy. There's no one trying to win me back. And before you even ask, no, I've never dumped anyone, so don't bother suggesting it's a get-even thing."

"You can't sit there and tell me you've never broken anyone's heart before!" He took a bite of her chocolate cake, thinking her cooking alone could break a heart.

"Not even a little crack," she assured him.

"I find that hard to believe." He cocked a skeptic eyebrow. Taking a generous sample of strawberry shortcake, he talked with his mouth full. "I'll need a list. Every man you've ever been romantically involved with, going back to pretty boy there in the tux."

"It's going to be a short list."

"Don't forget to list casual relationships. Sometimes the briefer the romance, the more likely the suspect. Unrequited love, and all that. Even undeclared love. It may be someone you only dated once or twice."

"Like I said, it's going to be a very short list. Embarrassingly short."

"I guess you're the type that believes in true love." His tone was condescending.

"To be honest, I haven't had a boyfriend in over two years!" The admission came with an embarrassed flush.

"Funny, I didn't take you for the type who put her career before true love," he murmured. Even he could hear the disappointment in his voice. After being involved with two independent women, he thought he could spot the type. For some reason, the desserts didn't taste as appetizing as they had.

"My dates and I seem to have a difference of opinion on how to end an enjoyable evening. I don't take relationships lightly."

"In other words, you don't indulge in casual sex."

"Do you always ask such personal questions, Mr. Sterling?" she asked, even as her face warmed.

"Please, please. We're discussing sex. Call me Lange," he drawled in a dry tone.

"Okay, Lange, do you always ask such personal questions?"

He set aside his dessert plate, suddenly all business. "In cases like this, you bet I do. You can't hold anything back from me. You can't rule someone out because 'they don't seem the type' or because they have nice eyes or the hair on your neck doesn't stand up when they're around. Someone is stalking you, someone just sent you a dead goldfish, and I'd bet you this condo it's someone you know."

"Fine, I'll get you a detailed list." Her tone was cool and brisk, only a few degrees less severe than his.

"Tell me about the other tenants here."

"Verbally, or on the list?" she clarified.

"Both."

"There are six apartments in all. The two downstairs are ground-floor units. Mr. Parnell, our landlord, has the unit on the right, under mine. Although I guess landlord isn't the right term, since we all own part of the house." She digressed with a slight frown. "Building super is more the word, since he takes care of most of the maintenance and such. Dear, sweet man. Getting quite forgetful, though. The house has been in his wife's family since the original Dr. Daisy had it built in the mid-1800s for his new bride. Mrs. Parnell passed away a few years ago, and the house was too much for just one, so he came up with the idea of condos.

"Anyway, the couple on the other side, Mr. and Mrs. Harris, have been here from the first. They're probably in their seventies, active, have children and grandchildren that come to visit quite a bit. Sweetest people you ever met in your life."

"Upstairs?"

"Front right, Unit 3, is Jason Madison. He's a professor at the university. Rather quiet, seldom participates in any group activity we have. Front left is Jasmine; I never can pronounce her last name correctly. She's a gorgeous Asian lady, late thirties I'd say, but it's hard to know with skin as smooth as hers. She's a buyer for one of the major department stores, so she travels a great deal. I think she's in Milan right now. Or maybe it's Morocco."

When she puckered her brow in thought, Lange sensed they might get off-track again. Steering her back on subject, he asked, "The professor. How old is he? Has he ever shown any interest in you romantically?"

Ashli squirmed uncomfortably in her seat. "He's probably late thirties, early forties. He has asked me out a few times, but I never accept. Well, once I did have dinner with him."

"Either you went, or you didn't," he pointed out.

"I went," she conceded. "There was no graceful way to avoid it. But I didn't have a good time, and I didn't consider it a date."

"Did he kiss you good night?" he asked.

"He tried."

"Then it was a date. Be sure you include as much information as possible on your list. What he teaches, what he drives, that sort of thing." He reached for his wine glass but found it empty. Ashli was up instantly, fetching the bottle from the table to pour them another glass. "That still leaves the apartment across the hall. Tell me about that tenant."

"Todd and Katelyn Evans. Cover-story power couple, probably mid-to-late forties, both career oriented. She travels quite a bit and is seldom home. Todd travels some, too, but not nearly as much. He's in real estate; the legal side, I think."

"Happily married, would you say?"

"I suppose. I've never given it any thought." She shrugged, taking a sip of wine. Growing thoughtful, she tucked her legs beneath her. "But I will say it has to be hard, both working demanding schedules like that, and with her always gone. You would need a strong marriage to withstand that, don't you think?"

"I'm hardly an expert on marriage." The words sounded strangled, squeaking past his heart.

"Have you ever been married, Mr. Sterling?" she asked.

Thoughts of Lauren, along with the wine, made him feel lightheaded. He rudely ignored her question, asking one of his own as he struggled to keep the conversation professional. "Has Mr. Evans ever shown any romantic interest in you?"

"No, of course not."

"You said something about group activities?"

"Sometimes we have get-togethers. In the summer, we might barbecue, or watch outdoor movies, or have potluck down on the back veranda. A couple of times a year, I make a big cake, and we have a communal birthday party. It's especially nice for Mr. Parnell and the Harrises."

"The birthday parties were your idea?" he guessed.

Hearing the skepticism in his voice, she couldn't help but go on the defensive. "I suppose. The first one was a surprise for Mr. Parnell. Everyone seemed to enjoy it so much, we decided to make it a tradition."

"Who has ownership to the balcony joining your space?" He was jumping topics so fast her head spun.

"Jason Madison."

Lange eyed her for a long moment, until she grew uncomfortable and squirmed. "What, Mr. Sterling?"

"I thought it was Lange," he murmured. "And I was just thinking of how your tone changes when you talk about Mr. Madison. You had nothing but glowing things to say about everyone else in the house, but very little to say about him. Why is that?"

In her best imitation of a Southern belle, Ashli batted her lashes. "As I was always told growing up, '*Sugah*, if you can't say something nice about somebody, just don't say nothin' at all.'"

Her honeyed drawl melted over him like warm molasses. His breath stalled in his chest as he recalled that flash of pink silk . . . He struggled to keep his face stoic, camouflaging the ridiculous and immediate response of his traitorous body. He had to think of her in a professional manner only.

"You dislike Mr. Madison?" he managed to ask in a reasonably flat voice.

"'Dislike' is a rather strong word," she hedged. "But no, he's not my favorite person."

Lange practically growled. This time, his frustration was aimed at her. She refused to believe anyone she knew could be evil. She refused to say anything unkind about anyone. She refused to believe in her own beauty, or that any man could be obsessed with her. The woman was a freaking saint. A delusional one, at that.

"Get me the list, Miss Wilson," he ground out.

"I thought it was Ashli," she replied with excessive sweetness. "How soon do you want it?"

"This morning would have been nice."

A background check would have been nice, too, he reminded himself. Maybe if he had done his homework, he wouldn't be sitting here now, wondering what he had gotten himself into. Aloud, he added, "I'll need names, addresses and phone numbers if you have them, and brief descriptions of your relationship with each of them."

"Between my cell phone and my address book, I can get all of that for you right now, if you'd like."

"I'd like."

As she left the room, her back stiff with resolve to be just as tough as he was, Lange leaned back against the tapestry sofa and sighed. He was so dog tired. He wanted nothing more than to go to bed and sleep for two days, or six hours, whichever came first. Maybe while she was upstairs, he could catch a few winks . . .

CHAPTER FOUR

"I've got that list for . . ." Ashli stopped in mid-sentence as she came down the stairs and found the man sound asleep on her sofa.

He was sprawled over the antique frame, one leg resting on the floor, the other dangling from an arm rest. His hand was flung across his face, shielding his eyes from the overhead light, leaving only his sensual mouth exposed. Relaxed in sleep, his jaw seemed less severe, his tight mouth more generous. As Ashli ventured closer, she saw his chest rise and fall in the steady rhythm of sleep, and something within her softened. He looked so vulnerable as he slept, so peaceful, nothing like the hard, cynical ex-cop she had seen before. It would be a shame to wake him.

She tiptoed over to the built-in bookcases and pulled a quilt from her collection. Carrying it back to the couch, she very carefully eased it down, covering the scuffed cowboy boot dangling from the arm rest. She pulled the quilt up slowly, covering his incredibly long legs and the lean, flat belly where his other hand rested. Light as a feather, she eased the cover up onto his chest, noting the width of his shoulders and the muscles visible beneath the clinging knit of his shirt. Drawing the cover up to his chin and carefully releasing it, she gazed at his handsome face for a moment, wondering if his mustache tickled when he kissed. Her eyes studied his lips, full and smooth and parted in relaxed slumber. What would those lips feel like on hers? Would he be as masterful with kisses as he looked?

Shocked at her own thoughts, Ashli jumped back, stepping against the coffee table in her haste to move away before she did something stupid, like kiss him. When he started slightly and mumbled an incoherent protest, she held her breath in dread that he might wake up.

What would she say to him if he did awaken? That he looked so lost and vulnerable, like a small boy alone in the world, that she couldn't bear to wake him?

That he was so handsome he stole her breath away, that just watching him sleep was a treat within itself?

That she was afraid she would embarrass him if she woke him twice in one day, especially since this time, it was her couch he was sleeping on?

Or what if she just admitted that he made her feel safe? Despite her brave words of not believing she knew her stalker, she was petrified at the mere prospect. Could she be so close to someone so sinister and not even know it? That thought was almost as frightening as the thought of being stalked.

Tiptoeing away, Ashli turned off the lights and secured the door. She paused when she got to the top of the stairs. There wasn't even a door she could lock between them. Was she taking too big of a risk?

After the slightest hesitation, she went to bed and slept the best she had in weeks.

* * *

Lange awoke to the first hint of morning light filtering through the wooden shutters. This wasn't his bed. It wasn't Diane's, or else she would be sleeping here beside him. And it wasn't the cold leather couch in his office.

As he lifted his head and looked around his shadowy surroundings in confusion, his nose brushed against the cover. There in the pieced patches of fabric he could smell the trapped scent of sunshine freshness and suddenly, he knew exactly where he was, for it held her scent.

Ashli's.

Lange fell back onto the couch and stared up at the high ceiling, wondering if yesterday had been a dream, or if the woman with the white-blonde hair was for real. Could anyone be so beautiful and domestic and so ridiculously sexy, all at the same time?

As the new day hovered in the shadows of early dawn, a strange feeling passed through the darkness of his heart. Certain that he was alone in the shadows with his thoughts, Lange allowed himself to steal a few moments of pleasure simply by thinking of her.

There was no denying how beautiful she was. Beautiful and zany and apparently quite intelligent, despite his first impression of her. He had never known a woman quite like her, a successful businesswoman who was independent yet somehow still so . . . domestic. She was the epitome of a true Southern lady, with her gracious ways and her warm hospitality. She made him think of home and evenings by the fire. She made him think of his grandmother. She almost made him forget about Lauren.

Lange threw the quilt aside as he swung his feet to the floor. And then it dawned on him . . . she had covered him with a quilt!

His forehead creased in a scowl. She was babying him, treating him like some lost little boy who had wandered in out of the rain and fallen asleep on her sofa. She had fed him and pampered him and then covered him in a quilt, one she had probably made herself. It was the same thing his grandmother would have done, and somehow, her thoughtfulness made him angry.

Made him angry because somewhere, deep beneath the hardened shell of his heart and his gruff exterior, the thoughtful deed touched some starving part of him, the part that still needed a home to return to and the loving arms of a woman to hold him. It had nothing to do with sex; it had everything to do with need.

Though he had sworn to never care again, he could already feel the stirring around his heart, a feeling that both hurt and felt good, all at the same time. He couldn't remember the last time he looked at a woman and felt that swell of emotion.

Angry to have confronted such confusing emotions he thought long buried, Lange jumped to his feet and started for the door. He had to get out of here, and fast. He had known the lady for less than twenty-four hours, and already she had stirred up feelings dormant for over five years.

No one had to tell him that getting involved with Ashli Wilson was nothing but trouble.

CHAPTER FIVE

Lange bypassed his apartment, intent on reaching the office. The sooner he could start this case, the sooner he could find the culprit and wash his hands of one Miss Ashli Wilson.

Early morning traffic was just getting started as he drove downtown. His mind was already whirling with details he needed to check, and leads he needed to follow through on. Squinting from the glare of the morning sun on his windshield, he searched the dashboard for sunglasses but came up empty-handed. Trying to avoid the reflection bouncing off the shiny side of the metro bus beside him, Lange sped up, only to have the light turn red and force him to a halt.

As he waited for the light to change back to green, he drummed his fingers on the steering wheel and glanced at the bus beside him, trying to think of anything but a certain blonde-haired beauty who kept invading his thoughts. Good Lord, he had to get a grip. He could conjure her image up, simply by thinking of her. He could swear that was her face beside him.

But sure enough, there it was. Ashli Wilson's face was plastered across the bus, larger than life but every bit as beautiful. She was flashing that megawatt smile of hers, holding a whisk in her hand and wearing a bright yellow apron.

Dumbfounded, he just stared at the image, even as it rolled away. An irate driver blasted his horn behind him, startling him out of his stupor.

"Oh, *hell*, no!" he muttered. With a jerk of the wheel and another angry horn blast, Lange whipped his pickup truck around in the middle of traffic and headed back toward Daisy House. Ashli Wilson had some explaining to do.

He made it back to the house in record time. Jabbing an angry finger at her buzzer, he repeated the action until she answered groggily, "Yes? Who's there?"

"Lange Sterling. Open the damn door, Ashli!" he ground out.

He took the steps two at a time, not pausing to admire the grand structure this time. As he pounded on her door, a blond man in a three-piece suit came from the front apartment, a scowl on his face. He looked as if he was about to speak, when Ashli opened the door.

"Did you forget something?" she asked, her voice still husky with sleep. Her hair was tousled, and she clutched a terrycloth robe together over her pajamas.

If he thought she was beautiful before, it was nothing compared to how she looked now, fresh from bed. God, he wished it was his bed she was crawling out of. The thought staggered him, almost as much as the raw surge of desire that flared through him.

Ashli glanced over his shoulder, to the man in the hallway. It was minuscule, but Lange saw the change that came over her face, and the way her body stiffened. The man, obviously Jason Madison, responded with a smirk and a weighted glance between the two of them.

Ignoring him, Ashli took hold of Lange's shirt and literally pulled him into the apartment. She made a distasteful sound as she firmly shut the door on her now-frowning neighbor.

"Did you forget something?" she asked again, heading toward the kitchen.

"No, but obviously you did!" His anger returning, Lange refused to be swayed by the sight of her, barefooted in the kitchen. "Why the hell did I see your face splashed across a metro bus? This changes everything! Did you think that wasn't an important little detail to share with me?"

"I can't think without my coffee," she muttered, selecting a pod for her single-cup brewer and punching the button to ensure a strong cup of coffee. "What are you even talking about?"

"I'm talking about your face, plastered all over the side of a bus, for Christ's sake! Why didn't you tell me you advertised on the side of a freaking bus?"

"I know, I know, it's atrocious, isn't it?" she groaned. "Do you have any idea how I feel, seeing my face all over the place, like a hundred times bigger than what I see in the mirror? And the way they had me wear my hair. It's all Mitch's fault, you know," she grumbled, wrapping both hands around her mug and blowing on the steaming liquid. "It was his idea to begin with. His and his photographer girlfriend's."

The first question out of his mouth wasn't the one he should have asked, but it slipped out before he could stop it. "Greenway has a girlfriend?"

Ashli rolled her eyes. She took a fortifying sip of coffee before answering. "How many times do I have to tell you, we're just friends. Yes, he has a girlfriend. No, we're not involved. We're colleagues. He's my producer, actually."

"Producer? Why the hell do you need a producer?"

"For my television show?" She made it a question, sounding as if he should already know this.

"Your *WHAT*?"

Ashli sighed, putting a hand to her forehead. It was barely daylight outside, and already she had a splitting headache, thanks in large part to the man standing in her kitchen, yelling at her. She motioned to the coffee maker on the counter and said, "Help yourself to coffee. Hang on, let me get a little into my bloodstream."

He waited impatiently while she gulped down several sips of what had to be scalding coffee. He scowled as he made himself a cup, back to berating himself for not having done a background check to begin with. No wonder the only search he had time to conduct kept throwing out a television celebrity.

"Start talking," he said, whirling back toward her with renewed ire. Damn, he hated surprises.

"Mitch produces the cooking show I host on the local cable channel, *Ashli's Kitchen*."

"Damn it, Ashli, you have a television show, and you're just now telling me? How the hell did that not come up before?" he thundered.

"You never asked. All you asked about was my love life, sad little story that it is." She reached past him to hand over his cup and brew her second one.

Lange took a deep, steadying breath. As much as he would like to blame her, he knew he had no one to blame but himself. He should have done a background check. He should have been more concerned with following his own strict protocol, and less concerned with screen legend voices. He had never let personal feelings get in the way of his professionalism before, so what was different this time? What in the hell was the matter with him?

Even without the background check, he should have been asking more pertinent questions, ones important to the case.

"Miss Wilson," he said, trying to keep his voice calm. It came out stern and irritated. "Ashli. Miss Wilson." He needed to steer them back onto strictly professional terms, which was difficult to do, given she was standing there in her nightclothes, looking utterly adorable. There was nothing sexy about the flannel pajama pants and terrycloth robe she wore, but there was something incredibly hot about her uncombed hair and her bare toes. "Miss Wilson," he repeated, keeping his voice sharp, "I need to know about this television show. How many viewers does it reach, how often does it air, where is the market exactly?"

"Local markets, every Thursday at four, not all that many viewers." She answered the questions in reverse order as she reached for her coffee. "This is only our second season, so it's not like we have a huge following strung out over the country. I'm hardly Rachael Ray."

"But you do realize this changes everything. We just went from a relatively small pool of suspects to an entire ocean!"

"Hardly an ocean. More like a lake. A small one, at that. Honestly, it's not that big a deal."

He saw the hesitation that crossed her face, just before she hid it behind her coffee mug. "What?" he demanded.

"Actually, we've had an offer. We're going into syndication. That's what Mitch and I have been meeting over so much lately, discussing the offer."

"When will this take place?"

"We'll sign contracts within the next few weeks, then start taping, but the shows won't air until the new fall schedule starts."

"At least that's something," he muttered. "Good Lord, Ashli, I can't believe you didn't tell me this."

"It never occurred to me."

He shook his head in disbelief. "I still can't decide if you are for real."

She stiffened. "I think I may hear an insult in there somewhere."

"Hardly an insult."

"Then what are you talking about? It's too early in the morning for riddles. And I'm only on my second cup of coffee."

"I can't decide if you are only pretending to be this modest, or if you don't have a clue. Here you are, a gorgeous woman, sexy as hell with your knockout body and your husky little voice, with your own business and your own television show, but you act like you can't imagine a man being obsessed with you. You didn't even demand special attention because you're some hotshot celebrity. Hell, yeah, I wonder if you're for real or not!"

"It's not the first time I've been called clueless." She sighed. "And I'm no hotshot celebrity. I stand in front of a camera and do what I love best, cooking. I'm sorry I didn't think to tell you about it, but honestly, it's not that big a deal."

"It didn't occur to you that your stalker might be one of your viewers?"

Ashli looked truly surprised.

"I take that look as a no," he said.

She shrugged. Somewhere along the way, her robe had fallen free, exposing the little camisole top she wore with the flannel pants. He tried hard to keep his eyes above its intriguing lace edge as she admitted, "I still tend to think of most of our viewers as middle-aged housewives, even though demographic studies prove that's not true. What with digital recorders, the internet, live streaming, and such, I know afternoon television 'isn't just for the afternoon'." She said the last with a flourish, then explained with a wry smile, "One of our advertising campaigns. The one before the bus escapades."

"Have you mentioned your stalker to the television station?"

"I've told Mitch. He says there's nothing the station can do, unless the person makes himself, or herself, visible, and then only if they clearly identify a threat to the station or their entities, in this case being myself." She used her best rote voice. "They can offer legal counsel if I ever wish to press charges, but at this point . . ." She left her sentence hanging, much as her life seemed to do these days.

"I take it that was Jason Madison in the hallway."

"Yes. Ugh. Did you see that smirk on his face? You know good and well what he was thinking. I have a feeling I'll hear plenty more about it."

"You're making a third cup of coffee? Do you think that's a good idea?"

"Already stunted my growth, what else can it do?" She grinned, passing a hand over her head to indicate her short stature. "I know, I know, too much caffeine can give you the jitters and cause sleeplessness and probably cause the latest cancer scare. Sue me."

Blinded by the megawatt grin she flashed him, Lange struggled to get back on track. He suddenly wasn't angry anymore. Her playful grin turned his entire mood around, along with his thoughts. "What do you think you'll hear out of Madison?"

"You know the type. He'll think if I let one man stay the night in my apartment, then I'm open for others, namely him. As if I'd ever be *that* desperate!" she muttered.

He smiled. "I think that's the first unkind thing I've heard you say about someone."

"See, I obviously haven't had enough coffee yet. Forgotten my manners."

"Good to see you're human. Even this caffeine addiction makes you seem a little more real. Hyper, maybe, but real."

"Hey, I have a long day ahead of me. I need all the caffeine I can get. I've got a private luncheon at noon, a meeting at two, and a taping this afternoon. I won't be home until late." She glanced at the clock and sighed. "Okay, I gotta get a move on."

He took the cue to leave. "How late is late?" he asked.

"Who knows? Depends on how many takes we need. At least nine o'clock, probably ten. Thirty."

"Do you have an alarm system?" Another question he should have already asked, instead of being so interested in her love life.

"No. But visitors have to be buzzed in at the front door."

"But apparently not onto the balcony," he reminded her.

"Point taken. I'll check into getting an alarm system."

"See, you're not so clueless, after all."

This time, Ashli was the one blinded by the beauty of a simple smile.

CHAPTER SIX

Six days later, Lange still wondered if Ashli Wilson were for real.

Could anyone be as damn perfect as she appeared to be? Experience told him no. Almost everyone had a secret to hide, and after six days, he thought he had discovered hers.

Keeping her under surveillance was one of the easiest assignments of his career. He watched her one morning, as she came out of her house like a ray of sunshine, dressed in a bright green dress the color of spring's first grass. He watched as she offered her sunny smile to everyone she met, and as she stopped to visit with an elderly man tending the flower beds. He watched that afternoon, as she came home from work with her little yellow boxes and carried them around to people in her condo, and to neighbors down the street. She shared not only her food, but her golden smile. From his parked truck, he could occasionally hear the rippling sounds of her laughter, carrying on the wind. Like a breeze on a summer day, it whirled around him and refreshed his tired soul, teasing at his senses.

As he watched her, he saw no evidence of a stalker, but he wasn't ready to dismiss the possibility of one. If someone was following her, he felt certain they were dealing with the attentions of an admirer, not an enemy. He could find no evidence of anyone even remotely unhappy with the beautiful Ashli Wilson.

Her business was one of Richmond's finest. Despite the fact she had a staff of eight, Ashli insisted on preparing most of the food herself, then on strolling through the dining room, greeting guests and attending to their needs. A visit to Ashli's Tea Party was much like a visit to her own home, a fact most patrons found the most delightful of all.

As for her television show, it was a certified hit. The woman was magic behind the camera, coming across the air every bit as natural and charming as she did in person. Lange spent an entire morning watching taped episodes of *Ashli's Kitchen,* understanding why the show was going into syndication after only one season.

Everyone, it seemed, loved Ashli's Tea Party. Everyone loved *Ashli's Kitchen.* Everyone loved Ashli Wilson. No matter who Lange interviewed, they had nothing but praise for the woman with the white-blonde hair and the whispery voice.

After following her for almost a week, Lange was exhausted by her constant deeds of kindness and her perky disposition. He felt the resentment growing inside of him, even as his admiration for her grew. Hell, the woman was practically a saint!

But no one could be as perfect as she seemed to be. There had to be a flaw somewhere, or at least a secret she hid. As he checked out the few names on the list she had given him, it didn't take long to clear each man's name of suspicion. With little else to go on, Lange thought he might have stumbled upon the deception, and he was headed to her house to confront her.

The last thing he needed on this case was another surprise.

* * *

"Are you sure this looks okay on me? I don't have your peaches and cream complexion, you know." Rachel Reese stood in front of the bedroom mirror, modeling one of Ashli's pink sweater sets.

"No, you have that wonderful dark complexion that no amount of sun or spray-on tan could ever give me," Ashli told her best friend. Both women were roughly the same shape and size but were opposites in coloring. "The pink looks great on you. Definitely in the 'pack me' pile."

"Of course, if you came with us, we could just work out of one suitcase. Or three."

"Rachel, even best friends aren't welcome on second honeymoons!"

"We'd love to have you, and you know it. Well, as long as you had your own cabin." She grinned, wagging her eyebrows.

"Thanks, but I couldn't possibly get away right now. There's that banquet we're catering, berry season coming up, this syndication deal with the network . . . I couldn't possibly leave, even if I wanted to crash your vacation."

"Are you sure I shouldn't stay and help? I feel so guilty, leaving at a busy time like this. Maybe we should postpone our trip . . ."

"Don't you dare! You and Kevin deserve a vacation. Molly can never take your place, but she's the best management trainee we've ever had. We'll do fine."

Still, Rachel was hesitant. "But with all the other things that have been happening." She pulled the sweater set off and tossed it onto Ashli's bed. "Maybe we should stay home. At least until this Peeping Tom incident is solved."

"Absolutely not! You're going on this cruise, if I have to truss you up like a turkey and stuff you inside a suitcase! This is an anniversary you're celebrating, after all."

"I can't believe it's been five years, can you? Time certainly flies by."

"I know. Here you've been married to the man of your dreams for half a decade, and I'm still looking for mine."

"No, you're not," Rachel argued. "You never even date."

"No one ever asks me out," Ashli countered. "Here, try this on."

"What about that Doug guy?" Rachel asked, wiggling her head out of a blue turtleneck. "He'd ask you out if you gave him a little encouragement."

"Doug? Who's Doug?" Ashli frowned.

"I don't know his last name. He drives the delivery truck for Flour Arrangements. The cute one that has a crush on you."

"He doesn't have a crush on me. Turn this way. Hmmm, maybe not the blue. Why don't you try on this yellow one?"

"He so does! He stammers all over his words when you talk to him. And yellow's not my color."

"The poor guy has a speech impediment. Here, try this lavender blouse."

"What about all the extra stuff he brings you, like extra flour and spices and things you don't even order? And why does he blush whenever he sees you?"

"He's just trying to keep my business. We're a big account for them, you know. He's just a nice guy, with a speech impediment and a stiff leg. He blushes because he's self-conscious about his limp."

"He blushes because you go out of your way to speak to him and be nice to him, and because he has a crush on you. Just like that lawyer guy that comes in with his partner, the redhead. That man definitely has a crush on you."

"That man definitely has a wife. He flirts with me because he's showing out for his partner. It doesn't mean a thing. Guys just aren't attracted to women like me."

"And what kind of woman would that be? The gorgeous type? The successful businesswoman type? Or the kind of woman who has her own television show? I'm a little confused here."

"You sound like Lange Sterling. He said the exact same thing."

"He called you gorgeous?"

Ashli blushed at the unintended omission. "Maybe. I don't recall his exact words." Hearing a knock downstairs, she said, "Hold on a sec, I think I hear somebody."

"What did you say?" Rachel asked, untangling herself from the lavender blouse.

"I'll be right back!" Ashli called over her shoulder, heading down the stairs.

She peered through the peephole, surprised to see who stood on the other side. They must have conjured the man up by talking about him. With a small frown, she opened the door.

"Mr. Sterling! I didn't realize you were coming over tonight. And I didn't buzz you in."

"Proof that not everyone uses the buzzer," he pointed out. He had followed a pizza delivery boy in. "There are a few things we need to discuss."

"Yes, of course."

As he moved into the living room, Rachel came bounding down the stairs, pulling on her blouse. "I didn't realize how late it was!" she said, her eyes on the buttons she fastened. "I'll get my suitcase later, if that's okay."

"It appears I have come at a bad time," Lange said, his dark eyes like daggers as he swung his gaze from one woman to the next.

"Oh my gosh, why didn't you tell me you had company?" Rachel clutched her blouse together, cheeks blazing.

"Rachel, this is the private detective I've been telling you about. Lange Sterling, my dear friend, Rachel Reese."

"Hello," Lange said, without extending a hand in greeting.

"Mr. Sterling! Ashli has told me all about you." Recovering from her acute case of embarrassment with lightning speed, Rachel practically gushed. "I am so relieved to know you're here to protect our dear Ashli." She put an arm around her friend's waist and beamed at her. "I just don't know what we'd do without her."

"Well, that's my job, ma'am, to see that no harm comes to your friend."

"Good, good. You take good care of her." She seemed not to notice his dry tone. "I'll go now, so you two can discuss business. Thanks, Ash, see you tomorrow."

After walking her friend to the door, Ashli joined him in the living room. "Did you discover something new?" she asked.

"I think I might have a new angle," he said, still standing.

"What? What did you learn? Do you know who is doing this? I know it couldn't have been any of the names I gave you."

"How can you be so certain none of the names you gave me could be the one?" he asked, his eyes narrowing.

"Well, just because," she said with a defiance that held just a pinch of uncertainty. "Because they're my friends, for one thing. Nothing like this has ever happened in the past, and I've known them for years. I mean, I don't know about that one man, Carl Simons, because we only went out once, but he seemed nice. I'm sure it's not him." As usual, she seemed to be talking to herself as much as she was to him. With a sudden impatience that Lange found almost amusing, given she was the one delaying his news, she demanded, "Well, are you just going to stand there, or are you going to tell me what you found out?"

"I've been watching you throughout the week," he began. He moved around the room restlessly, half afraid to even voice his suspicions, yet even more afraid of what could happen to her if he didn't know the whole truth.

"Yes, I could sense that you were watching."

"You could?" He looked up in surprise, marveling at how sweet and innocently seductive she looked in her dress of lavender jersey. It was a simple dress, with a scooped neckline and no shape, but it draped over her body in the most provocative way, clinging in all the best places, just as his gaze did.

"I would feel a sense of safety settling over me. A sense of security," she admitted in her breathless voice. "I knew it was you, and not him."

"I guess the hairs on the back of your neck didn't stand up." Last week, her 'proof' had sounded so ridiculous; today he thought he might see the logic behind the claim.

"No, they didn't." She smiled, knowing that he was tethering between making fun of her and teasing her. There was a big difference between the two, usually determined by the look in a person's eyes. His eyes were dark and sensual, so she took no offense, but her pulse did quicken. "I had a feeling of warmth when you were watching."

"A feeling of warmth," he repeated.

"I know you think I'm crazy, but yes, a feeling of warmth. I can't describe it, but I could tell you were watching me. It didn't make me feel scared or nervous; it made me feel warm and secure, like someone wrapping a blanket around my shoulders."

Blanket. He suddenly thought of the blanket she had placed on him, the sign of tenderness that he didn't want. The look in his dark eyes changed abruptly, and Ashli could have sworn she felt a blast of Arctic air in the room.

"While I was watching you," he said, his voice just loud enough and just gruff enough to break any spell that may have woven between them, "I saw that you had no dates."

"I already told you, I don't date very often."

"You had several female guests during that time. Two one evening, an entire houseful another."

"Yes, I invited some friends over for dinner one night. And the next night I had a Silver Sensations party."

"A what?"

"A Silver Sensations party. One of my friends just started selling it, so I hosted a party to help her launch her business. See, I got this gorgeous bracelet free, just for having a party." She held up her wrist and jangled multiple silver bands.

"Okay, so you had a couple of friends over for dinner one night, a hen party the next. What about tonight?"

"Tonight?" she asked in confusion.

"Rachel." He jerked his head toward the stairs, as if that explained everything.

"She came over to try on clothes."

"Do you share clothes with all your . . . friends?"

Sensing that something wasn't quite right when he hesitated over the word 'friend', Ashli narrowed her eyes and asked, "Exactly what are you implying? I don't understand this line of questioning."

"I'm simply trying to get to the truth, Ms. Wilson." He slipped back to formal terms, and to the title she always corrected him on. "If I'm to help you, you can't hide anything from me. I have to know everything."

"I told you before, I have no secrets."

He caught her arm and whirled her around toward him. "The truth, Ms. Wilson," he said. "I have to know the truth about everything."

"What?" she spat. "You think Rachel is my lover?" As her wild accusation hit its mark and she saw the truth of his suspicions in dark-hazel eyes, she gasped aloud. "You do! You think that-that . . . Oh! The sheer audacity!" She was so angry she couldn't even bring herself to finish her sentence. All she could do was stomp her foot in anger as her voice came out in a shocked whisper.

Lange had never felt a bigger fool than he did at that moment. He loosened his hold on her arm, but he didn't release her. He gazed down into her big, blue eyes and awkwardly tried to apologize.

"I-I'm sorry, Ashli. I didn't know, but I had to find out for sure. Your safety is at stake here."

"Why would you even think that? Rachel is my dearest friend in the world, and I do love her, but not like *that!*"

He stared down at her, wondering how he could explain it to her. What would happen if he admitted the truth, even to himself? The truth that he had to find something, anything, that would distance him from her, something that would stop him from feeling the emotions he already felt. What if he told her she had been too perfect, too nearly the woman of his dreams, back when he still believed in dreams? If she had been gay, he would have been safe, his heart would have been safe. How could he explain that to her, when he didn't understand it himself?

"As a private investigator, I have to explore every possibility," he finally told her, his voice low.

"You were wrong," she whispered.

His eyes slipped to her mouth, and, for the millionth time, he wondered what it would be like to kiss her. One kiss, he told himself. One kiss would get this crazy craving out of his system, and he could get on with business. He moved his hand to her waist and drew her closer, his other hand touching her cheek.

Ashli could see the desire to kiss her in his eyes. Her own eyes drifted shut as he lifted her face upward toward his. Lange pulled her closer, until first their bodies touched, and then their lips. And as she melted into the warm strength of his arms and felt the wonder of his mouth move on hers, Ashli imagined that their souls touched, as well.

It was a simple kiss, a gentle brush of one mouth against another, but it forged a connection between them. They pulled slowly apart, their bodies still close, and opened their eyes at the same time to stare at the other.

"I'm sorry, Ashli," he told her, his low voice uneven. "But I had to ask. I had to know."

"Do you believe me?"

He watched her lips as they formed the words, lips that tasted sweeter than he had even dared to imagine. Trailing his fingers over her cheek, he curled them through the strands of sunshine and gently tugged her face closer. Just as his mouth settled onto hers once again, he breathed the words huskily against her lips. "Beyond the shadow of a doubt."

This kiss was deeper, longer. Hungrier. As one hand gloried in the long tresses of her hair, the other moved over her back, caressing her in its travels. His hand roamed over her freely, from her shoulder blades to the gentle swell of her hips. Lange moved in a circular pattern, each time pulling with just the slightest more pressure, each sweep pulling her just a bit nearer, until Ashli felt as if his magic fingers were pulling her into his very soul. Leaning on the solid wall of his chest for support, she circled her arms around his back.

When at last he raised his dark head, he looked down at her with a strange sorrow in his eyes. Almost in anguish, he released her suddenly and swore beneath his breath. His reaction was at sharp odds with the poignant kiss. A blurted confession of undying love would have been more suiting than the way he now turned coldly away from her.

Finally, he spoke, his back still toward her. His voice was low and somber, but strong enough to carry across the room. "That shouldn't have happened."

Ashli made no comment.

"Damn it, Ashli, you hired me as your private investigator! This can't happen between a detective and his client!" He swung around, as if her silence was an argument.

Again, she made no comment.

"Stop staring at me like that!" he commanded.

"Then stop yelling at me." She finally spoke, her voice small.

Lange took a deep breath and reined in his anger, most of which was directed at himself. "Okay, I'm sorry I yelled." He spoke with tightly controlled volume as he stuffed his hands into his back jean pockets and silently glared at her.

"You can stop staring at me like that, too," she said, lifting her chin. "I didn't do anything wrong."

Again, he wanted to yell at her and say that she had made him kiss her, but he knew it wasn't true. He had wanted to kiss her, more than he had even wanted to breathe. God, he still wanted to. She was standing there looking at him like a defiant little girl, but he knew it was a woman's body that he held only moments ago.

He pulled his eyes away and forced himself to sound harsh. "No, but I did. I kissed you."

"You don't have to act like you contracted a disease, you know. It was only a kiss."

"A kiss that won't ever happen again." He said the words so defiantly, they both could hear the lie.

They stood staring at one another in challenge for a long moment. Lange was the first to break the gaze.

"Well, since we've gotten *that* out of the way," she said briskly, "maybe we can discuss my case. Have you learned anything new? Anything *real*?"

"I've watched you for almost a week now, and not once have I seen signs of anyone else doing the same. Have you heard anything else from him, seen him again?"

"No, not since the night you were here." With a weary sigh, she went into the kitchen and made coffee.

Lange followed and settled on a stool at the bar. "I found several vantage points where a person could sit and watch you from a distance. You'd never know you were being watched."

"Except for the hairs on the back of my neck," she reminded him.

He ignored that comment as he flipped open his little notebook. "Tell me about the bum behind the Tea Party."

She looked up in surprise, not realizing he knew about her friend in the alley. It seemed the man had done his homework this time.

"His name is Leon," she said, opening one of her trademark yellow boxes. She took out bacon-artichoke mini soufflés and pinwheel sandwiches. Dividing the offering on two plates she noisily rummaged through the cabinets for, she told him her story. "I found him out in the alley one day about six months ago, going through the trash. He ran away the first time, but I kept watching for him. When I saw that he was taking food, I realized he must be homeless. I waited behind the dumpster, until he came again, and I could talk to him."

"Do you know how stupid that was, waiting outside for a man like that? He could be dangerous!"

"Leon is as harmless as a fly. He's a nice man, just down on his luck. Occasionally, he finds an odd job or two, and when he does and he has the money, he leaves a few dollars for the food he takes."

"You leave something for him every day?" he asked, hand poised in mid-air as he devoured his second pinwheel.

"Well, I like to eat on a daily basis, don't you?"

"Yes, but I don't rely on the kindness of others to feed me!"

"You would, if you didn't have a home or a job. We never know what we would do in another person's position. My mother told me to never judge another Indian, until I had walked a mile in his moccasins," Ashli said in her soft, gentle voice.

"My grandmother always said the same thing," Lange murmured before a look of irritation crossed his face. Aloud, he asked, "Is there any chance this Leon character could be the one stalking you?"

"No, I'm certain of it."

"So far, you've been certain that no one you know could possibly be responsible, but someone *is* out there, Ashli. And I'd bet my last dollar you know the person."

"Maybe so, but it's no one we've discussed so far."

"Then give me more names."

Ashli sighed wearily. "Then what, Lange? Even if I give you the names of everyone I've ever known, what then? How do we know it's not some anonymous viewer? And do I just sit back and wait for him to make another move?"

"My guess is that you won't have to wait long." He hesitated, then was honest with her. "I don't want to alarm you, but I think you should be on your guard tonight. I think he might show up again."

"Why? How can you tell?"

"It was Monday two weeks ago that you reported a Peeping Tom to the police. Monday of last week that you got the note. There might be a pattern emerging."

She shivered visibly and hugged herself with both arms, losing her appetite.

"Is there someone who can come over and stay with you this evening? I would, but I have . . . plans."

She wondered if the plans were with a woman. Looking into his face, she was certain of it. Ashli convinced herself that she didn't care as she told him, "I was going out tonight. Ironically enough, I finally have a date."

"I don't think you should go," he said, and then wondered if his haste had more to do with his own jealousy than it did with her safety. But why on earth would he be jealous? He didn't want a relationship with her. The kiss had meant nothing, absolutely nothing.

"I'm not going to stop living, just because someone is stalking me." She lifted her chin in defiance. "So far, they've never threatened me or done anything to harm me. I see no reason for tonight to be any different."

"I don't know . . ." he said uncertainly. He hated to say too much, or he might frighten her unnecessarily. Yet too little concern could prove dangerous for her, something he knew he couldn't bear.

"I'll be fine, Lange. I won't be out late. We're just going for cocktails."

"Who is it?" Even to his own ears, his voice sounded like a growl.

"A friend of Mitch's. He's in town for the week, and we're meeting with Mitch and Allison for drinks."

"Tell me his name, I'll run it through the system."

"Seriously? I just met him this morning. His name is Brandon something, and he's from the network affiliate in Florida."

"Look, just to be on the safe side, make sure you have my cell number. If you see anything suspicious or if anything happens, I want you to call me." He handed her his business card, making her look at him. "Do you promise to call if you need me?"

She wondered how exactly he would define 'need'. Right now, she desperately needed to feel his strong arms around her. She needed a hug. But instead of revealing the truth, she merely said, "I promise."

"Okay, then I guess I do need to go." He glanced at his watch, knowing Diane was waiting. He tried to think of a reason to stall, a reason to stay here and forget his date with Diane and Ashli's date with the Florida pretty boy, but he could think of none that sounded plausible. He reluctantly stood and made his way to the door.

"Promise me you'll be careful tonight," he said.

"I will."

He stared down at her, wanting to take her in his arms and never let her go, wanting to stay and protect her, even if it meant staying forever. But the very thought scared the daylights out of him, making his dilemma all the harder.

Should he protect his heart, or protect her safety? Failing at either could be disastrous.

"You have my number?" he finally asked.

"Right here." She held up the proof.

"You'll call if anything happens, anything at all?"

"I promise." It was obvious that he was stalling, a fact that brought a smile to Ashli's lips. "Go on, Lange." She gave him a little shove. "You deserve a night off, especially if you've spent the last week tailing me. I must be the most boring person in Richmond. Go out and have fun tonight. I'll be perfectly safe."

He would have argued with her, but he might be tempted to prove his point that she was hardly what he called boring. Just the thought of how he could prove it made his blood stir, and he knew he had to leave, the quicker, the better.

CHAPTER SEVEN

"I take it you're not in the mood," Diane McIver pouted, as Lange rolled away and sat up in bed. Watching him closely through her tousled auburn hair, the woman beside him wondered what bothered him tonight. His mind obviously wasn't on her, or on making love.

"I'm sorry, Di," he said, running both hands through his own dark hair. "I guess my mind is somewhere else tonight."

"Want to talk about it?"

Out of habit, he turned his broad back to her, and she massaged the bunched muscles. She loved the feel of his skin beneath her hands, all hot and lean and tight.

"I have a new case I'm working on. My client thinks she's being stalked."

"What do you think?"

Lange released a long breath and admitted it for the first time aloud. "God, I'm afraid she might be right."

Diane was silent for a moment, kneading the powerful muscles as she mulled over the distraught tone in his voice. That tone and his strange mood tonight didn't leave her feeling very assured. "What can you do about it?" she finally asked.

"I don't know, but I swear I'll find some way to protect her."

Breath tangled in her suddenly aching chest, Diane managed to choke out the words, "Tell me about her."

"She's like a modern-day version of Doris Day," Lange said with a little laugh. He was unaware of the soft quality that slipped into his voice, but Diane heard it, and her heart broke. "I swear she sounds just like her, all hushed and breathless. Carries on like her, too, talking about things that don't even make any sense, and all without taking a breath between thoughts. You should hear her." He smiled and closed his eyes, thinking of how she carried on about the list of names she had given him, keeping him from getting a word in edgewise, all the while demanding he tell her what he knew.

"Doris Day was always your favorite old movie star, wasn't she?" Diane said, trying to keep her voice from cracking.

"I fell in love with her the very first time I saw her," he murmured as she continued to knead his back. It was a full moment before his eyes popped open, and he clarified his statement. "Doris Day, I mean."

Diane heard the guilt in his voice, even before he whirled around so she could see it in his eyes. She knew anyone moving that quickly and behaving that guiltily had something to hide, even if it was from himself. Her hands fell away, and she moved back to rest against the headboard, pulling the sheet with her.

"Diane," he said, and she knew what was coming next. He sounded too casual, too nonchalant, yet he wouldn't meet her eyes. "I've been thinking. Between this new case and the rest of my load, I'm going to be very busy for a while. I may not be able to see you much."

"That's nothing new," Diane said. "I'll wait."

"But that's what I've been thinking about. It's not fair to you, Diane. Just like the other night, when I missed that dinner party with your client. And the next night. And the two times this week. You shouldn't have to sit around, waiting on me. You should be free to make your own plans, without me messing them up."

Diane let the words settle between them before she asked, "What's her name, Lange? Who's this new client?"

"Since when did you start caring about my clientele?" he asked, reaching for his jeans from a nearby chair.

"Since when did you start caring if this relationship was fair to me?" she shot back. "You've been coming and going like the wind for almost two years now."

Lange paused as he stood to pull on his pants. Not bothering to zip the jeans out of false modesty, he turned toward her and raised a dark, shaggy brow. "Come on, Diane, we've been friends for too long to pretend this relationship was based on only my needs."

"You're right, of course. But what if I told you I wanted to make our relationship more permanent?"

Lange fastened his jeans and pulled on his shirt, leaving it unbuttoned as he sat on the bed to face her. His smile was one of affection as he told her with the honesty she once loved, but was now growing to hate, "Diane, you are one of the few people I call a friend. But you know it's too late for our relationship to ever be any more than it is right now."

"Because of her?" Her voice wavered with unshed tears.

Lange hesitated before answering. He and Diane had always been honest with one another, and he saw no reason to start lying now. He couldn't even lie to himself anymore. "Not entirely," he said. "But I do have to admit, she makes me remember feelings inside that I thought died long ago."

"You're just walking away?" This time her voice was harsh.

Lange sighed. Diane and her mood swings. She had gone from heartbroken to hateful in less than sixty seconds. So much for amicable breakups, the kind Ashli claimed to have.

"I'll still be around, if you need me."

"And I guess we can still be friends?" she sneered.

"I'd like for us to be," he replied.

"Well, you can just forget that, mister! I don't need friends like you! Friends don't waste two years — *two freaking years* — of a girl's life and then just walk away!" She picked up the remote control beside the bed and flung it angrily at his head.

Lange flinched and ducked, moving from the bed.

"I don't want a friend with some crazy-ass fascination with a movie star from fifty years ago! Get the hell out of my apartment!" She rose on her knees, throwing anything else she could get her hands on. A magazine landed with a thud at his feet, a water glass crashed against the wall behind him, a hurled pillow hit his knee. "And give me back my key, damn it!"

"It's there beside the bed," he said. The finality in his voice, in the very act of leaving the key before she even asked, made the ending even more bitter.

"Get out!" she shrieked again. "Get out and don't ever come back!"

As he turned to do as she asked, Diane fell over in a heap. "Get out!" she repeated, but the words were muddled with tears.

Lange hadn't wanted to end it this way with Diane, but she left him little choice. He knew now, beyond a shadow of a doubt, that their relationship was over.

"Goodbye, Diane," he said, before leaving her to cry alone in her empty bed.

CHAPTER EIGHT

Ashli stirred restlessly in bed, unable to find a comfortable position. Her body was tired, but her mind was wide awake. Random thoughts kept going through her mind — an idea for a new recipe, something funny Rachel had said, errands she needed to run the next day, the pros and cons of syndicating her cooking show — but all thoughts kept circling back to the one thing she was trying desperately to forget . . . the feel of Lange Sterling's mouth upon hers.

No. She wouldn't think about him, not tonight. For just one night, she would banish thoughts of the brooding private detective. She wouldn't think about how tall and lithe he was, how long his legs were. She wouldn't see those dark eyes of his, one moment snapping with irritation, the next smoldering with desire. The man did seem to be awfully intense, always agitated, never relaxed. She wondered why that was. Maybe he . . .

No, no, no, she wasn't thinking about him tonight! He had haunted her thoughts for the past week. Tonight, she banished him from her mind. She wouldn't even wonder, for the umpteenth time, whom he had a date with tonight. His personal life was none of her concern. In fact, she would think about her own date tonight.

Brandon had been perfectly nice. Handsome, too, if you liked the blond, made-for-television type. But his hands were so soft, she noticed, nothing like the callused palms of Lange Sterling's. His hair was perfectly coiffed, his teeth straight and white, his eyes a clear blue. She found herself comparing his flawless good looks to a more rugged counterpart; there was something about dark hair, worn just a little too long, about a sardonic off-center smile, something about dark, brooding eyes that seemed so much more attractive.

Brandon, she reminded herself sternly. She was thinking about Brandon. There was that witty little remark he had made about the network. He was a good conversationalist. And a real gentleman, unlike someone else she wasn't thinking about. He had been totally attentive, opening doors and pulling out her chair, making certain her drink was refilled. And he was an above-average kisser. Too bad she felt nothing special when he touched his lips to hers, nothing even close to what she felt when Lange kissed her.

Lange, again! Ashli punched her pillow into a new shape and slammed her head against it, hoping to dislodge all thoughts of Lange Sterling. She let out a low growl of frustration, but a sound from downstairs brought her up short. She lay still and listened.

Another muffled noise made her sit up in bed, straining to hear more.

Grabbing the phone and a long, heavy flashlight from her nightstand, Ashli eased out of bed and crept toward the stairs. She stood there for a tense moment, searching the shadows below, straining to hear what had awakened her. It was difficult to hear anything over the wild hammering of her heart, but it sounded like something — or someone — moving on her veranda.

She slid down the first few steps.

There was no movement from the shadows, but the noise came again, on the veranda.

Ashli squeezed flat against the wall as she ventured down another step, then two. With slow, stealthy movements, she eased down the remaining steps until she reached the bottom. Taking a deep breath, she peered around the corner into the kitchen.

Empty.

With her back still pressed against the safety of the wall, she scanned the rest of her apartment and found the shadows vacant and secure. As she eased toward the French windows, the frantic clamoring of her heart drowned out all other noise.

A cat, she told herself. It might be a cat.

She finally reached the windows. Her fingers trembled as, ever so slowly, she eased a wooden blind back a sliver of an inch.

She gasped when she saw the shadow on the other side. That was not a cat. It was a man, and he was moving slowly away, his back to her. After a few feet, he paused and started to turn toward her, presumably to retrace his steps. Not waiting to find out, Ashli flipped the porch light on.

She heard the man's hasty departure but didn't dare look out again. She dialed the phone as she jumped away from the windows.

"Lange!" she whispered when he picked up on the second ring. "There's someone outside."

He was awake instantly. Even as he spoke, he grabbed his jeans and jabbed a leg inside. "Don't open the door until you hear my voice. I'm on my way!"

It took him an eternity to get there. A full six minutes ticked away before she buzzed him in, another thirty seconds before he banged on her door. "Ashli! Ashli, it's me, open up!"

She opened the door and flung herself into his arms, much as she had done the week before. This time he was prepared for the attack, closing his arms around her and pulling her to his chest, even as he backed her into the apartment and shut the door.

"What happened?" he asked, his heart thudding in alarm.

"I-I heard a noise. I came downstairs and peeked out the blinds. I saw . . . I saw a shadow. A man. When I flipped on the light, he ran. Then I called you."

"Good, you did the right thing," he murmured into her hair, resting his chin amid the strands of sunshine. He held her for a moment longer, allowing her to soak up the strength and security of his embrace before he even attempted to step away. She felt so small and helpless in his arms, her head tucked tightly against his chest.

After several minutes, he spoke. "Why don't you make us some coffee while I check things out on the balcony? Do you have decaf?"

"Yes. But . . . do you think you should? Is it safe?" she asked, lifting eyes filled with concern.

"He's long gone by now," he assured her. "I could use that coffee."

Ashli moved reluctantly away but hurried to the safety of the kitchen as he opened the patio doors. Her hands trembled as she made two cups of decaffeinated coffee. She was just finishing as he stepped back inside, a bundle in his arms.

"What-what is that?" She was almost afraid to ask.

"Would you believe a dozen long-stemmed roses?" He was careful to lock the door behind him before bringing the flowers to the bar.

"Roses?"

"Twelve of them."

"But-but roses are so expensive!"

"Which rules out your friend Leon."

She sent him a look that said he had never been a suspect to begin with. Pulling away the tissue paper to see them better, she frowned in confusion. It was a beautiful bouquet of twelve yellow roses, interspersed with daisies. "From goldfish to roses? What does it mean, Lange?"

"I don't know. But there's a seal on the tissue paper, which means I can speak with the florist tomorrow and possibly find who bought these. This might be the break we've been hoping for."

Ashli looked skeptical as she handed him his coffee cup. He didn't miss the way her hand trembled. Not trusting her to carry the scalding liquid, he took her own cup from her as he suggested, "Let's sit in the living room. You can tell me exactly what happened."

Ashli curled her feet beneath her on the sofa, making room for him to sit next to her. She took the cup he offered and wrapped both hands around it for warmth.

"I got home around ten. Brandon saw me in."

"Did he come inside?" The words were guttural.

"No, we said good night at the door. I had an uneasy feeling that I was being watched, but of course, all the blinds were shut, and the curtains drawn, so no one could see in. I went to bed but had trouble sleeping. Just before midnight, I heard a noise and got up to see what it was. That's when I saw the shadow."

"What was he doing? Could you tell?"

"I couldn't tell, but I think he was moving back and forth along the windows, maybe pacing. I turned on the light, then ran to hide behind the sofa as I called you. I could hear him running away."

"You hid behind the sofa?"

She gave a sheepish grin as she admitted, "I never claimed to be brave."

"Well, bravery and stupidity sometimes go together. You did the smart thing, calling me."

"I was so scared. I just knew he could hear my heart clamoring on the other side of the glass. That's the first time I've seen the person. I've always known he was real, that he was there, but seeing him tonight makes reality hit so much harder," she confessed with a shudder. She ran a hand through her hair, tangling the golden-white tresses unmercifully.

Lange suddenly became aware of the night clothes she wore. On a taller woman, the ruffled hem of the baby doll gown would have been revealingly brief; on Ashli's petite frame, it offered modest cover. The matching robe wasn't much better. With her hair all tousled, it wasn't hard to imagine that this was what she would look like after he made love to her. Just the thought drove him wild.

Forcing himself to control his wayward thoughts, Lange stared at her a moment longer before dragging his eyes to the French doors. Knowing he had more important things to think of right now, it took a few seconds for any of those things to surface in his mind. Finally, he found one.

"Could you tell anything about the shadow? Was he a big man, was he tall, skinny, fat? Did he wear a hat? Tell me everything you remember."

Never guessing how the action distracted him, she toyed with her hair as she spoke, pulling on the long, silky strands through her splayed fingers, repeatedly. Working her fingers slowly from the roots to the ends, the old habit seemed to pull the thoughts from deep within. "You know how shadows are," she began. "They made him appear big and bulky, but somehow, I don't think he is. He might have had on a cap. And maybe boots. There was something about his feet . . ."

"What? What do you remember about his feet?" he pressed.

"I can't quite put my finger on it. But he didn't seem to move smoothly." She got up suddenly and went to the window, pacing alongside it.

"What in the hell are you doing?"

"I'm trying to remember what it was about his feet," she murmured. She closed her eyes as she walked, seeing the shadowed man in her mind's eye and allowing her own feet to mimic the image of his walk.

"He walked on tiptoe?" Lange asked.

"Shhh. I'm thinking." Never opening her eyes, she turned and retraced her steps along the door, this time trying a different step, a different interpretation. She would know when she got it right.

Lange sat on the sofa, staring at the woman who paced up and down her balcony windows with her eyes closed. She wore a look of utter concentration on her face, as she lost herself to re-creating the image that, just moments ago, had frightened her to even think of. She was a fascinating mix of contradictions and surprises, and even though he often wondered about her sanity, such as now, he suspected she had a brilliant mind beneath her zany actions.

It wasn't her mind, however, that captured his attention as he watched her pace the floor. The balcony light spilled through the blinds behind her, silhouetting the gentle curves of her body.

"I've got it!" she said, bringing his eyes open. "He walked like this."

"With his hips swaying?"

"My feet. Look at my feet." Her own eyes were still closed to keep her chain of concentration.

"You're dragging one foot. You're limping."

"Exactly!" She stopped her pacing and opened her eyes, bestowing him with a brilliant smile that could have blinded the sun itself. "He walked with a limp!"

Lange pushed off the couch and came to stand in front of her, taking hold of her arms. There was no mistaking the glint of excitement in his eyes. "Between this and the seal on the roses, we may be able to find our man." It was the first optimistic thing he had ever said to her.

"Oh, Lange, I hope so. I hope so!" Her trembling smile was hopeful as she threw her arms around his waist and hugged him. She squeezed him tightly in a quick, hard hug, but when she would have moved away, she found his arms had encircled her.

He held her loosely, two large hands placed on her back, as they stared into one another's eyes. He drew her closer, slowly, and slid one large hand along the silky sheerness of her gown, until it rested upon her hip. He folded her into his arms with sweet, deliberate slowness, staring down into her eyes so they both knew what was happening.

As her body slid up against his, he saw her eyes widen at the intimate contact that brought soft, willing flesh against hard, wanting flesh. His eyes offered a chance to pull away, now, before something happened that she didn't want.

Her tongue darted out nervously to moisten her lips; his eyes followed hungrily. His hands slowly caressed her, hesitantly at first, until her responding fingers moved across the wide breadth of his shoulders, leaving sparks of fire where they touched. His eyes returned to hers, dark and solemn in their quest; hers were alight with an eager response. His breathing quickened, then hers.

Still, he hesitated, as he struggled with his own emotions. She watched as a part of him won, a part of him lost. He told himself not to get involved, to stay aloof, but as she stood staring up at him, he knew his involvement was inevitable. He knew it the first moment he laid eyes on her. He knew it earlier in the evening when he kissed her for the first time. And he knew it now, as he held her in his arms and slowly lowered his mouth to hers.

The kiss was like lightning on a dry, parched prairie. There was the jolt of electricity when their lips met, then a spark of pure passion as the fire quickly spread. Faster than flames could ignite a dry prairie, the passion exploded between them and raced through their blood, consuming them both. Ashli wondered if his hands rushed over her body to control the blaze, or to fan it higher. She ran her own hands down the muscles of his back, feeling the heat of his skin and the response of his body, even harder and hotter than before. Time was scorched away.

Somewhere far away, Ashli thought she heard a phone ringing. Yet who could hear anything over the sounds of their fevered breathing and the blood rushing through her head? More than once, she thought she had heard her own whimpered pleasure, and the answering moan of his need, but nothing was certain except this man and this moment.

And then, from across the room, a voice penetrated their inferno of desire. It had the effect of a tidal wave, dousing the flame as they broke away in the middle of a kiss and listened to a man's voice coming across the answering machine.

"I guess you found the roses." The voice was low and raspy. "Next time . . ." The line went dead, leaving the unfinished threat hanging in the air.

Ashli slumped in Lange's arms. "Oh my God, Lange. What am I going to do? He said he'll be back."

His voice was gentle but fierce. "I swear, I won't let anything happen to you. I'm here, and I'm going to be here, and I'm going to keep you safe." He had the craziest urge to add the words 'forever and ever', but he bit them back just in time. He wouldn't make a promise he couldn't keep.

For the first time, she admitted, "I'm scared."

"There's nothing to be afraid of. I won't let anything happen to you." He squeezed her for a moment, pressing his promise into her heart. "Come on; let's sit on the couch. Just sit and relax."

"Don't leave," she said, clutching at his arm as he turned her toward the couch.

"I won't. Just come sit right here, I'll be right beside you." He spoke softly, soothing her as he guided her to the couch and sat her gently on the cushions. Seeing an afghan on the nearby chair, he grabbed for it with one hand, while keeping the other securely on her. He wrapped the warmth around her and drew her close.

"Next time. He said there would be a next time," she said, laying her head on the pillow of his shoulder.

"He won't be back tonight; I can almost guarantee it. And even if he does, you won't be alone. I won't leave you, Ashli."

"But I can't pay you to be here, twenty-four seven."

"This has nothing to do with money. I swear to you, I won't let that man lay one finger on you. I won't let him hurt you. I'll protect you."

Ashli chose to believe him, knowing in her heart there were a hundred reasons why he couldn't always protect her, even if he wanted to. She snuggled against him, absorbing the feel and scent of him, soaking in his strength and his warmth. At least in his arms, she felt safe, she felt protected.

For now, it was enough, she decided, as she closed her eyes and forcibly relaxed against him.

* * *

Three hours later, Lange stretched one long arm out, careful not to wake the sleeping woman in his arms as he consulted the watch strapped to his wrist. She had fallen asleep long ago, nestled close against his side, but he had only dozed on and off for the past hour. Each time, he had awakened to this same wondrous feeling of finding her in his arms, and each time, he had realized how habit-forming this feeling could become.

He stared down at her now, hating to wake her but knowing he had to move or lose circulation in the entire left side of his body. She looked so peaceful.

Lange carefully slid from beneath her, easing her down against the cushions without waking her. He felt his heart tug with emotion, and he had the strongest urge to run. He should go now, before it was too late, before he found himself doing something stupid, like caring for her.

Who was he kidding? There was no way he could leave her, and that, alone, was proof enough that he already cared. He had spoken the truth tonight, when he vowed to keep her safe. If it were humanly possible, he would never let any harm come to her. No matter what it took, no matter how long it took, he would protect her, even if it meant sacrificing his very heart and soul to do so. He suspected that even if his own life was in danger, he would risk everything to keep her safe.

What was it about this woman that made him feel this way? If it weren't so impossible, he would think he was falling in love with her. Little else could make a man ignore his own survival instincts, to spare a woman he hardly knew. But loving her — loving any woman — was out of the question. He had given up on love long ago, and there was no hope of him ever finding it again.

As he pulled the afghan over her, he remembered another woman he had cared enough about to protect with his life. He had covered her so many nights, too, when she had come in late from a stakeout or from pulling a double shift at the police station. Lauren had been the one love of his life, his one chance at happiness. Even though she had refused to marry him, he had been a devoted husband to her.

Lange would never forget the last time he had covered Lauren. He would never forget the heartache of pulling the sheet over her face, over her unseeing eyes, to cover her for the final time. Just the memory made his hand tremble now, as he tucked the afghan firmly under Ashli's chin. Because of this heartache, because of Lauren, he could never love again. When she had died, a part of him died, as well, the part of him that could love a woman and share a life with her.

Steeling himself to the memories and the tender feelings that stirred within him as he stared down at the blonde beauty, he swore that nothing would happen to Ashli. No matter what it took, he would find a way to keep her safe. He had failed Lauren, but he would find a way to keep Ashli from meeting the same terrible fate as his first love. And somehow, some way, he would find a way to keep himself from caring too deeply about her.

Lange stretched out on the floor beside the couch, as emotionally and mentally drained as he was physically exhausted. Ashli caught him at a vulnerable time; that was why he was so drawn to her. How could he defend himself when he was so dog-tired all the time? His defenses were down, his immunity was low, especially to the kind of pampering and caring that she offered, and to the kind of heroic protection she needed. Hell, the woman had covered him with a quilt, at just the time in his life when he needed someone to tuck him in. And then she turned to him with her huge blue eyes, and she asked him to protect her, to stay with her. No man could resist a plea like that.

Lange deliberately cleared his mind, determined to get a few solid hours of sleep in what was left of the night. He wouldn't think about love and caring and quilts. He wouldn't think about women.

Daisies, he thought sleepily. He would dream of daisies.

CHAPTER NINE

She knew Lange was awake, before she even heard him stirring. She felt his eyes upon her as she moved stealthily around the kitchen. His dark gaze traced her every move. Finally, she turned and bestowed him with one of her smiles of pure sunshine. “Good morning.”

“Morning,” he said, his voice coming out gruffer than he intended. Hell, let her think he was an old grouch in the mornings; anything so she wouldn’t guess what seeing her first thing in the morning did to him. It brought back lost memories of the only home he had ever known, and how it used to feel to wake up to one of Gram’s mouth-watering country breakfasts. It made him feel like he had come home again, despite the resolutions he had made to himself last night.

“Hope you’re hungry. I made you a huge omelet.” In one fluid movement, she tilted the skillet and slid her creation onto a plate, then presented it to him.

He wanted to protest, to tell her he rarely ate breakfasts in the mornings, but the tantalizing aroma wafting up from the omelet was too much for any man to resist. He concentrated on the melted cheese and bits of ham that oozed from its center, refusing to acknowledge the feelings of tenderness that oozed from his heart. When was the last time a woman had cooked him breakfast? Diane's idea of a morning meal was donuts and coffee on the way to the office; Lauren's hadn't been much better. Grams, on the other hand, had never let him leave the house without a 'decent breakfast' in his belly.

Trying to sidetrack his traitorous mind, Lange stepped into the kitchen and opened the refrigerator. "I'll get the drinks. O.J. or milk?"

"Juice is fine," she said, sliding a much smaller omelet onto her own plate.

Both noticed how well they worked together, but neither commented. "I suppose you've already had a gallon or so of coffee," he commented, getting his own cup.

"Working on it," she agreed with a grin, holding up her mug.

As they sat at the bar and began their meal, complete with fluffy biscuits, Lange told her his plans for the day.

"I'll check out the flower shop this morning and see if they can remember the man who bought the roses. If I know anything, I'll stop by the restaurant and tell you." In no way was it an excuse to see her later in the day.

A wistful expression crossed her face as she confessed on a sigh, "The first time a man brings me flowers in ages, and I can't even enjoy them."

"I thought it was old-fashioned to bring a girl flowers," Lange said, recalling something Lauren and Diane both told him.

"No, a lady always appreciates flowers," Ashli corrected him.

"And you're nothing if not a lady, are you?" he murmured, mesmerized by the look of shy pride that glimmered in the depths of her blue eyes. He stared at her for a long moment, realizing it was that very quality that set her apart from all the other women he had known, that made him think of his grandmother and home. More than anything else, it was part of what made her so special, part of what made his heart race in such a crazy pattern. It was part of what made her the woman of his dreams.

Dreams are for fools, he reminded himself harshly. *You gave up dreaming years ago, when your dream died in your arms. Lady or not, this woman means nothing but trouble.*

"L-Lange?" Ashli asked, a frown marring her forehead. At first, his look was so tender, so worshiping, it stole her breath away. But his eyes hardened now, even as she watched them, and a mask of indifference fell over his handsome features. Ashli reached out a hand and touched his. "Lange, what's wrong?"

He jerked away as if her touch was poison. He tore his eyes from hers, unwilling to see the concern written within them, unable to bear the pain he knew he put there. She couldn't possibly understand the change that came over him, and he couldn't afford to explain it to her. Let her think he was cold and uncaring, let her think he was mean and fickle. Let her think anything, just never let her know the truth. The truth about how much he already needed her.

"Thanks for the breakfast. I have to go." He pushed away from the bar and was already halfway to the door before Ashli found her voice.

"But-but you didn't finish . . ."

He paused at the door to look back at her. With her feet bare and a smudge of flour on her cheek and the morning sunshine streaming in behind her, Lange thought she had never looked more desirable than she did right now.

Instead, he muttered his reply gruffly as he opened the door. "Lady, I can't afford to finish anything with you, no matter how delicious it is."

* * *

The noon-day crowd thinned out as Ashli brought a tray from the kitchen, piled high with scrumptious desserts. She stopped at the first table and offered the confections with an irresistible smile, leaving two behind as she moved on to the next table. By the time she reached the third table, she could feel his gaze upon her, and she looked up to find her eyes locking with Lange's.

For a moment as their eyes met and clung, Ashli was reminded of their kiss. Gazing into his dark stare, she felt the warmth and excitement of his lips upon hers. Something about this moody man made her senses come alive and her heart beat to a new rhythm. It didn't matter if he held her with his gaze or with his arms; whenever he was near, she felt something she had never experienced before in her life.

Ashli pulled her head down out of the clouds and remembered why Lange was here. Forgoing a proper greeting, she hurried toward him and asked breathlessly, "Did you find out anything?"

"Can you spare a few minutes?" he asked.

"Let me finish serving these. Care for some coffee and dessert while you wait?"

"Sounds delicious." He turned his attention to the tray of delicacies before him.

Ashli rushed through delivering the desserts, not lingering to visit with guests as she normally did. She was eager to find out what Lange had learned at the florist. She grabbed a carafe of coffee and two cups before hurrying to his table.

Lange looked up as she returned, his bread pudding already half-eaten. He wondered why she stopped in front of him and waited before being seated, but his only comment was to raise a dark eyebrow.

With a sigh of frustration, she finally muttered in irritation, "Don't bother, I'll get my own chair."

Lange belatedly realized she was waiting for him to pull her chair out for her, just as she had done that first day he met her. Recalling a time, long ago, when he had practiced such manners, he chided himself for forgetting. Ashli was the kind of woman that deserved such conduct from a man.

"Sorry," he offered. What was he supposed to do, say that neither of the women he had been involved with in the last five years had appreciated his gentlemanly manners?

Should he have to admit he had forgotten how to act around a lady?

"Never mind the chair. Just tell me what you found out."

"That yesterday was some sort of appreciation day. Secretary or teacher or something like that. But it doesn't matter, because basically what it means is that hundreds of people flooded the florists yesterday, taking advantage of the special they had on long-stemmed roses."

"What you're telling me is that the florist had so many customers yesterday, they couldn't possibly remember one man who came in and bought my roses."

"Very perceptive." Seeing the frown that appeared on her forehead, Lange reached out to place his hand on hers. "Now get that look off your face. This isn't the end of the line, you know."

"But what now, Lange? What in the world will we do now?"

"I'm working on several avenues. They couldn't trace the call, but I have a buddy down at the police station who's analyzing the recording from your voicemail. They're dusting the paper from the roses for fingerprints, seeing if we can get a hit off that. I'm checking with local hospitals and clinics, seeing if anyone came in recently with an injured foot or leg, which could explain the limp. We can go through mugshots and descriptions of known criminals, check if any are listed as having a bad leg. They'll all take a little time, but they're not hopeless." He emphasized his last words with a little squeeze of the hand. "Don't give up. I swear, I'll find the man who is stalking you."

Ashli visibly shivered. "I don't like that word," she confessed. "It sounds so sinister."

"We can't rule out possibilities," was his only reply. He withdrew his hand and began to eat again, drawing her attention away from her troubles. "This is the best bread pudding I've ever had in my life."

"Thanks. It's my grandmother's recipe."

"Where would the world of cooking be if it weren't for grandmothers?" he pondered, holding a fork full of pudding up for inspection. "Mine had to be the finest cook in the world."

"I don't know about that," Ashli argued. "Both of my grandmothers were excellent cooks."

"Mine could make chicken and dumplings out of this world. And homemade yeast rolls. And fried corn, every Sunday. Mmm, I can taste it now," Lange said, allowing himself a rare stroll down memory lane.

"One of mine was famous for her homemade breads and cobblers and pies, the other for her chocolate cakes and fried chicken and meatloaf. And this bread pudding."

"I only knew one of my grandmothers. She raised me," he revealed, caught up in his memories as he continued to stare at the delicacy on his fork.

"Your mother . . . ?" Ashli prodded, curious to know but afraid of being nosey.

". . . was just a kid herself, too young to have a kid of her own. She left me with my father, who wasn't much older and certainly no more mature. My grandmother raised me." The moment the words were out, he wondered why he had revealed so much of his life to this woman who was little more than a stranger. But one look into her sympathetic blue eyes, and he knew she was no stranger, not to his heart.

"I'm sorry, Lange, I had no idea," she whispered, wanting to reach out and touch him but finding he had constructed the wall again, the wall of indifference and cool aloofness.

"Hey, the past is the past," he said, pretending it didn't matter that neither of his parents had wanted him. "And we were talking about bread pudding, and how good this one is."

"If you like that, just wait until you taste my berry cobbler," Ashli said, a twinkle in her eyes as she attempted to lighten the mood. "I'm going this weekend to pick fresh berries, so I can make my other grandmother's cobbler recipe."

"Where do you get the berries?"

"From my parents' farm. They live about an hour away, just outside of Petersburg, and they have blackberries that grow wild all over the place. Dad said there's a bumper crop this year, so I'll have my work cut out for me."

"You're not going alone, are you?"

"Oh, I'm sure my parents and my brothers will help me."

"No, I mean driving there. You aren't thinking of driving there alone, are you?"

"Well, of course I am. I go there by myself all the time. Why shouldn't I?" But the moment she asked, she knew the answer. The twinkle in her eyes faded, as tears of frustration welled up.

"You don't need to travel by yourself," Lange reminded her as gently as he could.

"But Rachel will be gone on her trip already, and if I don't go when the berries are ripe, I might as well not go at all."

"Ask someone else to go with you."

"I don't know anyone else to ask. Not without raising my family's suspicions, that is. They don't know about any of this," she admitted. "But I guess maybe I could take Mitch. They know him already and wouldn't think much of his coming. If Brandon's still in town, we could say it was a segment for the . . ."

"No!" he broke in. "Don't take Greenway."

She looked up in surprise. His tone was so adamant, his voice so sharp. Narrowing her eyes, she said, "Don't tell me you still suspect Mitch! I told you, that's preposterous! And Brandon was a perfect gentleman last night." She couldn't help but add, "He even pulled out my chair for me."

Letting her think he was suspicious of her friends was better than letting her know the truth — that he was insanely jealous at the very thought of her going away for the weekend with another man, much less two.

"I think it would be better if I went with you," he told her, surprising them both with his announcement. He didn't know how he planned to explain his outburst, but he certainly hadn't intended to invite himself to go!

"You?"

"Yes, me," he said, trying to convince himself as much as her. "Not only could I be there to protect you, but maybe I could find out some useful information. We never discussed the possibility of your stalker being from your hometown. Maybe he's someone you know from there."

"I doubt it," she said. "I grew up there and never had anything like this ever happen. And please don't start asking a lot of questions down there. I told you, I don't want my parents to know I've hired a private detective. I don't want them to know I've having problems."

"We won't tell them."

"And how am I supposed to explain your presence?"

"It's your family, not mine. You'll think of something."

"If I bring a man home with me for the weekend, my parents will think that we're . . . involved."

"Okay, so I'll pretend to be your boyfriend." He made the announcement quite casually, waving a piece of pudding around before stuffing it into his mouth.

"We can't do that! It would be lying!" she protested.

"Then tell them the truth, that I'm your private detective."

"I-I can't do that, either." Ashli hesitated for only a moment before conceding to his plan. "I suppose we could say we've been 'seeing' each other. It wouldn't be a complete lie."

"Oh good, I won't stay awake tonight with a guilty conscience."

Ignoring his sarcasm, Ashli frowned as she thought about their scheme. In a manner uniquely her own, Ashli argued with herself over the subject. "Knowing my mother, she'll be measuring me for a wedding gown the moment you walk through the door. I hate deceiving her like this, especially since her grand ambition in life is to see me happily married and with no less than a half-dozen grandchildren for her to spoil. But if she knew the truth, it would make her sick with worry, and I won't put my family through that

. . . Okay, so we'll do it. But not a word about why you're there, all right?"

"Whatever you say," he murmured, still a bit dazed at the way she started her argument so docile, then ended so adamantly.

Having made her decision, Ashli stood from the table and gave a final nod of approval. "Then I'll see you Saturday. And remember, not a word."

CHAPTER TEN

Ashli found a quiet corner table and sat with a vanilla latte and a slice of chocolate cheesecake. The dining room was all but empty, and the last of the afternoon coffee drinkers were clearing out. Ashli's Tea Party closed in less than an hour, another week at its end.

Ashli felt particularly pensive today. She had taken Rachel and Kevin to the airport, happy to know the couple were getting a well-deserved vacation but feeling just a bit envious of her best friend's fairytale life. Returning to the Tea Party, she found that Molly Robinson had everything under control, and there was nothing left for her to do. Or perhaps the real problem was that all she had to do now was think, and somehow her thoughts kept returning to one dark-haired, ill-tempered Lange Sterling.

Taking her first bite of the sinfully rich dessert, she savored the taste of carefully blended cream and rum, thinking the dark, swirling flavors reminded her of Lange's kisses. She was oblivious to the sharp clip of high heels on the marble until someone spoke from her side.

"Excuse me. Am I intruding?"

At the sound of the unexpected voice beside her, Ashli's eyes flew open. She flushed guiltily, then smiled in relief when she saw who caught her in such an unguarded moment.

"I'm sorry to disturb you, but I just wanted to drop by and say hello," the attractive redhead apologized.

"You're not disturbing me at all. In fact, I could use the company right now." Motioning for the other woman to sit, she said, "Please, join me."

"I'm not sure if you remember me. I've been in several times."

"Of course, I remember you. You're Diane, the lawyer. You're one of my most impressive customers." Ashli smiled as the other woman slid into the wrought-iron chair across from her.

"I'm not sure how impressive I am . . ."

"Oh, very. Even though I discourage tips, your clients always leave very generous gratuities." The twinkle in her blue eyes told Diane that her words were in jest. Feigning disappointment, she looked around and said in mock dismay, "What, no rich clients today?"

"Actually, they just walked out the door. And if I'm not mistaken, I think I saw Mr. O'Toole slip a crisp new twenty-dollar bill under the edge of his napkin," Diane assured her with a laugh. "I just saw you over here and thought I would drop by to say hello."

"I'm glad you did. Have you had dessert?"

"No, but—"

Seeing Molly a few tables away, Ashli called her newest manager-in-training and motioned her over. "Molly, please bring my friend Diane a piece of cheesecake. And make certain it's just as thick as mine. I can't stand the thought of gaining ten pounds all by myself."

"That's cruel!" Diane protested with a grin, as she settled more comfortably into her chair.

Molly returned, carrying a tray with cheesecake and a carafe of coffee.

"Thank you, Molly, you're an absolute doll. And you did an excellent job this afternoon while I was gone. Why don't you take off early this afternoon? I can close up here."

"Oh, I couldn't do that. I want to do everything that Ms. Rachel does. Besides, I promised her I wouldn't leave you here alone. I'm to walk out with you every day." Her skin, as dark and creamy as the chocolate dessert she served, glowed from Ashli's praise, but her dark eyes held the commitment of the oath she had made. It was obvious she didn't make her promises lightly.

Glancing at Diane and hoping the words hadn't registered, Ashli's smile widened, but her words brooked no argument. "I appreciate your dedication, Molly. You'll make an excellent manager here for us. But I insist that you enjoy the rest of the afternoon off. It's important to me that you know what a fine job you're doing. And take the rest of the cheesecake home with you; I'm sure George will enjoy it."

Still savoring her first taste of the heavenly confection, Diane murmured in appreciation. "And who wouldn't? This is absolutely divine."

When Ashli's only reply was a smile of thanks, Diane sensed that something was wrong. "Is everything all right? I think this is the first time I've ever seen you not beaming. You're always so cheerful and bright, but today you seem rather distracted."

"Ah, I see what makes you a brilliant lawyer. You're very perceptive." Ashli sidestepped the issue with a teasing smile.

"And very persistent. You didn't answer the question."

Toying with her food, Ashli wasn't sure how to put her strange mood into words. Finally, she settled on a partial truth. "I just took my best friend to the airport. She's going on a second honeymoon with the man she adores, and I've never even found a man to go on my first honeymoon with. I guess I'm feeling sorry for myself."

"I know exactly how you feel," Diane admitted with a long sigh. Suddenly losing her own appetite, she made idle designs in the cheesecake. "I just broke up with my boyfriend. Or rather, he broke up with me."

"Big fight?"

"No, nothing like that. He just came in and told me it was over."

"That sounds rather cold." Ashli frowned.

"You know, if we had had a fight, it would make it easier to accept, easier to deal with. I would have a reason to be mad at him, a reason to stop caring. But it wasn't like that at all. It was just . . . over."

"Did he say why?"

"I think he's falling in love with one of his clients," Diane admitted.

Assuming her ex-boyfriend was a lawyer such as herself, Ashli sympathized with her friend. "I've recently discovered that business and personal relationships don't mix very well. It's too hard to draw the line at where one ends and the other begins."

"Hmmm, I think I know what you mean. But it doesn't make the ending any easier. And it doesn't make the regrets go away. I keep thinking I should have been more domestic, more nurturing to his needs."

"And here I am, wishing I was a little *less* domestic, a little more exciting."

"More exciting than being a successful businesswoman and television star?" Diane asked. "And do I detect a man in there somewhere? Have you met someone?"

Ashli hesitated a moment before denying the truth that even a casual acquaintance could see. But the fact she *was* a casual acquaintance, someone she could confide in without answering to, made Diane somehow easier to talk to than Rachel, at least when it came to Lange Sterling. After all, Rachel didn't quite approve of her attraction to the handsome detective, but Diane didn't even know him. For the first time, she could admit her feelings without having them analyzed.

"He's way out of my league," she finally conceded.

"Why on earth would you think that?"

"Look at me. Here I am in my sensible flat shoes and my serviceable blue dress. And there you are in your fashionable suit and heels. Next to you, I look like chopped liver."

Her eyes alight with laughter, Diane pushed her uneaten cheesecake aside. "Girlfriend, I may not be Betty Crocker, but even I know what chopped liver looks like. And believe me, you're more in the league of prime rib. You just don't come with all the trimmings."

"Because I don't know what trimmings to use. It's . . . been a while since I had a man in my life," Ashli admitted.

"Is this man interested in you, too?"

"He kisses me like he is."

"Then you need to make a few alterations to your wardrobe. Necklines lower, hemlines higher. With your coloring, you would be dynamite in red."

"I'd probably look like a hooker!" Ashli laughed at the ridiculous vision she had of herself in the short, tight, daring red dress.

But when Diane said in a sultry drawl, "Now you're getting the general idea." Ashli's mouth went suddenly dry. Just the thought of an intimate relationship with Lange took her breath away.

"Listen to me," Diane said with a derisive sigh. "I'm one to give advice on how to catch a man. I couldn't even keep the one I had."

"Well," Ashli offered, wanting to return the favor of helpful advice, "if you think the way to your man's heart is through his stomach, I may have the road map you're looking for."

"I think I need an entire atlas but go on."

"You need to invite him over for a nice, hot, home-cooked meal."

"You must be joking. I can't even boil water without scorching the pan."

"But I know a terrific little bistro that specializes in nice home-cooked food," Ashli said with a twinkle of mischief in her eye.

"Why, you sneaky little thing, you. And you look so sweet and innocent. I love it!" Diane pronounced with glee.

Their appetites suddenly restored, the women finished their cheesecake with lighter spirits.

CHAPTER ELEVEN

He would never admit it, even to himself, but excitement stirred within Lange at the thought of spending the weekend with Ashli. He told himself it was the anticipation of a professional challenge, the rush of adrenalin he always felt when he was closing in on a case. He told himself it had nothing to do with spending two days in the company of the woman who occupied his dreams every night; he insisted that it had nothing to do with hair like sunshine and eyes as blue as the bluest sky.

But even he knew he lied.

He was at her condo early, ready to start their day. For the briefest of moments, he wondered what to wear to make the best impression on her family. But as quickly as the thought entered his mind, a rebellious anger had driven it away. It had been years — if ever — since he worried about impressing a girl's father; damn if he would start now! With a defiant streak of independence, he jerked on a faded denim work shirt, soft and frayed from countless washings. After all, he was going there to work, not to win the approval of Ashli's family.

Still, he wasn't sure he had made the right choice until he saw Ashli. And by that time, it didn't matter at all what he was wearing; all eyes would be on her. His were, at least. It was the first time he had ever seen her in jeans. And it was the first time he had ever felt envy toward a piece of fabric.

Yet there it was. A ridiculous yearning to be the soft faded denim that hugged her body in places he only dreamed of caressing. Even the simple pink T-shirt was draped across her body as sensuously as silk, drawing his eyes to her generous breasts and narrow waistline. The clothes she wore weren't tight, not revealing, not even suggestive, but his overactive mind had dozens of suggestions on ways to get her out of them.

Unaware of the scandalous thoughts he entertained, Ashli handed him one last bucket to load into the back of his pickup truck. "Okay, that should be enough."

"How many cobblers are you planning to make, woman?"

"Remember, the berries cook down, so it won't make nearly as many as you think." She absently wiped her hands clean by brushing them against the seat of her jeans, then tucked her hands into her back pockets.

Damn, she was a tease and didn't even know it! She struck an alluring pose, yet somehow managed to look like a little girl, with her hair up in a ponytail and a flush of anticipation on her face.

"It still looks like you're planning to cook for Lee's army," he grumbled, making room for the last bucket. "You'll have to put your suitcase in the cab, behind the seat."

Ashli started to lift the suitcase into the truck's interior, then stopped short. Seeing her hesitation, Lange sighed audibly and came around to where she stood.

"I forgot again, didn't I?" he muttered, reaching down for the case in belated gentlemanly fashion.

"No, it's not that. He's watching me. I can feel him watching me again, Lange."

"Are you sure?" His voice fell to a low whisper. Without turning his head, his eyes scanned the area.

"Positive." Her hand reached out to grab his arm for security.

"I want you to get into the truck and close the door. I'll take the suitcase around to my side. Lock the door behind you; unlock it for me after I get around."

"Lange, I'm scared," she whispered. Her wide eyes spoke for themselves.

"There's no reason to be. I'm right here. Walking around to the other side will give me a chance to look behind us. Can you tell which way he is?"

"No, just that he's watching."

"Okay, you get into the truck now and slowly close the door. We don't want to arouse his suspicions."

Ashli did as she was told, resisting the urge to look over her shoulder. Lange closed the door for her, for once acting the part of gentleman even though neither of them cared just now. As he carried the suitcase around to the driver's side, he scanned the neighborhood with keen, thorough eyes.

"Do you see anyone?" she whispered as he worked to fit the suitcase in. He exaggerated the close fit, which gave him more time to stand outside the truck, his eyes steadily moving.

"Not really. An elderly man watering the flowers, the paperboy on his bike, a couple of kids playing on the sidewalk. Up the street there's a car, but it looks like teenagers gathered around it, and none seems to be looking our way. I saw a person in the window across the street at the condos, a middle-aged woman, I think. No one else seems to be out this morning."

"He's out," she insisted, "and he's watching."

After stalling a few moments longer, Lange finally secured the suitcase and slid behind the wheel. "Okay, while I start the motor. Let me know if you can see anyone suspicious, anyone who's not normally out this time of day, that sort of thing. Try not to be too obvious."

Ashli saw nothing unusual on this beautiful late spring day. As the truck rolled slowly down the street, she lifted her hand in greeting to Mr. Parnell and Jimmy the paperboy, who returned her wave enthusiastically. No one else seemed to notice their departure as they slowly disappeared around the corner and soon, out of town.

"Tell me again," Lange said as they drove toward Petersburg. "Before the Peeping Tom and shopping incidents, had anything strange happened?"

Ashli pursed her lips, mulling over things she originally dismissed as being unimportant. She waded through some of those events in her mind, deciding which merited telling him about. "There were a few things," she admitted. "At the time, I didn't think much about them, but looking back, I have to wonder . . ."

"Like what? What sort of things happened?"

"Like one time, when I was taking my garbage out. I remembered something else I wanted to throw away, so I set the bag down outside and went back up. When I came back out, the garbage bag was gone. I just assumed it was Mr. Parnell or Todd being nice, but when I thanked them, they both denied knowing anything about it."

"Hmm. Okay, what else?"

"About a week later, I came home from work, and my door was unlocked. I could have sworn I locked it before I left, but there was nothing missing, nothing out of place, so I decided it was simply an oversight on my part."

"And when was this?"

"I don't know, about . . . three weeks before the first Peeping Tom incident, probably. Actually," she said, giving it more thought, "I know exactly when it was. It was the last week of April, right after we had our movie night. That was the night Mr. Parnell got so upset with Jason Madison. I actually decided that maybe he had gone in to check out my air conditioner and forgot to lock the door behind him."

"Jason Madison has a key to your apartment?" he asked.

"No, silly, I was talking about Mr. Parnell. No way would I give Jason Madison a key."

"Why did Mr. Parnell get upset with Madison?"

"We were having movie night, when we play old movies on the projector against the carriage house wall. It's the perfect canvas, by the way, a solid brick wall on the side facing the gardens. We pull up lawn chairs and pop popcorn and have a nice night outdoors, visiting and watching movies." By now, Lange was growing accustomed to her roundabout answers. "Mr. Parnell still has his old projector and lots of old movies, especially anything filmed by Doris Day. He's like her biggest fan. Which is fine by me, since I enjoy watching her, especially when so many people think I sound like her. Anyway, that night we were watching *Lover Come Back* with Rock Hudson.

"It came to the scene where Doris Day is considering changing into something 'more comfortable' and coming back to his room. Jason was joining us that night, which was unusual, but I think it was probably because Jasmine was home, and of course she is absolutely beautiful, a fact not lost upon dear Jason. Anyway, he made some snide comment to Jasmine about the scene, and they snickered. Mr. Parnell got upset. I mean very, very upset. He demanded an apology from Jason, as if he were protecting the honor of Doris Day. I don't remember what all was said, but it rattled Mr. Parnell. He was just . . . off for several days after that."

"What do you mean 'off'?"

"Not his usual jovial self. Very short-tempered. Forgetful, too. I know he's getting older and more forgetful, some days more than others, but for about a week after that, he was distracted. I didn't want to make him feel bad about not locking my door, so I never said anything about it to him."

"You don't know if he went in your apartment that day or not?"

"No, but he did go in at some point. About a week later, he told me everything looked fine, and I could start running the air."

"What did Madison say when all this happened?"

"Some rather unkind things. Called him old and made remarks about his obsession with Doris Day and with his garden, especially his daisies. I do have to say, the man takes great pride in those plants. Feeds them some special diet mixture that he stirs up himself. It smells awful, but it must work; our gardens are fabulous. Have you ever walked through them?"

"No," he admitted, thinking that was something he probably should have done. He made a mental note to explore the extensive backyard of Daisy House when they returned.

"The property line actually goes back all the way to the street behind us. There are some amazing flower-lined trails, and Mr. Parnell has a vegetable garden back there, too. Every spring and fall, the gardens are open to the public during the Richmond Home and Garden Show. We even shot a summer episode of *Ashli's Kitchen* in the gardens last year."

"You say it goes out to Redmond Street?"

"Yes. If you'll notice, there's what looks like an empty lot between the gingerbread house and the two-story brick on Redmond Street, but it's just the tree line behind the gardens."

"Hmm, I'll definitely check that out. That might be how your stalker is approaching the house."

"I hadn't thought of that." Ashli released a heavy sigh. "The gardens are so beautiful, especially the different varieties of daisies. Now I guess I'll have to think of those as sinister, too."

Hating the sound of dejected woe in her voice, Lange attempted to lighten the mood. "The old man has a thing for Doris Day, huh?"

"I suppose. He has all her movies and records and even some autographed photos of her."

"I was once accused of having a thing for her, too," he admitted, recalling Diane's tirade the night he broke up with her. Had that only been a few days ago? He hadn't given his former on-again, off-again lover as much as a thought since then.

"Which of her movies is your favorite?" Ashli asked.

"I like the comedies."

"Really?" Ashli cocked her head sideways and spoke in that whispery voice that sounded so much like the movie star herself. "I would have thought you more the *Midnight Lace* sort. Or a *The Man Who Knew Too Much* fan."

"Not when it comes to Doris."

* * *

They reached the farm about an hour later.

As they pulled into the white gravel drive, Ashli's sigh of relief was audible. She was home. She was safe here, away from the prying eyes of her stalker, away from the dangers of the city. There was no feeling in the world like the one she had now, this feeling of utter and complete security.

As her eyes eagerly roamed over her family's home, and she drew strength from its very sight, Lange's sharp eyes surveyed the scene before them. A neat, modest yard with blooming flowers and a covered porch swing. A sturdy old white farmhouse that had weathered the years and the elements and the people who lived there, sheltered beneath a half-dozen ageless old trees. He instinctively knew this was a home where love abided, where a stranger was always welcome. Lange felt something tug at his heart, stirring up memories of how it had once felt to have had a home, to truly belong. Those memories, along with the image of his grandmother's similar homestead, had been long buried within the empty pit of his heart but were awakened again by the sight of Ashli's childhood home.

"Now remember," she whispered as they walked up the cobblestone path to the front porch, "not a word about why you're here."

"Of course, sweetheart," he crooned, taking her elbow and giving it a gentle squeeze. "I am, after all, a professional."

The door opened before they reached the porch. Even without the introductions, Lange knew the smiling faces belonged to Ashli's parents. She took her coloring from her father, a fair-haired man with a fatherly countenance and kind, gentle eyes. Her features were those of her mother, a woman whose beauty had matured with age and whose smile could still turn a man's head.

After hugging both parents, Ashli made the introductions. "Mom, Dad, I want you to meet a friend of mine, Lange Sterling. Lange, my parents, Alice and Albert Wilson." Ashli was nervous, once again afraid of what they might read into his presence. She was even more afraid of how he might deliberately act to confirm their misguided suspicions.

"Nice to have you here, young man," Albert said, extending his hand. He liked the way Lange shook his hand in a firm, steady grip and the way he looked him right in the eye to speak.

"Thank you for having me, sir. Ma'am, nice to meet you. You have a lovely place here."

Ashli resisted the urge to turn around and stare. Was that Lange Sterling speaking in such cordial, respectful tones? She nearly stumbled over her own feet as she followed her parents inside, but Lange's hand caught her elbow in a firm, possessive grip. Had she not known it was only pretend, her heart might have melted right then and there when he looked down at her with tender concern.

Ashli soon discovered that when it came to keeping his cover, the man was a professional. No one could have guessed that his presence there was for business reasons only. For the first time, Ashli saw a glimpse of what she suspected might be the real Lange Sterling, a man of charm and grace and genteel breeding. There was no sarcasm in his voice when he talked with her two younger brothers Adam and Andy, no harsh, clipped tones when he visited with her parents. He appeared relaxed and at ease in the home she had grown up in, and if he noticed the dazed expression of disbelief that occasionally crossed her face, he never showed it.

Instead, he gently teased her, as if he found everything she said and did utterly fascinating, as if he were an adoring boyfriend who had come to make a good impression on her family. He didn't smother her with embarrassing kisses or clinging hands, but he played his part of a smitten suitor with great finesse. It was mostly in the way his hand touched hers, the way he hovered at her side without being intrusive, the way his eyes followed her when she left the room. It was the way he said her name, the way his eyes lingered on her lips when she spoke, the way a slow smile would spread across his face whenever her eyes lifted to his.

By day's end, the Wilson family was convinced Lange Sterling was the best thing that had ever happened to Ashli.

He was a hard worker, picking twice as many berries as anyone else.

Along the fencerows and down the small country roads, blackberries grew wild and thick, and it didn't take long to fill their buckets with the plump offerings. Lange carried the harvested berries back to the house, where he covered them with towels on the back porch to keep them moist and cool. When they broke for a light lunch, Lange insisted on helping Albert with a few chores around the house, and when they finished picking berries for the day, he asked for a tour of the farm. While he went off with her father and brothers to see their pride and joy, Ashli spent the time hearing how much her mother liked the young man she brought home.

"Mom, I know how much you want grandchildren, but don't read too much into this. I've only known him a few weeks, and I just brought him along so he could help with the berries," Ashli warned her mother as they sat in the kitchen peeling vegetables.

"Your father used to look at me like that," Alice said, a faraway smile on her face. "We had only known each other for a few days, but somehow we knew we would spend the rest of our lives together. Your young man reminds me of your father at that age, so dashing and charming. And so handsome. His eyes are so dark and mysterious . . ."

Ashli murmured a denial, but the truth was, his eyes were dark and mysterious. And despite herself, she found it impossible not to be affected by those eyes and the way they followed her every move. She knew it was all pretend, that Lange was just keeping his end of the bargain, but for the life of her, she couldn't keep her heart from fluttering when he acted out the part of the adoring boyfriend. She found his dark, watchful gaze as tantalizing as any kiss he might give her, his light touch as possessive as any grip he might hold her with. The man truly was a professional, attacking his assignment with a thoroughness that left her nerves distraught and her heart badly out of rhythm.

When the men returned, Ashli found a moment to pull Lange aside and whisper a warning to him. "You're going just a little overboard on this thing, aren't you?"

"Why, darlin', I don't know what you mean," Lange drawled, his eyes tracing the curve of her lips with infuriating fascination.

"Stop it!" she hissed, her heart thudding in a way that made her angrier. "Just stop it!"

"But honeybunch, I thought you wanted your family to think I was your boyfriend, not your bodyguard." He reached out to encircle her waist with his arms and drag her up against him. His voice was low, the tone a murmured caress so no one could ever guess what he said.

Knowing her family was already gathering around the dining room and could easily see into the living room where they stood, Ashli tried her best to look relaxed in his embrace. "The way you're acting, they're going to think we came here to announce our engagement!" she whispered in exasperation.

"I told you I was a professional," he said, finding her discomfort amusing.

"Yes, but I thought you meant private detective, not a professional gigolo!" she hissed.

When he chuckled, she could feel the rumble of his chest against her own. It occurred to her that today was the first time she had ever heard him truly laugh, and she cocked her head to one side, wondering for the hundredth time about his past and who he was, deep beneath the rough exterior.

"Have I done one thing to suggest anything but respectful intentions? I thought I was being a perfect gentleman. Besides, I think your family likes me."

"I know they do. How will I explain your behavior a month from now, when this mess is all cleared up? They'll want to know why you never came back, why we aren't still dating, why we're not married by then, for heaven's sake! You've done such a convincing job of being my boyfriend, they'll never believe our breakup!" she complained in a hiss.

"We'll say the fresh air and sunshine went to my head, and I was temporarily intoxicated," he teased. Yet when he lowered his head to nuzzle the blonde strands, he knew the joke was on him.

God, he was intoxicated. He was intoxicated with *her*, with her very essence, her very nearness. Today had been the easiest assignment of his life, pretending to be falling in love with her. Even though he knew it was impossible, that it could never and would never happen, it was easy to pretend otherwise. All he had to do was pretend that he still had a heart, that he still had the capacity to care about a woman. That he still believed in love and dreams and being part of a family.

"Just remember," she warned, reaching up to smooth away an imaginary wrinkle from the breadth of his shoulder, "I have to live down whatever you make up."

Her touch seemed to take him by surprise. When her hand lingered for a moment too long, she could feel the sudden pounding of his heart. Stunned, she looked up into his eyes and felt her breath catch in her throat. The teasing light was gone now, replaced by a glow so tender and so new, she knew it had to be real. There was nothing 'pretend' about the shudder of realization that passed between them, settling somewhere in the weakened support of her knees, echoing poetically in the ragged intake of his breath.

"God, so do I." The words could have been spoken aloud on a sigh or held forever silent in his eyes. She tasted the words on his lips, as ever so slowly, his mouth descended upon hers. He kissed her slowly, and the act was so sweet and reverent, Ashli felt a bittersweet longing seep into her heart. Even as he kissed her, she wondered how something could feel so beautiful and so painful, all at one time.

It wasn't a passionate kiss, not like most they had shared. This kiss was a cool drink of water on a warm summer day, a long draw of bourbon on a cold rainy night. It was warmth and shelter and a place to come home to. It was slow and meaningful, and it was intoxicating.

In the drunken euphoria that followed, they pulled slowly apart, both trembling. A silly smile broke between them, making words unnecessary. It was perhaps the single most beautiful moment in her entire life, but its magical spell was broken when Ashli's mother called them for dinner.

Lange ate his meal with a healthy appetite, but it wasn't the food that held his attention. It was the family gathered around the dining room table. It was the laughter and good conversation. It was the feeling of belonging. Watching Ashli argue good naturedly with her brothers, Lange wondered what it would have been like to grow up with siblings and not as an only, lonely child. He wondered what it would have been like to have parents who smiled at you with pride in their eyes. He wondered what it would be like to raise his own family, to have his own children gathered around the table for a family meal. A table where Ashli joined him.

An intense longing swept over him, stealing his very breath away, shattering his aloof shield of indifference. Just for a moment, the raw need to belong was revealed in his eyes, ones that searched out the face of the woman responsible for his vulnerable state of mind. He realized then that she had been watching him, that she had seen his deepest, innermost thoughts, that he had been naked before her. What was that in her eyes, compassion?

Or was it pity?

Hell, he could stand anything except her pity. He didn't want her to feel sorry for him, he didn't want her to coddle him like some little boy without a mother. In that instant, as he struggled for control of his emotions, he convinced himself he didn't want *anything* from her, that he didn't need her at all.

A defiant light flared in his eyes as his gaze suddenly turned cold. He knew that his abrupt change would take her by surprise, even before he saw the shock register on her face. He knew he was hurting her, even before he saw her eyes turn a clouded, murky blue. He knew he was being cruel, but it was his only choice. Let her think he was a cold, uncaring fool.

Just don't let her pity him.

CHAPTER TWELVE

Ashli's family was oblivious to the sudden strain that erupted between her and Lange. Andy and Adam became involved in a heated debate about football and wanted Lange to settle their argument. He went along with their request, his demeanor toward her family not changing, but Ashli now knew him well enough to detect the tightness around his mouth and the clench in his jaw. Both belied his relaxed attitude.

It was a relief when the meal was over. Her brothers excused themselves, citing plans in town, and Alice recruited Albert's help with the dishes, which left Ashli alone with her silent, brooding guest.

With an entire evening stretching out before them and her parents expecting them to spend time alone, Ashli decided to take Lange on a historical driving tour of her hometown. It was too late to go inside many of the places, but she drove him past Farmers Bank that had been built in 1817, pointed out the Siege Museum, drove through the historical district of Old Towne and past many of the fine old homes that graced the city. Finally, they ended up at the National Battlefield, where she parked her mother's borrowed car near the ranger's station and proceeded to take him on a tour by foot. As darkness hovered, they found they were the only visitors in the park at so late an hour.

A hush seemed to fall around them on their self-guided walking tour. It was near twilight, a peaceful time of day when even the birds seemed to pay reverence to the shrine of human sacrifice. Only an occasional whippoorwill broke the stillness of the evening, somehow making the battlefield of so long ago come alive with its misery and pain. When they reached the crater, they stood near the sunken earth that had meant death for thousands of brave soldiers and listened to the chilling account of war as it was related in the automated recording. Even now, it was difficult to look at the pit where 4,000 Union soldiers had perished in a grave of their own making. The winds of war had blown away, the passage of years had mended the deep rip within the country's fabric, yet the deep cavity in the earth remained.

Staring into the sunken remains, Ashli shivered, and Lange turned cynical.

"That's what happens when people get too confident, when they think they have outsmarted the enemy. The minute they let their defenses down, the minute they get careless — bam — the enemy strikes again. And this time, he wins." His voice was cold and bitter, leaving Ashli with a chill.

"You're not talking about a hundred-and-fifty-year-old battle, are you?" Ashli asked. He spoke with such vengeance, Ashli suspected it had something to do with his strange mood, something to do with the wall he had constructed around himself. She glanced up at him questioningly, but his face was closed.

"I'm talking about life," he snorted, pushing away from the fence surrounding the mouth of the hole. He turned and headed for the car, leaving her no choice but to follow.

If he thought their 'date' was over, Lange soon was to discover differently. Leaving the battlefield, Ashli drove to the Blandford Church and cemetery. She stopped to show him the beautiful stained-glass windows of the church, then drove down the many rows of dirt paths that checkered the cemetery as twilight crowded near.

"Louis Comfort Tiffany created the church windows," Ashli explained. "Each window was donated by a different Southern state in memory of the sons they had lost. Over 30,000 Confederate soldiers are buried here; this entire side of the cemetery contains graves from the Civil War. There are even some tombstones here dating back to the 1700s, including some of my ancestors."

"Why are you pulling over? Where are you going?"

"I like to look at this monument that honors each of the Southern states and their losses. Just beyond it is the grave of my great-great-grandfather. He was killed during the fall of Petersburg."

Lange glanced around, uncomfortable being in a cemetery. He followed her reluctantly as she began to read aloud the tribute to the fallen states and the brave soldiers who had died.

"How can you read that? It's getting too dark to see," he grumbled.

"Mostly from memory," she admitted. "I've been reading it since I was a little girl."

"Hasn't anyone ever told you it's morbid to play in cemeteries?" he muttered, following her lead to the old tombstone beyond.

Ashli knelt beside the old headstone, ignoring Lange's overall attitude. She lightly ran her fingers over the inscription as she mused aloud. "He was only twenty-eight years old. That's so young to die. So young to give up his life, simply out of honor for a cause."

Was it Lange's voice that spoke in the gathering darkness, so soft and low and reverent? "It was something he believed in, something he was willing to die for."

Ashli moved from beside the grave to gently perch upon the stone. Her voice was little more than a whisper on the wind as she asked softly, "Who was it, Lange? Who did you lose?"

He was silent for a moment, staring out at the thousands of stones that marked the loss of life. He felt the loss in his own heart, as if each of the graves held a piece of him. The stones glowed an eerie white in the twilight, reflecting in the darkness of his eyes when at last he spoke.

"It might be easier to name who I didn't lose. My father died when I was just a kid, and God only knows if my mother is still living. To me, she's always been dead. My best friend died when I was nineteen, my grandmother just six months later. And Lauren . . . Lauren died five years ago."

Ashli bit her lip as she listened to the changes in his deep voice. The bitterness when he spoke of his parents turned to sadness at the loss of his grandmother and friend, but when he spoke of his Lauren, there was pure heartache in his voice.

"Who was Lauren?" she whispered. A part of her wanted to know about his past, yet something in her heart begged her not to ask, knowing the truth might be too painful to hear.

When he didn't answer, she guessed. "Your wife?"

"We didn't have a piece of paper, if that's what you mean. But yes, we were married, in all the ways that mattered." He took a deep breath, and then the words just seemed to tumble out as he stared out into the cemetery, no longer seeing. "She didn't believe in the roles of marriage because she said love should be free and unbinding. I used to tease her that she was just afraid of becoming a housewife. She couldn't cook to save her soul. We ate out mostly, and we had a maid to come in once a week because she hated to clean house. To say the least, she wasn't very domestic." A faded smile appeared on his face, wavering as he drew in a long, unsteady breath.

"She had big brown eyes that snapped with anger whenever I tried to pamper her. She was, to put it lightly, very independent. But for all her unconventional independence, she was one hell of a cop. She put everything into her career." He paused for a significant moment before adding, "Including her last breath of life."

"What-what happened?"

"She was on the force, and she died in the line of duty. She had just done a brilliant piece of work on organized crime, and the big boys were behind bars. But their payroll still walked the streets, and the minute she let her guard down . . . She walked right into their ambush. And I wasn't there to help her, I wasn't there to protect her." If she heard heartache in his voice earlier, it was nothing like the sheer anguish he revealed now.

"Oh, Lange, I'm so sorry," she whispered. She moved toward him, wanting to offer comfort, but the moment her hand touched his arm, he jerked away. The look in his eyes was more chilling than any she had ever seen before.

"Don't!" he commanded. Just a hint of desperation crept into the bitterness of his words. "Don't you understand? My heart lies in another cemetery, in another grave. When I buried Lauren, I buried a part of myself. The part that knows how to treat a woman, the part that knows how to care." His words were harsh. "I'm dead inside, Ashli. I go through the motions of living, but I don't have a heart, not anymore. Don't waste your time trying to mend a heart that doesn't exist. And don't forget why I'm here in the first place," he added. "That kiss earlier meant nothing. I'm only doing a job."

Silence surrounded them. Ashli knew no words to say that could comfort him, no words that would comfort herself. She was devastated by his brutal denial of their kiss. There was a long, tense moment when they both struggled to get their emotions under control, but finally she spoke.

"I'm sorry I brought you here," she said.

Neither spoke as they walked to the car and drove back to the farm. But when they reached the house, Lange took her arm in the shadows of the porch and stopped her before she went inside.

"About what I said in the cemetery . . ." His voice was low and a bit hesitant.

"Forget it, Lange. I understand."

"I didn't mean to sound cruel."

She didn't quite meet his eyes. "It's okay. I was prying. I shouldn't ask so many personal questions. It's just that . . . today . . ."

"Today was make believe. Today we were pretending." His voice was so low and so deep, it had to scrape past his heart to come out.

"I know." Her whispered voice held an emptiness he had never heard before. "It's just that . . . you know everything about me, and I know nothing about you."

"You're my client, Ashli. It's my job to know all about you."

"I know."

"I can't get personally involved with my clients. I might lose my objectivity." His voice, still low, had lost its gruff edge.

"I know that, too." Her voice, still whispered, no longer sounded so empty; now it sounded as if it were filled with pain.

He forced the next words out, husky and deep. "We could never be involved, Ashli."

"No, never."

* * *

The ride home on Sunday was the longest of Ashli's life; one hour of pure agony as they drove into Richmond, neither speaking. It was easier to pretend she was sleeping, even though her senses were very much awake in the small confines of the truck. It was impossible to ignore the handsome man sitting behind the wheel, impossible not to smell the clean, masculine scent of his cologne, impossible not to remember the way it felt to be held within his strong embrace. But with her eyes closed, it was at least possible to keep the tears from blurring her vision when she thought of how he had said their kiss yesterday meant nothing.

Oh, but it had meant something! It meant something magical was happening to them, something beyond either of their control. It meant a new fairy tale was being born, that somewhere a new poem was written, a new song sung, a new masterpiece painted. A new treasure had been discovered, and it was safely tucked into the sacred secrets of their hearts.

Her heart, at least. Ashli spent most of the trip wondering how she could have misunderstood that kiss so completely.

Once back in Richmond, Lange helped her deliver half the berries to the restaurant, half to her apartment. He insisted on going in each place first and checking out every room in her apartment before letting her past the door.

"It looks like everything is in order here," he told her as he brought in the last of the buckets. He glanced around again, seeing a perfectly normal setting. Yet there was an awkward silence in the apartment, a silence of their own making. He looked slightly uncomfortable as he took a retreating step toward the door. "I guess I'll shove off."

Ashli's smile was deceptively bright as she avoided meeting his eyes. "Sure, I can manage from here just fine. Thanks for bringing in the berries."

She turned away to rummage through her cabinets for colanders to wash the berries. Lange hesitated, repeating himself unnecessarily. "Then I guess I'll go."

When still he lingered, Ashli had little choice but to finally abandon her task and look at him. His eyes, however, dropped the gaze she turned upon him. He seemed to study the floor between them, searching for a clue on what to say next. "Be careful," he finally said, his voice oddly strained.

"I will."

"Lock the door behind me."

"Okay."

He turned away at last, his hand on the doorknob, but still he hesitated.

"Lange?" Her whispered soft voice reached across the silence of the room, causing his heart to jump.

"Yeah?" He dared not turn back, for fear of how beautiful she would look.

"Thank you for going with me this weekend. I appreciate all the work you did, picking berries and all."

"It's been a long time since I picked berries. I enjoyed it."

"Well, I-I just wanted to say thank you. Especially for not letting on to my family about why you were there. Thank you for keeping my secret and playing along."

He opened the door, speaking without turning around. "Problem is, I enjoyed that, too."

The words, hastily spoken, seemed to choke from his throat. He rushed quickly out, without even saying goodbye.

CHAPTER THIRTEEN

After a restless night, Ashli's day started out badly and continued to get worse.

When she stepped out on the veranda to water her plants that morning, she found a single rhododendron bloom lying near the door. Resisting the urge to call Lange in a panic, she struggled to convince herself it was a hapless accident. Obviously, Mr. Parnell had been trimming the plants and somehow a bloom had inadvertently ended up on her patio. A high wind had blown it there, or someone — probably Jason Madison — found it and tossed it up toward her window. There was no significance to the flower, she was sure. And she certainly wouldn't call Lange first thing this morning, not after all the things he had said.

Still, discovery of the flower worried her as she drove to work. What if it had some significance to her case? What if the stalker had put it there? Did it mean he had been to her apartment over the weekend? Should she call Lange, after all?

She had little time to ponder the questions once she arrived at the Tea Party. Two workers called in sick with stomach flu, and the internet was down, interrupting credit card sales and all online business. By the time the long day at the restaurant was finally over and she got to the studio where more troubles ensued, the flower was completely forgotten. Technical difficulties delayed filming, and frazzled nerves made for terse, awkward scenes. It was well past ten o'clock when Ashli left the studio and almost eleven when she arrived home.

She was looking forward to a long hot bath and a glass of wine, but the moment she opened the door to Daisy House, Ashli knew neither would happen anytime soon. She found Mr. Parnell in the lobby, looking particularly vulnerable. His gray hair stuck up in all directions as he paced the floor with an uneven gait, mumbling to himself. Ashli had seen him like this on only two other occasions, but neither time was as drastic as this.

"Doris? Is that you?" the old man said when he saw her come through the door.

Ashli's heart went out to him. He was confusing her with his late wife again. "No, Mr. Parnell, it's me, Ashli."

"Ashli?" He stared at her with an empty gaze.

"What can I do for you, Mr. Parnell? Can I help you to your apartment?"

"No. I need to water the daisies. I need to mix more fertilizer."

The old man was clearly confused. Ashli sighed as she set her load down on the stairs and went to aid her friend. "Why don't you wait until the morning to do that, Mr. Parnell?" she suggested, though her voice was loud so he could hear. "It's too dark outside to get much done tonight. I think you should wait till morning."

"Dark?" He seemed surprised to hear that.

"Yes, sir. Why don't I help you to your apartment? Have you had supper tonight, Mr. Parnell? I'd be happy to fix you a bite to eat."

"No, no, Doris will have supper cooking. I saw she had a nice pot roast in the oven."

"Mr. Parnell, maybe I should call your nurse."

"Nurse? Why do I need a nurse?" He looked even more confused. When he frowned, wrinkles swallowed his forehead. "Am I sick?"

"You have a nurse to keep you well." Ashli took his arm and tried to gently tug him toward his apartment door. "Let's get you settled in, and I'll call her."

The old man allowed her to lead him for a few steps, still murmuring about his wife and the dinner she had cooking. Despite his advanced age, he was hardly frail. At over six feet tall, his shoulders were only slightly stooped, and his arms were still muscled and strong. Ashli knew that if he balked, there was no way she could guide him into the apartment.

"My fertilizer . . ." he protested, coming to an abrupt halt.

"Yes, sir, your fertilizer is stored away in the shed, safe and sound." At least, she hoped it was. "You can put it out first thing tomorrow."

"But I've got to mix it up first!"

"You can do that tomorrow, too. Remember, it's too dark to see tonight."

"Is it night already?" He looked toward the door in surprise, searching for daylight.

"Yes, sir, and time for bed. Let's get you inside and all settled in."

"No! No, you can't come in!" he said with sudden vehemence. They had reached the door, and he stopped in front of it to bar her way.

"Are you sure I can't come inside and fix you a bite to eat?"

"No. Doris don't allow no one inside her kitchen but herself."

"Mr. Parnell, I think I should call your nurse."

"Why? Doris don't allow her in there, neither. Both of you best stay out of Doris's kitchen, if you know what's good for you."

Perplexed by his sudden defiance, Ashli wasn't sure what to do. She hated to leave him alone when he was so clearly confused, but he was adamant about her not coming into the apartment. It had been a long day, and she was in no mood to argue with him. Since she had the number for his home healthcare nurse programmed in her cell phone, she would simply call Veronica and let her handle him.

"All right, Mr. Parnell. I won't come in tonight, if you'll promise me you'll go on inside and get ready for bed. Can you do that for me?"

He smiled, suddenly looking like his old self. "You know, Miss Ashli, I think that's a good idea. I am a might tuckered out. Good night, now, and you sleep well."

"Good night, Mr. Parnell."

She waited until he entered the apartment and closed the door, then found her cell phone and scrolled down to Veronica's name. She made the call to the nurse as she ascended the stairs, trying to keep her voice low so she wouldn't disturb her neighbors. As she neared the top of the steps, she could see Jasmine's door open.

"Thank you, Veronica," she said into the phone. "I hated to disturb you this late, but he seems terribly confused. If I can help you at all, I'll be up for a while yet. I'm going to stop in and speak to my neighbor, then I'll be in my apartment if you need me . . . Okay, be careful coming over. Thanks again. Bye."

She ended the call and readjusted the load she carried, debating on going first to her apartment and unloading, or stopping to visit with Jasmine now. But even as she pondered what to do, a frown settled across her face. Something didn't look right. The door was open, but the lights were off inside the apartment. Forgetting about the heavy bulk in her arms, Ashli crossed the hallway to approach the front unit.

She then noticed Jasmine's foot, lying in the doorway, a fashionable heeled sandal strapped on her ankle.

"Jasmine?" she called, her heart thudding. Gripping her purse and assorted paraphernalia closely to her chest, she ventured closer. She paused near the door, overcome by a fierce sense of foreboding. Chiding herself for being frightened when her friend might need help, Ashli pushed gently on the door.

The scream started low in her throat and gained momentum when she saw what lay — or, what didn't — on the other side.

* * *

"Ms. Wilson, are you ready to speak with me now?" the young policeman asked inside Ashli's apartment. His nametag identified him as Detective Sullivan.

"It's Miss," Lange corrected him. He stood behind Ashli, one hand at the small of her back in moral support. He stood a modest distance away, but close enough so he could catch her if she fell, which was entirely possible given the way she still trembled. Even a cup of coffee and a blanket around her shoulders did little to ease the violent chills still wracking her body.

"I-I think so," she said.

"What time did you find the foot, Miss Wilson?"

She shuddered, reliving that horrible moment when she first realized there was no body behind the door. "About an hour and a half ago. I was just getting home, a little before eleven."

"And you had been . . . ?"

"At work. The restaurant until just after four, then down at the television station."

"You work at the station?"

"No. We were filming a segment for *Ashli's Kitchen*."

The young officer's head snapped up, and a smile spread across his face. "That's where I know you from! You're her, aren't you? The girl on the busses. The one who cooks."

Ashli sighed, snuggling closer into the blanket. "Yes, that's me."

"I hear your show alone has pulled the television station from the edge of bankruptcy."

"I don't know about that," she protested with modesty.

"I do! I heard your ratings are through the roof! There's—"

Lange cleared his throat and glared at the young detective. "You were asking about a timeline?"

"Yes." It took a moment for the man to blink the stars from his eyes and refocus on the notepad in his hand. "You say you arrived just before eleven?"

"Yes. I can tell you an exact time if I look at my phone. I was just hanging up when I saw her . . . it . . ."

"And what did you do?"

"I saw . . . I saw Jasmine's foot—" her voice wavered as she spoke her neighbor's name — "in the open doorway. I thought maybe she had fallen, or was hurt, so I called her name and went to . . . went to see if something was wrong." She took a deep gulp of air. "When I saw . . . when I saw there was only . . . a foot . . . I started screaming. I backed away and almost fell over the railing. I called Mr. Sterling, then nine one one."

"And why did you call Mr. Sterling—" the detective glanced up at Lange with a slight frown on his face — "before you called nine one one?"

Ashli leaned into the strength of Lange's arm without being too obvious. "Instinct," she said.

"You two are . . . involved?" Something about the question, or perhaps the look in the young officer's eye, led Lange to believe the inquiry wasn't entirely for professional reasons. Damn, did she have this effect on every man she met?

"Miss Wilson hired me to look into some problems she is having with a stalker," Lange informed him.

"A stalker? That sounds like a matter for the police."

"That's exactly what I thought," Ashli said, "but your superiors thought differently. I reported it to the police, but no one took me seriously, so I hired a private detective to find the person responsible."

"And have you?" Detective Sullivan asked, glaring at Lange.

"Not yet." His confident tone suggested it was only a matter of time.

"I'd like to talk to you more about this stalker, Miss Wilson, but now I need to discuss tonight's events. Did you see anyone else when you came home this evening?"

"Just Mr. Parnell. He's the building supervisor. The poor thing, he was terribly upset this evening. I wonder . . . I think he might have been the first to find Jasmine."

"And why do you think that?"

"He was extremely disoriented. I've never seen him so badly confused, or so upset. I called his nurse and asked her to come over and settle him down. That's who I was speaking to when I saw . . . the foot." Each time she said the words, her voice faltered. "Poor Mr. Parnell. I can only imagine what all the lights and sirens and people have done to him."

"I spoke to the nurse downstairs. She said he was so upset she had to sedate him."

"That's why I wonder if he had already found . . . the foot . . . and that was why he was so rattled."

"We'll have to wait until morning to speak with him. But you saw no one else?"

"Not until my other neighbors ran out to see why I was screaming." Ashli looked at the policeman directly. "Detective, is Jasmine . . . dead?"

"Nothing has been confirmed at this time, Miss Wilson. We haven't found her body, but I would say the odds are not in her favor," he told her.

"Was she . . . did it happen here?"

"There's no evidence to support that, no large quantities of blood or signs of a struggle. More than likely, the crime occurred somewhere else, then the foot was dumped here."

"But why? Why would someone deliberately leave that sort of evidence behind?"

Even before the detective answered, Lange slid his arm around her waist. He pulled her firmly against his solid form and held her tight in support when Detective Sullivan replied, "That's a very good question, Miss Wilson. Maybe now's a good time for you to tell me more about this stalker of yours."

* * *

The police were finally gone. In the absence of red and blue strobe lights, darkness was even blacker. Quiet settled into the old mansion like a lethal injection.

"Are you sure there's no one who can come and stay with you?" Lange asked Ashli once again.

"I'll be fine," she lied. "It's almost three in the morning. I'm not about to call someone and ask them to come over and stay in a house where a murder possibly took place."

"She wasn't killed in her apartment," Lange said, to dispel all doubts. "The foot wasn't even severed there. Someone brought the foot back to her apartment to be found." He hesitated for only a moment before deciding. "Gather up a few things. You're coming with me."

"Where to?" He could hear the skepticism in her voice.

"My apartment. At least we can try to salvage what's left of the night."

She stiffened. "I don't think that's a good—"

He cut her off before she could protest further. "The next couple of days won't be pleasant around here. There will be policemen, detectives, investigators, not to mention the media and all the nosey neighbors from a seven-block radius. Unless you want to deal with the reporters sticking a camera in your face every time you come in or out of the house, you might as well resign yourself to staying somewhere else for the next few days."

"Then I'll go to a hotel," Ashli said.

Lange sighed, clearly exasperated. "And then I'll have to go to the hotel, to keep an eye on you. It will be a lot easier if you just stay at my apartment. At least for tonight."

"Fine. But you better not bill me for it, since I'm actually saving you the trouble of staking out the hotel." She gave a saucy toss of her head before she whirled around and headed upstairs to pack a bag.

While he waited, Lange sank onto the couch in exhaustion. He had hardly slept a wink the night before, and tonight didn't promise to be much better. And if he had to share an apartment with her, his traitorous body would be way too stimulated to even consider sleep for the next several nights.

Not that his mind would shut down long enough for sleep. Right now, a thousand thoughts rushed through his brain, demanding he consider each possibility it threw out. But no matter what lead he considered, no matter what scenario he played out in his head, one thought kept circling in his mind, one thought made him feel physically sick to his stomach: it could have been Ashli tonight.

Lange rubbed a weary hand over his face, thankful she wasn't there to see how badly his hand trembled.

CHAPTER FOURTEEN

Lange lived in a trendy neighborhood in a revitalized part of downtown. Once a warehouse, the old brick and glass structure was now home to twenty or so residential lofts. A service elevator took them up to the fifth and top floor, where Lange led Ashli to a corner apartment.

"It's not much," he said by way of apology as he unlocked the door, "but you'll have privacy from the media."

To say the loft apartment was sparsely decorated was a gross understatement. It wasn't even fashionably minimalist; it was practically empty.

What could have been a spacious but intriguing room was simply a vacant backdrop for the few pieces of furniture deposited there. A sleek black leather couch and chair, both of obvious quality, were the only seating choices. Their companions, an end table and a low bench serving as a coffee table, were old wooden pieces with an industrial feel. A massive chest with multiple drawers, its wooden surface scarred and dinged and marked with age, held an oversized flat screen television, both of which were dwarfed against an impressive brick wall. The saving grace of the sparse room was the floor-to-ceiling windows, which created the outer walls of the corner apartment and revealed a spectacular view of the glittering city beyond. Other than the view, there were no pieces of artwork, no offer of color, no personal effects.

Ashli looked at her host questioningly. "Have you lived here long?"

Lange shrugged, tossing his keys onto the one other piece of furniture in the massive room. Tucked along the wall beside the door, the narrow table was practically lost in the big space. The only thing seeming to anchor it down was a wooden bowl where his keys now rested. "Three years. Ever since I came to Richmond."

He avoided looking her in the eyes. Until right now, the sparseness of his home had never bothered him. It was just a place to eat and sleep, after all. It wasn't like he ever had company. The few guy friends to come over — and they were very few and far between — never seemed to notice anything other than the more-than-ample television screen. Ashli was the first female to ever step through his door; he had never even allowed Diane to visit. He didn't bother to ponder the significance of that fact as he carried Ashli's meager luggage across the room, silently bidding her to follow.

The living room flowed into the kitchen, which was impressive with its gleaming stainless-steel appliances, dark mahogany lower cabinets, and open glass shelf uppers, suspended on metal pipes. The few dishes on display were a snappy shade of bright blue and were the lone bit of color in the room. A round dining table and four chairs occupied a mere fraction of the space available in the large window-wrapped kitchen.

The right side of the kitchen was banked with a wall, which was bisected by a short hallway. Lange pushed open the door on the left, revealing his bedroom. Compared to the other rooms in his apartment, this one was packed; it sported a king-sized bed, nightstand, a chest of drawers, a smaller chest at the foot of the bed, and an upholstered chair. The bed covers were unmade and rumpled, piled up in a heap of blue and green tartan plaid. Like in the other rooms, electronic shades covered the wall of windows, but in here was the added layer of dark-blue drapes.

"You can put your things in here," Lange said, swinging her suitcase onto the foot of the bed.

"But . . . this is your room. Where will you sleep?"

When she raised big blue eyes to his, all sorts of wicked thoughts flooded through his mind, but none of them involved sleeping.

"There's a guest room across the hall. We'll have to share the bathroom, though."

"No, I wouldn't dream of taking your bed. I'll take the guest bed."

"I'll sleep in the guest room," he insisted. He didn't bother telling her the guest room was an office. At least it had the added comfort of a couch, buried somewhere beneath all the boxes. He opened a drawer and took out a few articles of clothing, which he carried with him to the door. "Towels are in the bathroom cabinet. Bathroom is at the end of the hall."

"Really, Lange, I don't want to take your bed," she protested.

"I insist. End of discussion."

He left without another word, leaving Ashli alone in his bedroom. She was still reeling from the night's gruesome events. Running a hand through her hair, she wandered over to her suitcase. She stared inside for a long moment, forgetting what she was looking for. Oh yes, night clothes. She pulled out a T-shirt and jeans, then frowned at her selection. A second foray brought forth a skirt. Trying once again, she rummaged through the rest of her clothes at least twice before her brain registered on its task. She finally found a pair of capri pajama pants and fresh panties.

As she turned away from the suitcase, a trio of framed photographs caught her eye. The first was of Lange as a teenager, leaning against a gleaming red and white vintage Mustang coupe. There was another young man standing beside him, probably the best friend he had spoken of at the cemetery, and both wore the carefree, lighthearted smiles of youth. It was a look foreign to the one he now wore, and just for a moment, Ashli wondered what that Lange must have been like, the one who believed in dreams and a future and the simple pleasures of life. She wondered if the car had anything to do with the happy look on his face.

Her eyes moved to the next photo. Apparently taken just a few years later, Lange appeared slightly older in this shot. He still looked young and happy, but there was a shadow in his eyes. The smile on his face didn't seem to come quite as easily, but it seemed sincere as he stood with his arm around an older woman with greying hair. Her blue eyes sparkled with pride, her smile warm and wide and just a little mischievous. Just seeing her photo, Ashli knew she would have liked his grandmother.

Almost with reluctance, her gaze slid to the last of the photos. She knew it would be a picture of Lauren, but seeing the dark-haired beauty took her by surprise. The woman in the picture didn't look a thing like any of Ashli's pre-conceived notions. Lauren was tall and robust, her full figure clad in jeans, biker's boots, and a clinging V-neck sweater was partially covered by a worn leather jacket. She posed provocatively astride a motorcycle, holding her helmet and dangling a set of handcuffs from her long fingers. The look in her eyes was one of defiance, the slight smile on her face one of challenge. Even though she was fully dressed, the sensual photo could have easily passed as a professional layout for a racy calendar or a men's magazine. Only the disorganized background and a smear in the corner of the photo — most likely Lange's finger — marked it as an amateur's work.

Ashli stared at the other woman's image for a long moment. Her hair was long and dark and straight, her mouth full and sensual, her eyes dark and snapping. Even through the photographer's lens, she could tell Lauren had possessed a passion for life. She looked dark and exotic and slightly dangerous. She looked . . . exciting. No wonder Lange had loved her so. She was everything Ashli was not.

Turning her back on the photos, particularly the one of Lauren, Ashli quickly undressed and slid into her night clothes, then wandered into the bathroom for her bedtime routine.

Face scrubbed clean and teeth brushed, she exited the bathroom and saw the light spilling into the hall beneath the closed guest room door. The rest of the apartment was dark.

Like a beacon, the light guided her forward, where she stopped in front of the door. Her mind, her body, her frightened soul, screamed at her to push the door open and find solace in the arms of the man inside. But pride kept her hands glued at her side.

He didn't want her. Perhaps his body did, but not his heart. It didn't matter that he brought her into his home tonight. 'Home' was just a shelter, a place to store his belongings, not his heart. There was nothing personal about his invitation, nothing personal about his house. Nothing personal about *them*.

Ashli turned away from the closed door, wishing she could close the door on her heart just as easily, but she knew it was too late for that. Lange Sterling had already invaded her heart and soul.

She wandered through the darkness toward the living room, drawn to the huge wall of windows. The lights of the city twinkled back at her, thousands of tiny illuminations breaking through the black cover of night. If only something could break through this terrible, heavy blackness in her heart.

Her frozen mind had begun to thaw, and reality was so much more frightening without the numbness. At least shock had held the horrifying thoughts of Jasmine at bay. But as the horrors of the evening replayed in her mind, her body trembled, and tears flowed down her cheeks.

Jasmine, her beautiful and elegant friend, was probably dead.

And it was all her fault.

* * *

From the shadows, Lange watched her against the windows. She hadn't seen him there on the couch, and he hadn't alerted her to his presence. He was still reeling from the scene in the hallway that he had witnessed. Ashli hesitated for a long moment at his door, clearly wanting to go inside. His body reacted instantly, desire swarming his senses. He almost went to her, but just as he rose from the couch, she turned away.

His heart reacted instantly to that, too. It practically stopped beating.

He watched as tears ran unbidden down her beautiful but stricken face. He ached to go to her, to hold her, but he was the one who demanded they remain uninvolved. They were playing by his rules, *his* lies. If he went to her now, he would only confuse her with his offer of comfort.

He knew the exact moment she re-lived finding the severed foot; a look of horror replayed on her face, the shock as fresh and real as it had been four hours ago. He knew the instant she realized her friend's fate; she bit her bottom lip and shut her eyes in overwhelming grief. She cried silently, her entire body wracked with sobs, as she re-lived the horrors of the night, alone in her misery and grief.

The hardest of hearts, not even the empty shell that resided inside his chest, could ignore the sheer agony she suffered. Before he could think better of it, Lange was off the couch and reaching for her.

Having no idea he was even in the room, his sudden presence scared her. She jumped away at his touch, a scream on her lips.

"It's just me, Ashli," he assured her, reaching for her again. "It's just me."

She fought against him, trying to free herself from his hold. Shadows and demons merged together, fogging her senses. Hysteria rose within her chest, pushing her breath out in small clumps as her heart hammered in a wild staccato. The harder he tried to pull her into his arms, the harder she pushed away.

"It's me, Ashli. It's Lange."

She stopped fighting, but she was stiff and rigid as he tried to gather her near. "Shh," he said, "it's just me."

Just for a moment, she allowed him to hold her. She ached to stay there against his chest, absorbing his strength and his warmth, seeking comfort in the safety of his arms. She wanted him to hold her more than anything she had ever wanted in her life. She *needed* him to hold her.

But he didn't want her. The frustration of the weekend, of their entire relationship, added to the overwhelming grief she felt and gave her renewed strength to shove against him. "Let me go! Get away from me!"

"Dammit, Ashli, I'm trying to help."

"I don't-don't want your help!" she insisted, pushing hard at the wall of his chest. "Get away from me. Don't touch me!" With a final wrestle that gained her freedom, she spat out, "It's what you wanted, so . . . Don't. Touch. Me."

They stood three feet apart, both gulping for air, both glaring at the other. Tremors still ran through Ashli's body, causing her slight form to shake, but she stood her ground against the dark giant. He didn't want her. She kept reminding herself of that, even as she craved to hurl herself into the safety of his arms.

Lange was the first to give. He closed his eyes, unable to hold her heated glare any longer. "Please, Ashli," he said, his low, gravelly voice just short of begging. "Just let me hold you."

"I can't." Her whispered words were a bequest of their own. Couldn't he understand? If she allowed him to hold her, if she allowed herself to depend on him, to believe in him, to believe in them . . . Couldn't he see that just those few moments of comfort could destroy her? She squeezed her eyelids together, holding back fresh tears.

Lange stepped closer, closing the distance between them. This time, she allowed him to tug her rigid form into his arms. "Let me hold you." His voice had an odd break in it. "I need to hold you," he admitted in a rough whisper. He gathered her up close to his chest and buried his face into the strands of sunshine framing her wet cheeks. He didn't question why his own cheeks felt damp, pressed against the clinging silk of her hair.

They held each other in silence, both fully aware that it could have been Ashli lying on that floor tonight. Now wasn't the time to argue. The rules of their relationship were of little importance in view of what could have happened. Each lost in their own thoughts, Ashli wept again while Lange held her with a fierce gentleness that took her breath away. They absorbed the other's nearness, the other's weakness, the other's strength. Together they forged a strength that was greater than either of their own métier.

After a long time, Ashli spoke. "Tell me the truth, Lange. Do you think I was the intended victim?"

"There's no reason to even think that."

Ashli pushed out of his arms. "Except for the fact someone has been stalking me. And now my neighbor winds up . . . mutilated, and most likely dead, and the killer brings evidence back to our house. I see only two possibilities. Either he's trying to make a statement, threatening me about what's to come, or else he made a mistake and killed the wrong person."

Lange smiled gently down at her face, all splotchy and red, and yet still so unbelievably beautiful. "From what I understand, Jasmine was an Oriental woman in her late thirties, five foot seven, with short dark hair. You barely stand five three, you have long hair so blonde it's almost white, and you're ten years younger. She was definitely not mistaken for you."

"Then he's sending me a message. I'm still responsible for her death."

"*If* it's her foot," he reminded her. "We'll have to wait for prints and DNA to know for certain." He hesitated before adding, "And that may not be the only explanation."

Ashli stared up at him with piqued interest. "What are you talking about?"

"I didn't mention it to the police, and obviously Sullivan is too green to have recognized the connection, but tonight's incident is reminiscent to a string of disappearances that happened here well over thirty years ago."

"You mean like a serial killer?" she asked.

The woman was too smart to be called clueless. "They didn't call it that back then," he said. "And they weren't necessarily murders. Even though the women were never seen again, the rest of their bodies were never found. But back in the late seventies, early eighties, several young women went missing. The only thing ever found was their foot. Most were confirmed as belonging to the missing women, but science back then was hardly what it is today."

"What are you saying? We have a serial killer who's been mutilating women's bodies for over thirty years?" She moved to the couch and plopped onto its leather surface.

"More than likely, we have a copycat. Someone who's read about the old case and decided to emulate his style. The odds of one person, killing and mutilating bodies for over three decades and getting away with it, are very slim."

"And why do you know so much about a thirty- to forty-year-old case?"

Lange shrugged as he sat beside her. "In my spare time, I work cold cases. I've solved a few, but this one is still as baffling as it was from the first day. No signs of the remains, no connections between victims, no clear reasons of motive. Just seven feet, from seven different women."

Ashli raked her fingers through her hair, unconcerned with tangling the blonde tresses. "You're telling me to look on the bright side, it may not be my stalker that's responsible for Jasmine's dismemberment. We may just have a crazed serial killer on our hands, copying a thirty-year-old mystery." Her voice was as heavy as her heart. "Somehow, that's not very comforting."

"I never said there was a bright side. I simply said it wasn't your fault." He pushed a strand of hair away that was stuck to her cheek. "We can talk about all this in the morning. Why don't you try to get some sleep? Tomorrow's going to be a long day."

"It already is tomorrow. And I doubt I can sleep," she said, glancing toward the bedroom with obvious reluctance.

He couldn't blame her for not wanting to go in the room alone, any more than he could blame himself for not letting her out of his sight. With a sigh, he settled back against the cushions of the couch and lifted his arm. After the slightest hesitation, she curled beneath the haven he offered. He held her without words, without kisses.

Eventually, they both fell asleep.

CHAPTER FIFTEEN

With a heavy heart, Ashli went through the motions of a normal day, but it was far from being life as usual that following day.

She awoke stiff and sore from sleeping on the sofa, even if it had been for only a few hours. Lange was already up and in the shower, so she made her way into the kitchen in search of a coffee pot. She was on her second cup when Lange appeared in the doorway.

"I see you found the coffee," he said, lifting a dark eyebrow.

"If I find nothing else, I always know where the closest coffee pot is."

She looked so gorgeous sitting in his kitchen, her hair still mussed from a restless night's sleep. On purpose, Lange turned away from the image of perfection as he brewed his own cup. "I liked your pot so well I got one for myself," he commented.

He seldom offered even the tiniest sliver of information about his own life, but this morning, Ashli failed to notice. She was staring out the kitchen's wall of windows, wondering if the rest of Jasmine's body was out there somewhere, waiting to be discovered.

"I'll drop you off at work," Lange said. "What time do I need to pick you up this afternoon?" When she just looked at him with a blank expression of confusion, he elaborated. "Remember, we left your car at Daisy House? I'll have to drive you to work."

"Oh. Well, I guess we could go by and get my car."

"Not if you want to avoid the media."

Ashli sighed. "I wonder how Mr. Parnell is this morning. Poor thing, he was so disoriented last night."

"I'll go by today and try to speak with him."

It wasn't until she finished her coffee that she answered his original question. "I'll probably work late this evening," she said. "I didn't get to start on the berries last night because we were filming. You can pick me up around nine."

"You need to get in bed early tonight. I'll be there at six."

"I have a lot of berries to process. And I doubt I'll be able to sleep. Nine or so is fine."

He tried a different tactic. "Okay, I need to get in bed early tonight. I'll be there at six."

The day seemed to drag out forever, but promptly at six, Lange pulled up at Ashli's Tea Party. He waited for her to find a good stopping point with her berries, even helping her transfer buckets back to the step-in cooler. It was closer to seven when they finally left the restaurant, so when he suggested they go out for supper, she didn't protest. Even though she wasn't hungry, for once, she didn't feel like cooking.

It was their first time to go out to eat, but it was hardly a date. When Ashli's phone wasn't ringing, what little conversation they had was centered on her case. Lange didn't seem to mind when her parents called, but his expression tightened when Detective Sullivan called to "check on her". After watching his thunderous expression during Mitch's call, Ashli decided it was best to turn her phone off for the remainder of the meal.

"Was Mr. Parnell any help today?" Ashli asked as she slipped her phone into her purse.

"None at all," Lange said in frustration. "When I went by this morning, he was sleeping. I went back this afternoon, and he was still groggy from the sedation and a little hard to understand."

"Yes, sometimes I have trouble making out some of his words, too."

"One thing came through loud and clear. I asked him if we could mount surveillance cameras around the house. He was adamant about not allowing it, saying something about disturbing the true spirit of the house, whatever the hell that means. Seeing as it's a condo, I'm not sure he can make that decision on his own. I'm going to ask a lawyer friend of mine if he has that authority." At least, he hoped Diane would take his call.

"It might help me find my Peeping Tom, but it won't help poor Jasmine," Ashli murmured, as tears pooled in her eyes. "Detective Sullivan said there was still no sign of the rest . . . of the rest of . . . her body."

"It hasn't even been twenty-four hours yet. But you do realize there's a chance they'll never find it, don't you?"

Ashli nodded, her eyes downcast. "For her family's sake, I hope that's not the case. I can't imagine what it must be like never knowing for certain, like the families of those seven girls." She looked up suddenly, catching his eye. "Lange?"

"Yeah?"

"Do you think I could see the files on those old cases?"

"Why? Another sense of morbid curiosity?"

"Maybe I'm just playing amateur sleuth, but I keep thinking maybe there is some connection between those cases and Jasmine's, something a fresh set of eyes might see. I just feel so helpless right now, and I'd like to help in some way. What could it hurt?"

"Some of the information is classified," he hedged.

"But some of it isn't."

Lange hesitated, weighing the consequences of letting her get embroiled in the old case. He could understand her need to be involved in some way, but he couldn't risk putting her in any more jeopardy than she was already in. He doubted there was a connection; he only brought up the possibility to deflect some of the guilt she heaped upon herself. There was no danger in letting her look through a few old files on a thirty-five-year-old crime. Finally, he gave a slight nod. "I'll see what I can do."

"Thank you, Lange," she said, the breathless quality in her voice once again recalling his favorite screen legend.

"Tomorrow I'll see if I can get your car for you. I didn't even bother today, with all the media there."

"Was it bad?"

"I've seen three-ring circuses with less chaos," he said.

"I know I wasn't very gracious about it last night but thank you for getting me out of there. The last thing I need is for the media to make the connection that I live at Daisy House. Thank you for that."

"No problem." He brushed off her thanks, all the time knowing that he lied.

It *was* a problem, having her in his home. Now that she was there, he realized how empty it had been. In fact, he realized his life had been empty, until he met her. And now he feared neither would ever be the same, especially when this case was through and it was time to say goodbye.

"We can stop by the market on the way home and pick up a few groceries," he said, changing the subject. "I know my cupboards are bare."

"I don't want to be a bother. As long as you have coffee, I can manage." She flashed a smile, but it lacked her usual brightness.

His only reply was a loud snort. After he called for the check and insisted on paying for their meal, he drove them to a nearby supermarket.

It was such an intimate gesture, walking together through the grocery store aisles with a shared buggy, especially so late in the evening. Ashli noticed how the other shoppers looked at them, assuming they were a couple. The women eyed Lange with appreciation and Ashli with envy. She kept reminding herself they weren't a couple, even when she asked him what he would like for supper the next evening.

"You don't have to cook," he said.

"It's the least I can do. And it will keep my mind occupied. It's sort of like therapy."

The thought of her cooking for him, in his own home, was so tempting that it scared him silly. If he allowed her to cook for him, how could he ever eat another meal there, all alone, once she was gone?

"Don't worry about it. I've got plans tomorrow night, anyway."

"Okay," Ashli said, wondering why he was so terse. She put the box of noodles back on the shelf. It was obvious he didn't want her cooking for him, and she could eat her meals elsewhere.

Lange knew he was being brusque, but the intimacy of their shopping venture wasn't lost upon him. Even he and Lauren had seldom shopped together, mostly because they never ate together, at least not at home. Another reason he had to keep Ashli out of his kitchen.

"Then this box of coffee is all I'll need." She took it from the buggy, symbolically separating them even further. "I'll wait for you in the car while you finish shopping."

"I'm done," he said, even though there were only a handful of items in the cart.

They walked stiffly toward the checkout counter; any thread of intimacy now snapped free.

Back at his apartment, Ashli took a long hot bath and went right to bed, even though sleep was slow in coming. As if thoughts of Jasmine and Lange's moodiness and Lauren's overseeing eyes weren't enough, she had to endure the lingering scent of Lange's cologne on the bed sheets. Snuggling into the covers and imagining they were his arms around her, she finally fell asleep around midnight.

The next morning, Ashli packed her suitcase and informed her reluctant host she would be staying with Molly for the rest of the week.

* * *

By Friday, Ashli was back at home. A bomb threat at an area high school whisked the media away from Daisy House. Already, the investigation there was growing cold. There were no new leads on the case, no witnesses to interview, no body to be discovered, and forensics had yet to confirm if the foot did, indeed, belong to Jasmine. Without a story to report, the media soon lost interest, and no one was happier about that fact than Ashli.

Even without the horror surrounding Jasmine and the interruption of her life, Ashli had a busy week. Relocating — twice — meant losing precious time from her tight schedule. By Friday evening, Ashli made up for lost time.

The enticing aroma of warm, sweetened blackberries scented the entire house. Every surface in her kitchen was covered with some aspect of berry cobbler — berries, flour for the crust, chunks of sweet butter, and an assortment of baking dishes and utensils. When she heard the intercom buzz, she frowned at the interruption and wondered who dared to disturb her at a time like this.

"Yes?" she asked, hurrying to answer it on the third buzz.

Her heart did a strange little flop when she heard the quiet voice on the other end. "It's Lange. May I come up?"

She hesitated for a moment, glancing into the kitchen. She didn't have time for this, no matter what 'this' was; with Lange, it was always complicated. The seeds of Southern hospitality, however, rooted deep within her. It was rude to refuse such a request. With a resigned sigh that came across the intercom, she buzzed him in.

When he reached the door, it took her a few moments to answer his knock. He wondered idly if she was primping for him.

"Sorry," she said as way of greeting when she finally swung the door open. She brushed a strand of mussed golden-white hair away from her cheek, leaving a smudge of flour in its place and dispelling any fantasy of primping on his account. Still, it took great discipline not to reach out and brush the smudge away with his fingertip. Or, better yet, with his lips.

"Cooking something?" He sniffed the fragrant air.

"I'm catering a banquet tomorrow night and getting a jump on some of the baking," she answered. She headed back to the kitchen, saying something about a cobbler in the oven. Lange shut the door behind him and followed, trying to keep his eyes off her gently swaying hips.

He tried to brace himself for the powerful image she made in the kitchen, her face flushed as she straightened from the hot oven and stirred a couple of pans on top of the cook top. She wore another of her uninspired dresses, her feet were bare, and an apron wrapped around her tiny waist. Lange knew there was no bracing his heart from the devastating effect that her domestic beauty had on him. What was it about this woman? He couldn't resist her any more than he could resist breathing the air around him. The air scented with her cooking, her fragrance. Her very essence.

It had been only two days since she left his apartment. Two long, lonely days. How could he have missed her so much? His voice came out a bit husky with emotion, even though he was trying to sound sardonic. "It looks like a berry bomb went off in here."

"I know, it's a mess, but I'm running way behind schedule. This week didn't turn out quite the way I had planned." She picked up a bowl and stirred. "What's with the computer?"

"I brought my laptop so we could log onto the criminal database. I thought maybe you could look through a few mug shots, see if anyone looks familiar." He set the computer and a stack of files on the counter, then helped himself to a seat on the stool.

A tiny frown wrinkled her forehead as she dropped her eyes and concentrated on mixing the ingredients in her bowl.

"What?" he asked, seeing the look on her face.

"I don't know. It's just the thought of being stalked by a known criminal . . ."

Lange sighed heavily. "You refuse to believe it's anyone you know. Now you don't want it to be a total stranger!" He threw his hands up in exasperation.

"More than a stranger, a criminal, someone with a track record, someone who's done mean things before to other people and who might want to do those same mean things to me now!"

As always, it amazed Lange that she could say so much in one breath. In spite of himself, one corner of his mouth lifted in a smile.

"What, you think it's funny?" she demanded.

"No. But I think you're going to beat to death whatever is inside that bowl." He nodded to the furious way she was stirring the mixture with her wooden spoon.

"Oh, for heaven's sake, look at what I'm doing!" she muttered. "This is dough for another cobbler, and it's going to be as tough as a leather boot. Look what you let me do!" She sputtered and muttered to herself as she deftly sprinkled a handful of flour onto the counter, then turned the bowl of dough onto its surface. After dividing the dough in half, she took her rolling pin and spread one of the lumps into a thin, flat circle.

Just for a moment, Lange was lost in the pleasure of simply watching her work. He could remember doing the same thing with his grandmother as a child. Even then, he was fascinated with how a lump of flour and water could be maneuvered into a smooth work of art and transformed into a mouth-watering masterpiece made just for him. Knowing how well he liked the flaky crust, his grandmother always saved a few strips of dough and baked them separately so he could enjoy the special treat.

He watched silently, mesmerized by the deft, sure movements of her hands as Ashli expertly rolled out the dough.

Soon, his mind was taking a path of its own, wondering how it would feel to have her hands kneading the muscles of his back, the same way she kneaded the dough; wondering what it would be like to have her smooth away the knots of frustration and fatigue, as easily as she smoothed out the dough.

Pulling himself out of his reverie, he forced his mind onto business. "You said you were catering a banquet?"

If she noticed his sharp, abrupt tone, she didn't mention it. She continued to work with her dough until it suited her, then lifted it in one large sheet and eased it down into a large glass baking dish. To Lange's amazement, it was a perfect fit, with no excess dough around the edges. She completed her task before she bothered answering his question.

"Yes, I'm serving a party of thirty-five tomorrow night at the Tea Party. It's an awards dinner for a small insurance company."

"Why didn't you tell me about this earlier?" he asked.

"I didn't think it was important." She shrugged. She filled her crust with plump, freshly washed blackberries.

"Didn't think it was important? Damn it, Ashli, have you forgotten why you hired me in the first place? You can't be breezing back and forth at night into empty buildings and empty apartments without telling me!"

"I think you're being a wee bit melodramatic," Ashli insisted. She coated the berries with a generous amount of sugar as she brushed away his concerns. "First of all, I have no intentions of serving thirty-five people all by myself. My staff will be there to help, so the building will hardly be empty. And second, I come home to an empty apartment every single day without clearing it with you first."

"You come in at four thirty in the afternoon, not at midnight. There's a big difference. And don't tell me you won't be the first person in at the Tea Party to set up for the dinner."

"Okay, so maybe you're right. I'm sorry I didn't tell you before. And in answer to your question, no, I haven't forgotten why I hired you in the first place. It would be impossible to forget, even though I would love to!" With a toss of her head, she grabbed her rolling pin and rolled out the second ball of dough.

"What time is the banquet?" he growled.

"From seven until nine thirty."

"What time will you go to the restaurant?"

"Probably around four thirty."

"I'll be there waiting for you."

Ashli sniffed her disapproval. "You don't have to act like you're making an appointment to have your teeth pulled."

"I had planned to work on another case tomorrow afternoon, but I guess it can wait. I don't want you going there alone. I'll be back at ten to escort you home." He watched as she took out a pastry cutter and rolled it over the smoothed-out dough, cutting it into strips with zigzag edges.

Lifting the strips with care, Ashli placed them carefully over the top of her cobbler, creating a lattice pattern. As she dropped pats of butter strategically over the top of her creation, she sighed dramatically. "Then I guess I'd better tell you about next Saturday night. There's another banquet, but I'll be attending this one as a guest."

"With whom?" He hoped the barked words didn't sound as accusing and jealous as they felt while stabbing into his heart.

Her shrug was casual. "I don't know. I haven't thought about a date, but I guess you're right. I do need an escort. Most of the other people will have dates, and I don't want to be a fifth wheel." She seemed to be unaware of how her rambling words of taking a date were eating right into the flesh of his heart. "Although I do remember that last year Grace Henning came without a date. She sat at our table and—"

"Ashli," he broke in, sensing she was about to lose the thread of the conversation. "What kind of banquet is this, and why are you going?"

"Because everyone who's anyone in the restaurant business will be there." Going over to the double ovens, she bent over and retrieved a bubbling cobbler from the depths of the lower chamber. She spoke from over her shoulder, not turning to see how his gaze had slipped to caress the view of her nicely rounded bottom. "It's the annual RRR banquet, and I go every year." When she straightened with the pie and brought it over to the counter near him to cool, she glanced up and caught his eye.

"Looks delicious." He glanced down at the dish, but something in his innocent act made her suspect his words weren't geared toward the cobbler.

"Well, anyway . . ." she said, retracing her steps with the unbaked pie and bending once again to slide it and another pan into the oven, "Ashli's Tea Party has been selected as one of the top five finalists. It's a huge honor and one I fully intend to enjoy. Don't expect me to cancel my plans, even if this banquet will draw a lot of publicity."

"What kind of publicity?" he asked, his mind snapping back to attention.

"Newspaper, television, that sort of thing. Each finalist will be featured in a full-length newspaper article, and we'll have a group interview on *Wake Up, Richmond* on Friday morning."

"What kind of banquet did you say this was?" He realized he hadn't been listening, not when presented with the view of her very lovely little upturned bottom.

"The Richmond Restaurant Review. It's an annual event, where all the area restaurants are honored. The top five are given special awards and are featured in travel guides and national magazines. It's wonderful publicity. I'm honored to even be a nominee; I never dreamed they would choose the Tea Party!"

"Sound like a big shindig."

"It's the Oscar Awards of the local restaurant business."

He didn't comment as she tended to the pans on top of the stove. While she brought two small plates to the counter and scooped out generous helpings of the cobbler, Lange considered the crazy thought inside his head. Did he dare?

"Ashli?" he began.

"Yes?"

She made asking so much harder. She looked up at him with a question in her eyes, looking as young and innocent as a high-school beauty queen. Hell, it even felt like he was back in high school, trying to get up the nerve to ask for a date for the prom! When she licked her thumb, sticky and red with berry juice, his pants became too tight, and his palms became sweaty. He greedily followed the movement with his eyes, feeling as young and eager as a high school stud on his first date.

Somehow, he managed to sound nonchalant as he made his suggestion. "I was thinking . . . maybe it would be best if I took you to this banquet."

She looked surprised at his suggestion, then doubtful.

"What, you don't agree?"

"Do you mean take me as in drop me off or take me as in be my date?" she asked, dropping her eyes.

Shifting uncomfortably on the stool, he cleared his throat. "As your escort. That way I could be there to protect you without being obvious." Hell, he couldn't be any more obvious than he was right now!

"I'm not sure that's such a good idea, Lange." She set the plate of cobbler in front of him and followed it with a cup of coffee, yet she never quite met his eyes.

He never considered the possibility of her turning him down. It felt like she was rejecting his invitation to the prom, and he never dreamed it could smart so much. Not that he had ever bothered with stupid things like proms and high school parties, and not that it mattered to him now. It had just been a suggestion.

Still, he had to know why. "You have someone else in mind?" he asked.

"No, it's not that."

"Then, what?"

Her answer was slow in coming. She turned away to stir another pot, then bent to get a pan from the oven. She seemed to give its contents a great deal of attention as she slowly walked back to the bar. Finally, she looked up at him, her words as clear and distinct as her beautiful blue eyes.

"This banquet is very important to me. It represents a personal victory I'm very proud of. And you have made it perfectly clear that you want nothing to do with any aspect of my personal life. Thank you for the offer, but I won't be needing your professional services that night."

Lange found it difficult to hold her gaze. She stared at him with complete honesty, making him painfully aware of the fact he hid behind a lie. He had been lying to her, lying to himself, when he claimed their kiss meant nothing. What would she say if he were honest and admitted his offer had nothing to do with his professional services, and everything to do with personal involvement?

He looked away, diverting his gaze to the pan she set between them on the counter. And when he saw the thin golden strips of extra crust, just like the ones his own grandmother used to bake, a sharp ache began in his heart and brought the sting of moisture into his eyes. "I-I can't believe you baked extra crust," he murmured.

The change of topics threw Ashli a little off guard. "Oh, that." She shrugged. "My mother used to cook the extra crust for me and my brothers. It's very good."

"I know. My grandmother used to bake the extra crust for me, too."

Hearing the odd ache in his voice, Ashli glanced up. He wore that same look of longing on his face she had seen at her parents' table. His obvious turmoil was so intense she forgot her own grievances with him. "Tell me about your grandmother, Lange," she said.

He didn't even stop to think about the implications of sharing his feelings with her. He was lost in a memory as he softly spoke. "She was the only mother I ever knew, the only real family I ever had. She was everything a grandmother should be . . . good food and good advice, all wrapped up in a hug and a kiss. Looking back, I see that I gave her a lot of hell, but she never complained. She was the only person who ever thought I would ever amount to anything."

"She sounds wonderful," Ashli said, encouraging him to continue.

"She was a gentle woman, softly spoken, but she would fight like a mother bear when the other kids picked on me. She taught me to defend myself and not take flak from others if I knew I was right. She taught me about honor and trust and all those things that grandmothers know so much about."

"Your grandfather?"

"He died before I was born. It was just Grandma and me. We didn't need anyone else. I didn't want to share her with anybody else. She was the one thing, the one person who was mine." He lifted a strip of crust and examined it as if peering into a picture of the past. "I remember one time when she was baking a cobbler and didn't have enough dough for extra crust. She took one look at my face and decided that the lattice on her cobbler was too 'fat'. She took off every single piece and trimmed them down, until there was a whole pan of extra crust, just for me."

"I think I would have liked your grandmother," Ashli decided with a smile.

"I never thought I'd ever meet another woman like her. I thought she was too perfect to be like anyone else in the whole world."

"And then you met Lauren?" she guessed.

"Lauren was as different from my grandmother as day and night. Truth is, I don't think Grandma would have approved of Lauren," he confessed. He frowned slightly as he studied the piece of crust one last time. Then he slipped the morsel into his mouth and let it melt upon his tongue. Savoring the taste with his eyes closed, he could picture being a child once more in his grandmother's kitchen.

When he opened his eyes, Ashli was looking at him, her beautiful face filled with compassion. It wasn't pity; he knew that now. It was just Ashli's amazing ability to care about other people and share their emotions. It was part of what made her so damned irresistible, part of what fueled this incredible weakness he had for her.

"You," he said in a strangled voice. The word peeped out of his heart, squeezing past the lump in his throat. "My grandmother would have liked you," he managed in a voice raspy and gruff. "You're so much like her."

The heartache he exposed himself to was worth the pain. Her smile was all the reward he needed for willingly breaking off a piece of his heart. Her smile was like the very first rays of sunshine after a gentle spring rain; slow and hesitant at first, gaining confidence as it peeked through the clouds, then bursting into its full, brilliant glory. Seeing her smile, Lange felt his heart swell and threaten to burst.

"I think that's the nicest thing anyone has ever said to me," she whispered, tears in her eyes.

Lange stared at her for a long, hungry moment, his own eyes not quite dry. But as he realized what had happened, his head rolled back in weary defeat. He cursed the ceiling he stared at, but there was no real anger in his voice. "Damn it, Ashli, you've done it again. You've got me telling you things I have no right to say to you."

She made no reply, just stared down at the remaining strips of crust in a brave effort to keep the tears at bay. "You're right. I'm sorry."

"Then why are you crying?"

"I-I'm not."

"A mere technicality, at best," he chided. "You look like a kinked water hose, about to burst."

Unshed tears thickened her whispered voice. "Maybe I'm just dense. Maybe I am clueless. But I don't understand. What has telling me about your grandmother got to do with protecting me?"

"We've been through all this." His voice was low, rough.

"But this has nothing to do with me, nothing to do with the investigation."

Silence followed, one that stretched into the sound of two hearts in pain. At last, Lange spoke in a voice so low it was a rumble. "I thought I had explained this to you. I can't get involved with you."

"Would it be so terrible, Lange?" she asked, hurt creeping into her voice. He made caring about her sound so detestable.

"Yes, Ashli, it would. If I let myself get too close, I might lose my objectivity. I can't do that. I've already stepped over a line that I should never have crossed."

"Aren't you being a little hard on yourself? It's not like the man slipped through your fingers while you weren't looking."

"How do I know that? All I can see is you, Ashli." He made the admission in a voice raw with vulnerability. "In every color of blue, in every ray of the sun, in every dream. The man could be right under my nose, and I wouldn't even see him because I can't take my eyes off you!" He slammed his fist down onto the bar, rattling his pie plate with the force.

It was difficult to be flattered by words that obviously caused him so much pain, but somewhere deep inside her, new warmth spread through Ashli's heart and gave her hope. "Maybe . . ." she said slowly, quietly, ". . . maybe you should go with me to the banquet."

"No, you were probably right."

She looked up at him, her eyes shimmering with such a beautiful blue, Lange knew she could hear his heart thundering. In a tactical move, she touched him. She reached out and laid her own small hand upon his on the bar. Looking straight into his eyes, she said one simple word.

"Please."

It didn't matter then if she asked him to take her to the banquet or to the moon; if humanly possible, he would do whatever she wanted. Under her gentle touch, he was as pliable as pie dough.

"Do I have to wear a tux?" he asked, not wanting her to see how deeply her touch affected him.

The thought of him in a tuxedo was titillating. No matter what he wore, he would be the most handsome and exciting man there. "Not if you don't want to," she finally answered.

He looked down at her hand still covering his own, resisting the urge to curl his fingers around hers. What he wanted to do was to curl his fingers into that gorgeous hair of hers and pull her into his arms. He wanted to pull the apron and that horrid brown dress away from her body, and he wanted, more than he had ever wanted anything in his life, to make love to her. He wanted to wake up in the morning with her in his arms, and he wanted to come home to her again tomorrow night. And the night after that, and the night after that. Damn it, he wanted to be here a year from now, ten years from now.

A knock on the door broke whatever mood had been created. Lange pulled away quickly, almost guiltily. "Are you expecting anyone?"

"No," she said, frowning. Whoever it was had lousy timing. And they hadn't used the intercom.

"Wait before you open it," Lange cautioned. He hurried to the door, slipping behind it to hide.

Ashli peered through the peephole, relaxing when she saw the familiar face on the other side. Despite Lange's frown, she swung the door open.

"Mr. Parnell, what a surprise! How are you this evening?"

"Fine, missy, fine. Just wanted to bring up this mess of okra."

"Oh, from your garden?"

"Grew it myself." He beamed. "Thought you might enjoy a fresh mess for dinner."

"How sweet! And I've been wanting some okra but refused to pay such a high price for it at the supermarket. You couldn't have brought me a nicer gift, Mr. Parnell."

Clearly pleased with her reaction, the old man gave a cackle of delight. "Seein' that smile of yours is all the thanks I need, little darlin'. Think of me when you eat it, you hear?"

"I promise, I will. Wait here just a second while I get something. There's a berry cobbler sitting on my counter right now, just begging to be had for supper. You wait right here." Her own eyes twinkled as she thought how his gift had come at the perfect time, when she could reciprocate.

As Ashli scurried off to the kitchen, her neighbor wandered inside the apartment. Lange remained behind the door, watching as the old man strained his neck to see into the other rooms where Ashli had disappeared. He lingered at the hall table, idly fingering through her mail, then wandered over toward the dining area. When he glanced up and saw Lange standing behind the door, a startled expression came to his wrinkled face.

"Young man! You gave me a fright!" he chided, his voice taking on a hardened tone.

"Sorry about that, sir." Lange extended his hand in greeting.

Mr. Parnell studied him for a long moment before taking the proffered shake. "Why are you hiding behind the door, young man?"

"I wasn't exactly hiding." Lange defended himself. Again, he felt like a high school boy, being confronted by an over-protective father on prom night.

"Then come on out here so we can see you. Doris don't like people sneaking up behind her."

"Doris?" Lange asked in confusion.

Ashli came back into the room with a generous helping of cobbler in a disposable container. "Here you go, Mr. Parnell. That should be enough cobbler to last you a couple of meals."

"Thank you, missy. Thank you. Sure does look and smell delicious." He threw Lange a withering look as he moved slowly toward the door. "You best watch out, little darlin'. Always check behind doors and around corners. You never know what's on the other side."

"That's good advice, Mr. Parnell," Ashli said, but her brow was creased in confusion. The old man ambled through the door, missing the frown she threw to Lange, who merely shrugged his shoulders in reply. "Thank you again for the okra."

"Anytime, little darlin, anytime. Take care now, you hear?"

"Yes, sir, you too. Enjoy that cobbler."

"I will, I will. I'll be thinking of you when I eat it for supper."

"Good night, now," Ashli called, then closed the door behind him. Turning to Lange, she asked, "What was that all about?"

"Who the hell is Doris?"

Ashli sighed. "Doris is his late wife. Poor thing, what did he say now?"

"He accused me of lurking behind the door. Said Doris didn't like people sneaking up on her."

"I guess seeing you startled him so badly, he got confused again."

"That, or the way you flirted with him got him flustered. You ought to be ashamed of yourself. He's old enough to be your grandfather."

"Flirted? I did no such thing!" Ashli denied with shocked indignation.

Putting a dramatic hand on his hip, Lange imitated her Southern belle voice and batted his eyelashes with blatant exaggeration. "'There's a pie on my counter, just begging to be had for supper!'" he mimicked.

"I didn't say it like that!"

"You most certainly did. 'Begging to be had'? It sounds like you're offering more than a pie!"

"How dare you! Mr. Parnell is just a kind old man who enjoys doing nice things for others. He always brings me fresh vegetables and flowers from his garden, does little odd jobs for me. I repay the favor by cooking for him, running some of his errands, dropping in to visit occasionally. It's what friends do, and I wasn't flirting!"

"Yeah, I bet he went down and took a cold shower after your idea of 'not flirting'," Lange muttered.

"Lange! He's an old man!"

"He's breathing, isn't he? You seem to have that effect on every man, young or old. Don't think I didn't notice the same kind of reaction out of Detective Sullivan. By the way, why did he come by here this afternoon?"

Stunned by Lange's accusation and then by his angry demand for an explanation, Ashli spun on her heel and went back into the kitchen. She chose to ignore him as she busied herself, turning off pots and taking the last of the cobblers from the ovens. Lange sulked from his perch on the stool, watching her every move. She worked with her back toward him, her movements jerky and stiff. He finally grew tired of her cold treatment and turned his attention to his uneaten cobbler. Still slightly warm from the oven, it was both sweet and tart, and it melted in his mouth the way Ashli melted in his arms when he kissed her. Lange made a supreme effort to think only of the cobbler, and not the woman who made it.

When she finally finished banging her way through the cupboards and had the pots emptied and the cobblers cooling on the counter, Lange figured her anger had run out of steam. Pushing his emptied plate away, he caught her eye as she finally turned toward him.

"If you've finished, can you take a look at these files now?" he asked.

"I guess," she said, in no real hurry to look at the faces of criminals. She made them each a cup of coffee as Lange logged onto the database and entered his clearance credentials.

"Take your time and look at the faces," he advised. "If anyone looks familiar, click on them to bring up more information."

For an hour, Ashli dutifully looked through face after face of known criminals. Many of the faces had scars and cuts and visible signs of a violent lifestyle, but just as many, if not more, were just ordinary faces of what appeared to be ordinary people. It was perhaps that fact — the hidden danger that lurked behind the average eyes and the average faces — that sent a shiver of apprehension rippling through Ashli's slight frame. She thought of Mr. Parnell's warning about not knowing what lay hidden behind a door; apparently the same held true for inside a person's soul.

"You okay?" Lange asked, seeing her shudder. He cupped her shoulder in a show of moral support and returned to the stool beside her.

"Yes. It's just that . . . there's so many. So many faces, so much evil." She shivered again.

"Maybe you should take a break."

"No, I want to get this over with," Ashli said with determination. She clicked on a new page, bringing up a dozen more faces to consider. She swallowed hard when her gaze fell upon one particularly horrid face. Unconsciously, she leaned closer toward Lange and grabbed the hand that still rested on her shoulder. She squeezed his fingers as she stared at the deep, jagged scar where an eye should have been.

It seemed so natural to simply turn his palm upward. Entwining his fingers with hers, Lange leaned in so she could rest against him. Ashli continued with the perusal of each photograph, studying each thoroughly before moving on to the next. Periodically, a truly repulsive photo caused her to cringe, and she would squeeze his hand for support. She never said a word, merely leaned closer bit by bit, until she was cradled beneath his protective arm, seeking security against his warm chest.

Finally, she spoke. "No one," she sighed. "No one looks even vaguely familiar, besides those three men I clicked on."

"One's dead, one's in prison, and the other is now a quadriplegic." His sigh matched hers. "There're still a few more pages to go. Maybe you'll see someone in them."

"I'll probably have nightmares tonight," she mumbled with a shudder.

He bit back the offer to stay with her and keep the evil dreams at bay.

"Does this happen often?" she asked, rubbing a thumb across his fingers as she clicked on another set of photos.

Distracted by the feel of her huddled against him and the gentle way she caressed his hand with her thumb, Lange found it difficult to concentrate on her meaning.

Did she mean this wonderful chemistry that existed between them? No, it happened rarely.

Did she mean the way his body reacted to hers, the way he hardened as he thought of holding her throughout the night? Yes, it happened every time she was near.

Did she mean the way his mind whirled and his heart quickened, the way his thoughts and his feelings and his basic survival instincts warred within him, leaving him totally vulnerable to her special kind of charms? God, it happened all too often.

"Does what happen often?" he finally choked out, trying to think straight. With her in his arms, he knew he was fighting a losing battle.

"Are many people like me?"

"I have never, ever met anyone quite like you," he admitted, his voice low and raw with emotion.

But Ashli hardly noticed. Her mind was still troubled with the thought of so much evil in the world, particularly her own little corner of it. "I mean, are many people stalked? Do you see this sort of thing often?"

"Unfortunately, yes. With the internet and social media and the constant flow of information and interaction, stalking someone has become easier. There's no such thing as privacy anymore. There are thousands of people, primarily women, who have to go through the same kind of hell you're going through." The seriousness of the matter sobered him, causing him to forget his lustful wanderings for a moment. "But, in a way, you're one of the lucky ones."

"Because I have you?" She couldn't resist asking, her mouth curving into a smile as she bumped her shoulder against him.

"That, too." He couldn't resist smiling back. He grew serious once more as he answered in earnest. "Because your stalker has made no actual threats, no actual attacks. Sending a dead goldfish and buying you gifts and a dozen roses is disturbing, but hardly menacing."

"Unless Jasmine's dismemberment is connected to my case. That's certainly more than a threat."

"I've been thinking about that. I'm still having trouble connecting your neighbor's detached foot, found in her own apartment, to you. If your stalker was trying to send you a message, I think he would have placed the foot in your apartment, or someplace he knew you would be sure to find it. You just happened to be the first person to find Jasmine."

"Maybe," Ashli said. She sighed, pulling her fingers through her hair. "I don't mean to be making this all about me. What happened to Jasmine is so horrible, so inconceivable, and you're right, all I've had so far are a few harmless gifts. Maybe it is just a coincidence that I have a stalker at the same time my neighbor comes up . . . you know . . . but somehow I don't think so."

"We have to find some connection. Something that ties her dismemberment to your Peeping Tom."

Just the thought sent a shudder through her narrow shoulders. With new resolve, she took a deep breath and turned back toward the computer screen. "Okay, let's get this over and done with. Maybe I'll find the missing link in the last of the mug shots."

Lange nodded to the stack of files beside the laptop. "Those are the old case files you asked about. Who knows, maybe the answer is somewhere in there."

"You sound doubtful."

"It has been over thirty years since the last crime," he pointed out. "Finish with the mug shots, and I'll leave these files with you. They're my copies, so there's no hurry to go through them tonight."

While Ashli finished searching through the criminal database, Lange wandered into the kitchen. A disaster like this meant at least an hour or so of cleanup, and it was already late. He knew it was his fault for detaining her this evening, and she had to be tired. She was being such a trooper, bravely looking through face after face, searching for anyone vaguely familiar. Some of the faces were evil enough to make even him squirm.

In an act of caring totally foreign to him, Lange drew up a sink full of sudsy water and washed dishes. He didn't give himself time to think of the implications; he simply went to work cleaning up the mess. He glanced up every so often, making certain she was all right. Even though she sat just on the other side of the bar, she was so engrossed in her task, she didn't realize what he was doing.

When she did, her undoubted look of pleasure would be worth the pucker of dishwater hands.

* * *

An hour later, Lange paused in the doorway before leaving. "There's just one last thing," he said. "Why did Detective Sullivan come by here today, Ashli?" he asked. The question had been eating at him all night.

"Routine follow-up, he said. He wanted to make certain I was all right, after . . . after everything."

"And?" He could tell she was hiding something by the way her eyes avoided his.

"And what?" she hedged.

"He could have called you on the phone — again — to check on you. What else did he want?"

Ashli paid close attention to the doorknob beneath her hand. "He asked me if I would like to go to dinner some night."

"And?"

"And I thanked him for the invitation, but I told him I couldn't think about dinner dates just now."

"But later?" he pushed.

"I-I don't know." She looked up at him, her breath catching in her throat when she saw the look of thunder upon his face. "I made no promises."

Without warning, Lange's hand came out and cupped around her neck, pulling her face in close to his. "Just remember," he murmured against her lips. "You're going with me to prom." And then he kissed her, slow and deep and sweet, with just a faint taste of desperation. She was so dazed by the intensity of his gentle kiss that he was already gone and out the door before his words settled into her befuzzled brain.

"Prom?"

CHAPTER SIXTEEN

With the catered banquet behind her, Ashli took a few minutes for herself on Sunday morning. Since the incidents with the Peeping Tom, she avoided spending time outside, but this morning, she chose to make an exception. It was still early, before the sun heated up and the city came fully awake, the perfect time to enjoy a few moments of fresh air. There must be a rule somewhere that said even stalkers had to take Sunday mornings off.

As she stepped onto the smaller balcony off her bedroom, coffee in hand, she realized how much she had missed the simple pleasure of being outdoors. Later, she would be angry that the stalker had taken this from her. Right now, she would just enjoy the sights and sounds of the early summer morning.

Birds flitted through the trees, singing to one another in greeting. She watched a couple of squirrels run among the treetops, jumping from one limb to another, making their way across the lawn, one tree at a time. A light breeze ruffled the leaves and teased her hair and carried the sweet scent of dew-kissed flowers.

Ashli smiled as she looked out over the gorgeous grounds of Daisy House. The grass was lush and green, randomly interrupted with bursts of color from one of Mr. Parnell's many flower beds. From so high up, she had a better view of the far gardens than of the pergola and the flagstone patio closer to the house. She could easily see the carriage house turned potting shed, the delightful goldfish pond, the stone benches at the edge of the tree line, and the little trails that led off into the profuse floras at the back of the property. She missed wandering through the maze of trees, shrubs, and flowers that crisscrossed through the estate, so badly it was almost a physical ache.

Ashli made a second cup of coffee, then hurried back up to the balcony. She needed to be at the airport in an hour to pick up Rachel and Kevin, which left only a few more minutes to indulge in nature's vista. In just the few short minutes that she was gone, the morning had heated up, promising to bring a warm day. And the peaceful quiet of morn was now broken by the sounds of Mr. Parnell, tinkering in the gardens below. She could see him moving around near the potting shed, spraying some dark-colored concoction over the flower beds. Between the fertilizer and the weed killer, his concoctions always had a foul odor, but he was conscientious enough to spray in early morning, when normally no one was outside. Luckily, the wind was blowing away from him, keeping the morning air sweet and fresh from where Ashli soaked up the last few moments of solitude.

It would be a busy week, so she had to enjoy these stolen moments of peace when and where she could get them. She was anxious to look into the files Lange brought her on the disappearances of those seven young women, but now wasn't the time. In fact, now wasn't the time to think of mysterious gifts or stalkers or severed feet. It wasn't the time to think of Jasmine or those seven girls from the past, not even the time to think of Lange.

Right now, Ashli wasn't thinking of anything. She was simply enjoying nature and her few moments of solitude, high on her balcony on an early summer morning.

* * *

It proved to be the only solitary moment of the entire week. The rest was filled with chaotic schedules and surprise visitors.

Typical of a Monday, the county health department chose a particularly busy lunch hour to inspect. Though Ashli's Tea Party passed with a perfect score, their surprise visits were always stressful.

On Tuesday, reporters flocked to the restaurant for interviews and restaurant reviews. The publicity generated by the upcoming awards was terrific for business but hard on Ashli and her staff. She posed for dozens of photographs and had just herded the last of the reporters out the door when she spotted her new friend Diane McIver.

"Hi stranger!" She smiled. She hadn't seen the lady lawyer since their conversation two weeks ago.

"I only have a minute, but I was in the neighborhood and wanted to bring this by to show you. I heard there was some sort of fancy banquet this weekend, and I thought your Romeo might be taking you. Is he?"

"Yes." Ashli couldn't help but smile.

"Then I have found the perfect dress for you!" With a dramatic flair, she pulled an ad slick from her briefcase and presented it with a triumphant smile. "In this dress, you're guaranteed to catch your man!"

Ashli took the glossy paper from her friend and looked down at the dress featured. She gave a small gasp. "That's not all I'd catch! What about pneumonia?"

"It's not that skimpy. I've worn less to Christmas mass!" Diane quipped.

"And I've used more wrapping than this on a Christmas present! I couldn't possibly wear this out in public!"

"Why not?"

"It's too . . . sexy." That was the only word to describe the daring red dress.

"Exactly," her friend said with a sly smile.

"I don't know. I think I need something a little more traditional, a little more . . . sedate."

"You want to open his eyes, not put him to sleep! I may not be an expert on love, but I know what makes a man tick." She tapped the paper with a long red nail. "This dress right here."

"I'll think about it," was all Ashli could commit to.

"Good. But don't think this little tip comes without strings. I'm thinking of calling my ex and inviting him over for a 'home-cooked meal'. Be thinking about what you can whip up for me!" She grinned.

"I'll work up a menu and get back to you."

"Great. Look, I've got to go. Promise me you'll buy the dress."

"I promise I will at least look at it."

"Between this dress I've found for you and the meal you'll cook for me, we'll both get our man. And then we can see about a completely different kind of 'cooking'." She sailed out the door with a wicked smile, leaving Ashli with a very provocative advertisement in her hand.

* * *

Wednesday's surprise visitor was Detective Sullivan, who dropped by the Tea Party 'just to say hello'. Ashli used the opportunity to pump him for information about Jasmine's case, but nothing new had been discovered. Even though the crime tape was still across the door of her apartment, no one had been inside for days. The rest of her body had still not been found, and the case was growing colder by the minute.

Thoughts of Jasmine weighed heavily on Ashli's mind as she went dress shopping that afternoon. At Diane's suggestion, she visited the boutique to see the infamous red dress. Modesty wouldn't allow her to as much as inquire about the dress featured in the ad, but she did find another one, and somehow, she ended up buying it. When she tried it on again at home that evening, she blamed her temporary lapse in judgment on worry over Jasmine. The dress was hardly her style, and time was running out to find another one.

Again, thoughts of her friend and her own troubles with a stalker took some of the luster from Thursday's bright spot. It was a big day for her career, the day contracts were signed to launch *Ashli's Kitchen* into syndication. As a surprise, Brandon from Florida was on hand for the occasion. Of course, he was part of their group as they celebrated afterwards with dinner and cocktails. He pressed for an invitation into her apartment when he saw her home that night, but Ashli begged off, saying she had to be ready for an early morning interview on *Wake Up, Richmond.*

By the time Friday rolled around and Ashli spotted Lange sitting at one of the tables eating a late lunch, she wasn't sure she could handle one more surprise.

She didn't even say hello. "If it's bad news, I don't want to hear it," she said instead.

Lange looked up in surprise, gesturing to the papers in front of him. "Actually, I'm just here for lunch. This isn't even your case I'm working on."

Never mind that he could have gone to a half-dozen other restaurants closer to his office. It had nothing to do with the empty feeling gnawing at his gut all week long, or with the jealousy he had been dealing with, knowing that Sullivan and Pretty Boy from Florida had both spent more time with her in the last few days than he had. He was just hungry, pure and simple.

Yeah, right.

"Oh, sorry," Ashli said with a contrite shrug. "In that case, I'll let you get back to work."

"If you've got a minute, why don't you sit down? You look like you could use a break."

"You wouldn't believe me if I told you the half of it." She groaned wearily as she sat in the chair next to him.

"Too much partying last night?" he asked with a wry crook of his brow.

"I thought that was you!" she said with a triumphant lift of her eyebrows.

"You made me? I thought I was rather discreet."

"In all fairness, I knew you were there before I actually saw you."

"How did you . . . oh, I forgot. The warm blanket theory." His tone was dry, but a tiny smile tugged at the corner of his mouth.

"Hey, don't make fun of me. I was right, wasn't I?" Her sassy smile turned into a grimace as she slipped off her shoe and massaged her foot beneath the table. "Of all days for me to break in a new pair of shoes," she moaned.

"Busy day?"

"Busy week. Every day this week has been crazy. It doesn't help that I've been up late every night, reading those old case files you dropped off."

"Find anything?" Lange pushed his plate toward her, offering to share his potato chips. Neither seemed to notice the casual intimacy of the gesture. They were enjoying a rare camaraderie between them, a light flirtatious atmosphere.

Munching on one, Ashli rested an elbow on the table and sighed. "Not really. Like you said, they didn't seem to have a thing in common. All seven were different ages, different professions, different backgrounds. Four of them had blonde hair and blue eyes, but the other three were black or Hispanic. It just doesn't make sense."

"And Jasmine is Oriental. Even if it was a copycat, he's seeing a connection we obviously can't make."

"Hey, get this. I was reading through the files, and I noticed they had interviewed one of the local business owners. Apparently, some of the disappearances and/or the places where the feet were found were within a four or five block radius. At the time, there was a movie theater in the area, I think about where that Lee's Station strip mall is. You know, where there's like three jewelry stores, all in a row? Sparkle Station, some people call it. Anyway, you'll never believe who the owner of the theater was."

By now accustomed to her wandering way of telling a story, Lange just shrugged. "Who?"

"Henry Parnell."

"The old man from your condo?"

Ashli nodded, biting into another of his chips. She just realized how hungry she was; she hadn't eaten today. "I guess that's how he got all those Doris Day posters and autographed photos."

"Did you talk to him about it?"

"I tried, briefly. He said, and I quote, 'Little darlin', I can hardly remember what happened thirty minutes ago, much less what happened thirty years ago'." She gave her best imitation of his shaky old voice. "He did, however, remember what movies were top box office hits in the years of 1960, '62, '63, and '64. They were all Doris Day movies, by the way."

"What is it with that old man and Doris Day?" Lange muttered.

"Obviously a severe case of starstruck-itis that he never outgrew. Anyway, I don't think he'll be much help. If he didn't have any valuable information at the time of the murders, I doubt he could add something new after all this time, even if he could remember anything. Which, apparently, he can't."

"Maybe I'll try to talk to him, even though he doesn't seem to like me very much."

"He's a sweet old man."

"He's a control freak, if you ask me. He refuses to consider putting up surveillance cameras."

"You can't blame him. The house is a historic landmark. I think there are guidelines on what can and can't be done to the property."

"It didn't originally have electricity or fancy kitchens like the one you have but look at it now."

"You have a point. Maybe I could talk to him about it."

"Yeah, he obviously has a soft spot for you. Another reason I don't think he likes me. He was acting like an over-protective father the other night."

Ashli laughed aloud, thinking he sounded just like a sulking teenager. As another thought popped into her head, she sobered. "Oh, another thing. I saw an ad the other day about flowers and their meaning, so I did a search on rhododendrons. Took me three times to spell it correctly but turns out rhododendron means 'beware'. Do you think that has any significance?"

"Only if someone sent you a rhododendron bush," he said, shoving the rest of his sandwich into his mouth.

Ashli frowned. "Not a bush, but a bloom. It was on my verandah one morning. Didn't I tell you?"

Lange nearly choked on the last bite of turkey and rye. "Damn it, Ashli," he sputtered, coughing into his hand. He took a gulp of iced tea, his eyes furious. "When did this happen? And why are you just now telling me?"

She thought back to when she had found the flower. "It was . . . oh, yes, it was a week ago Monday. I didn't call you because I thought maybe it just blew up there by chance, and because . . . because that was the day after we came back from my parents.'" She didn't have to explain any further; he knew all too well how things were left between them that weekend. "That-that was the morning that Jasmine . . . Oh my gosh, Lange, do you think he was warning me about Jasmine? Do you think I could have somehow stopped it from happening? What if I could have done something, but didn't? What if . . . ?"

He pulled her hand away from her mouth and held it determinedly. "Look at me," he said. He waited until her stricken eyes were focused upon his. "You have nothing to feel guilty about. There's no way you could have possibly known what was in store for Jasmine, so there's no way you could have stopped it. Even if you had told me about the flower that morning — which you should have done — there's no way either one of us would have made the connection between a flower blossom and a severed foot. Get that frantic look out of your eyes. This isn't your fault. End of story."

"Maybe I couldn't have stopped what happened to Jasmine," Ashli agreed. The light mood they had enjoyed, so rare between the two of them, was totally dark now. "But I definitely think he was sending me a message. Beware, because I just might be next."

CHAPTER SEVENTEEN

It was Saturday evening, and Ashli stood in front of the full-length mirror. "Good Lord, what was I thinking?" She tugged and pulled, attempting to cover more skin. "I think it shrunk," she muttered. "What on earth possessed me to buy this dress?"

Not that it wasn't a beautiful dress. The material was a fine cut of fire-engine red silk, the design stylish and sophisticated. On anyone else, she would have thought the dress stunning. On her, it seemed somehow scandalous.

It was a strapless bustier affair with an alluring sweetheart neckline and a tight, trim waist that flared into a silk caress around her hips. Much shorter than anything she normally wore, the material swayed provocatively around legs that looked long and shapely and unusually bare in silky sheer nylon.

Even her hair was different tonight. She had curled it on hot curlers to give the ends bounce and body, then had taken a section of hair and twisted it into a glamorous swirl, securing it with a glittering barrette of red and silver. Her only jewelry was a slender silver chain, its ruby-studded pendant dangling just above a generous show of cleavage.

The intercom buzzed as she applied a sheer matte gloss to her lips. She carefully maneuvered the stairs in her red high-heeled pumps, praying she didn't make a fool of herself tonight. Why, oh why, had she listened to Diane and bought this dress?

What if Lange didn't like the dress? What if he thought she looked like a tramp? What if . . .

She opened the door, and all thoughts flew from her mind.

She had never seen a more beautiful man. The tuxedo jacket showcased the perfection of broad shoulders and chiseled chest; the pants accentuated flat hips and long, lithe legs. Against the crisp white shirt, his skin was tanned and rugged. He looked like the full-color version of a golden Adonis statue. Dark hair brushed his collar, soft stubble shadowed his squared jaw, and his eyes . . . oh, his eyes. Hazel orbs, dark and steamy and alight with a fire she had never seen before. He was gorgeous. And so outright sexy. Something hot swirled inside her body, making her ache somewhere deep, deep inside.

It was a long moment before she remembered to breathe. Why didn't he say something? He just stood there and stared at her. Was the dress that bad?

She had no way of knowing, but he was unable to do anything else. Seeing her in a truly inspired creation for the first time, Lange felt his knees threaten to buckle.

This was an Ashli he had never seen. This was Marilyn Monroe, not Doris Day. Sultry. Sensuous. And oh, so sexy.

She was absolutely intoxicating. There was no other way to describe it. His pulse surged, his ears buzzed, his mind slowed. She completely flooded his senses, inebriating him with her beauty.

Lange knew it was useless to deny their attraction any longer. After all the times he had managed to resist her, it came down to this. A little red dress.

Even as he admitted defeat, he felt oddly victorious. Drunkenness did that to a man.

"I-I'm dressed all wrong, aren't I?" she finally whispered in dismay, mistaking his silence for disapproval.

"No." His voice was little more than a croak.

"But . . ."

He could hear the uncertainty in her voice. He stepped closer, bringing his long, tall body within inches of hers. Despite her heels, he was tall enough to gaze down into her upturned face. The deep timbre of his voice curled around her, caressing her entire body, but he resisted the urge to reach for her. "I have never," he told her, "in my entire life" — breathlessly — "seen a woman as beautiful as you."

The air between them crackled. Sexual tension swirled thick, stealing the air from their lungs. A long, pregnant moment purled around them. The sweet ache deepened, tightening low in Ashli's belly. Lange struggled to keep this overwhelming wave of passion in check. With breath ragged and uneven, they stared at one another, battling the urge to reach out and touch the other, fighting the crazy flame of desire that threatened to burn them both.

"Thank you," Ashli finally whispered. Her words were nearly drowned out by the hammering of their hearts.

With obvious effort, Lange swallowed hard and forced his drunken mind to function. "Are we ready?" he managed to ask.

"Uhm, I haven't heard from Rachel yet."

Right on cue, her phone rang. She struggled for normalcy as she spoke to her friend. Her fingers were clumsy as she hung up and slid her phone into a small sequined bag. "The limo is here. They're waiting for us downstairs."

"Let's get this party started." There was already a wild party happening in his head. His own hand fumbled on the doorknob as he opened the apartment door. "After you, my lady."

* * *

It was a magical evening.

As a nominee for the prestigious award, Ashli received star treatment. A stretch limousine waited to transport them to and from the event, where she and seven guests had a special table in the front of the hall. The limited space meant not everyone from Ashli's Tea Party could share in the spotlight, so Ashli had done the next best thing — she had bought a ticket for each employee to attend the night's gala and offered the last seats at the head table by way of random drawing. Along with all their dates, Amanda Kline, one of the baristas in the coffee shop, sat with Rachel, Molly, and Ashli at the front table.

Once again, Lange played the part of the perfect gentleman. He was charming and attentive, remembering to open doors and help with her chair. He even stood each time she did, which turned out to be quite often, given her many nominations for awards that night. Handsome, intriguing, and seemingly captivated by her every move, Lange was the perfect date. His attention just short of possessive, Lange stayed near her side the entire night, his hand on her waist, his eyes never straying far from her.

The excitement of the evening — and of the man — heightened with the steady flow of champagne. There was a toast each time the Tea Party or Ashli's names were called. Another toast for the winner. Too nervous to do more than nibble on the elegant meal served, Ashli felt the spin of alcohol go to her head. It swirled down and around, tempting and delicious, twining its way through her belly, down to secret places that were now heavy and throbbing with need. Maybe it wasn't the champagne. Maybe it was the man.

Just before the final award of the evening, Ashli excused herself and slipped off to the restroom. She stared at her reflection in the mirror, noting the high color in her cheeks and the undeniable gleam in her eye. Pressing a cool towel to her cheeks and the back of her neck, she willed herself to cool down. She pressed the other hand to her abdomen, where a swarm of butterflies had taken flight. Champagne and passion made for a queasy stomach, but *Lordy*, was it exhilarating!

While she straightened her hair and reapplied lip gloss, a woman joined her at the sink. "Mmm, mmm. I don't know who your date is tonight, girl, but I half-expect to see you go up in a puff of smoke! That man is H-O-T, and the looks he's been giving you are absolutely sizzling!"

Startled, Ashli shifted her eyes to the other woman in the mirror. She vaguely recognized her as a manager at another restaurant in town. Seeing her expression, the woman simply laughed. "Don't pay me no never mind, girl. I've done got all hot and bothered, watching your man stare at you all night with that look in his eyes." She laughed again coarsely as she opened the door. "*My* man is definitely getting lucky tonight!"

"Don't pay Shanitra any attention," another woman advised as she approached the sink. "I think she's had a little too much to drink." Her smile was warm. "Congratulations on all the awards tonight, especially 'Most Innovative Entrepreneur'." Her eyes twinkled as she added, "And on the smoking-hot date, too. Shanitra was right, you know. That is one fine date you have tonight."

"Uhm, thank you, Grace," Ashli murmured. Let her decide which comment she was accepting praise for.

As she left the restroom and made her way across the room, Ashli had a clear view of their table. Lange, her smoking-hot date who created such a stir among all the ladies, engaged in easy conversation with her friends. She watched in wonder as he tossed back his dark head and laughed at something they said.

Marveling at the change she saw in him tonight, Ashli paid little attention to her surroundings. She clumsily bumped into someone's arm.

"I'm so sorry," she murmured. "I wasn't watching . . . Doug! What a surprise! I didn't know you were here this evening."

The nice-looking deliveryman seemed more than pleased to have her bump into him. "Had to come s-s-support my favorite r-restaurant," he said with a nervous smile. "You're doing gr-great s-s-so far."

"Why, thank you, Doug, how sweet of you to say so. And to come tonight." Her pleasure was genuine.

"I hope you win the big pr-pr-pr-pr . . ." He swallowed hard, then chose a different word. "Award."

Ashli pretended not to notice how he stuttered over certain sounds. He was a military hero and deserved the utmost respect. Putting a hand on his arm, she squeezed gently and smiled. "Thank you so much. It's about time for them to announce it, so I'd better return to my seat. I'm sorry I nearly ran you over. I'll see you Monday for delivery?"

"S-s-sure."

Lange stood when she reached their table. He leaned close as he gently pushed her chair forward. Greedy hands lingered on her shoulders. "Who was that?" he asked.

She should have known he would notice. "One of the delivery guys from Flour Arrangements."

"You got more flowers?" he asked.

She laughed aloud, causing the others at the table to look her way. She motioned for him to take his seat. Leaning into him, she whispered, "No, silly, not flower, f-l-o-u-r."

"Was he on the list?"

"Doug?" she asked in surprise. "No."

"Why not?"

"I guess I never thought about him. He's a super nice guy. A veteran from the Iraq war. He was wounded in action, and it ended his military career."

"I don't like the way he looks at you," Lange said. "He keeps staring at you."

"So do you. People are noticing."

He seemed unbothered by her hissed statement. "What are they noticing?"

"That indecent gleam in your eyes. There!" she hissed again, as his eyes strolled over her. "That one right there."

"Can I help it if I can't take my eyes off you?" he murmured.

It was the truth. He tried repeatedly to settle his gaze elsewhere, but his traitorous eyes and lustful wonderings kept returning to her. As embarrassing as it was, he felt like a randy teenager tonight, attending his first prom. And with the Homecoming Queen, no less. He was spellbound. Dazzled. Completely intoxicated on her essence and barely capable of putting together a coherent thought. It was ridiculous, the way his mind churned thick and slow, mired with pure, unadulterated lust.

Or, maybe it wasn't so pure. The only thoughts that managed to break through his stupor were downright dirty.

"I'm serious, Lange, people are starting to talk about us."

"They're just jealous," he murmured. "They know."

Her heart tripped a beat, seeing the scorching look in his dark eyes. For the life of her, she couldn't look away. "They . . . they know what?" The question was little more than a whispered breath.

He didn't stop to think. Didn't stop to censure the words that tumbled from his dazed brain. He muttered the truth, his voice a low rumble in his chest. "That I can't wait to get you alone. That I can't wait to strip that beautiful dress from your body, one piece at a time."

She should have gasped. Should have been embarrassed. Appalled by his lack of propriety. Insulted by such a private revelation, in such a public place.

Instead, she was mesmerized. Fascinated by the images that popped into her mind. Singed by the bolt of electric sex pulsing between them. Trapped in the flames by her own desire.

The air around them crackled with sexual tension. The rest of the world fell away as they stared at one another.

"Ashli! Ashli, it's us! They called our name!"

As if from far away — well past the passion that clouded her brain, past this crazy surge of desire that was so thick she could taste it, outside the realm of a world where only she and Lange existed — Ashli heard Rachel calling her name. Her friend shook her arm to get her attention.

"We won, Ashli! Ashli's Tea Party won!"

The remainder of the evening was a complete blur. Ashli shook herself from Lange's hold and stumbled to the microphone, frantically trying to remember what the award even was. Oh, yes, Best of the Best, the ultimate award among her peers. She made a rambling but endearing speech that brought laughter and applause from the crowd, and she called her entire staff up for recognition. Ashli insisted they deserved the award as much as she did.

After the speeches, Ashli was swept away to stand in a receiving line. There were hands to shake and people to greet and pictures to take. Surrounded as she was by her colleagues and peers, Lange kept to the sidelines. Ashli told herself it was for the best. She didn't need the distraction he created, no matter how delicious it might be. Tonight was about *her*. Her career, her employees, her years of hard work and dedication. An honor such as this deserved her full attention.

A good thirty minutes after she accepted her award, Lange finally made his way to her side. He came up behind her and quietly slid his hand around the curve of her waist, his voice deep and sincere.

"Congratulations, Ashli. This is a well-deserved honor."

He had once accused her of being clueless. He thought she was an airhead. A classical, stereotypical blonde. Early on, he realized how wrong he had been, and tonight only confirmed it. Ashli Wilson was a brilliant woman, a successful businessperson, and an innovated leader in the community. She deserved this award and so many more.

As always, her brilliant smile dazzled him. "Thank you."

He touched a curl near her cheek, testing the feel of silk on his fingers. His gaze slipped to her lips. "I wish I could kiss you right now," he admitted.

She raised her smiling face to his. "Then why don't you?"

Her smile fell away when she heard his reply, raw and honest. "Because I might not stop."

Just like that, the fire was rekindled.

* * *

"You're sure you won't come with us?" Molly asked as they all piled into the limo.

"This new nightclub in Shockoe Bottom is supposed to be a happenin' place," her husband George said.

"Come on, Ashli, you gotta go," Rachel encouraged. "How cool will it be, pulling up at the hottest new nightclub in the city, in a stretch limo?"

"Dancing in these shoes?" Ashli laughed. It was the first excuse she had come up with when their group suggested they all go clubbing.

"We'll wait on you. You can change shoes and join us." Rachel wasn't giving up so easy. "The night's still young, and we've got some serious celebrating to do!"

Lange had been mostly silent, allowing Ashli to make the decision of what came next. As much as he wanted to stoke the fire that burned between them, this was her night. If she wanted to go clubbing, they would go clubbing. But she had begged off from the nightclub, several times now.

Were her friends so dense? Couldn't they see he and Ashli wanted to be alone? They could hardly keep their eyes — or their hands — off each other. The air around them sizzled with sexual tension. Surely, the others felt it.

Or did they simply disapprove of him that much? Rachel, Lange knew, wasn't his biggest fan. Was she so desperate to keep him and Ashli from being together? Was he that wrong for her friend? Resentment pooled in his gut. Doubt formed in his mind, penetrating the fog of drunken desire.

But then Ashli darted him the look. It was a silent plea for help, a request to convince their friends, once and for all, to go on without them.

Someone poured champagne and passed glasses around the backseats of the limo. Lange snagged a flute and lifted the bubbly to his lips. He spun the glass and tipped the rim to Ashli's mouth, so she drank from the same spot as he. Keeping his eyes fastened hungrily to hers, he turned the glass again. The rim was still wet from her lips. His tongue traced the area as slowly and thoroughly as his eyes traced the outline of her mouth.

The erotic scene wasn't lost upon their friends.

"Don't worry," Lange assured them, his voice deep and sensual. "We definitely plan to celebrate."

Nothing else was mentioned about them going to the club. The laughter from the other couples was a little too loud, a little too high-pitched, the color in Ashli's cheeks a little too pink, to be completely natural. By the time the limo reached her house, Lange's smoldering gaze rendered her a quivering mess.

As the car pulled away and left them alone on the front veranda of Daisy House, Lange looked down at her and asked quietly, "Are you sure?"

They both knew what he was asking. He was giving her a chance to change her mind, not just about the club, but also about being alone with him.

With a nod, Ashli drew a nervous breath and whispered, "I'm sure."

Instead of reaching for the door, Lange reached for her. "I've wanted to do this all evening long," he murmured, lowering his mouth to hers. Her arms still held the trophies of the night; his held the trophy of a lifetime. He couldn't pull her close, couldn't deepen the kiss the way he wanted to, but for now, it was enough.

This wasn't a kiss of passion; this was a kiss of promise.

In a sudden hurry to open the door and get inside, neither of them noticed the person at the end of the veranda. The person sat in the shadows, watching them kiss, slowly crushing the bouquet of daisies held in their hand.

* * *

Lange kissed her again when they stepped inside the foyer, a quick peck of his lips on hers. He repeated the kiss at the foot of the stairs, which drew a giggle from her. Playing along with his game, she climbed halfway up the staircase, then stopped for a kiss. This time he chuckled, a deep throaty sound that sent shivers of delight along her spine. This kiss was a bit longer, more than just a peck. Ashli hurried up the remaining steps, clumsy in her high-heel shoes and her eagerness. They both laughed as he chased close behind, and when he, too, stumbled. There was another kiss at the top, this one longer than the last.

By the time they reached her doorway, their kiss was long and lingering. With her hands still full, he had to get the key from her purse, and he did it with his arms around her, his mouth still on hers. Neither minded that it took several attempts to hold the purse still and fish the key from within. They laughed and kissed, trying not to make too much noise in the hallway.

He finally got the door open, and they fell into the room, their mouths and laughter still fused. When Ashli stumbled, Lange murmured against her mouth, "I think you might be drunk."

"I think I might be, too," she giggled.

Lange reluctantly released her to shut and lock the door. Ashli broke free and emptied her arms.

"Here, let me help you," he said. She struggled to keep from dropping the entire load on the dining room table. Spoils of the night included two beribboned bottles of champagne, another of wine, a gift basket piled high with goodies, commemorative programs, a dozen long-stemmed roses, and a gold-plated trophy.

"Thanks. All that was getting heavy." She flexed her arm to restore blood flow. "I need to put my roses in water. Why don't you select a wine and pour us a glass?"

"More wine?" He cocked an eyebrow.

"You, yourself, said we still have some celebrating to do." She ran a playful fingertip up his chest, then sashayed off to the kitchen to put away her roses. Lange's hungry gaze followed her.

She arranged her roses in a cut-glass vase and carried them to the trunk that served as her coffee table. She felt Lange's hot gaze on her as she bent over, the short hem of her dress exposing dangerous amounts of skin. He came quickly into the living room, carrying two glasses of wine.

"Let's have our wine out on the veranda," she suggested. Ashli saw the frown that came with his hesitation. "Oh, come on, Lange, just this once," she begged. "I used to sit out there almost every night, but since the whole stalker thing began, I've been cooped up inside. At least for one night, let's go outside and enjoy the stars and the breeze and the smell of the flowers."

She knew he couldn't deny her. As they stepped out into the warm night, he mumbled something about the heat and no breeze, but he followed her just the same. She walked all the way to the far railing, where she stopped and looked out over the landscaped backyard. Light from the lampposts spilled over the colorful flowerbeds, and solar lanterns twinkled from tree limbs and along the paths that wound through the gardens.

"Let's go for a walk in the gardens," she said, whirling toward him.

"Tonight?" he asked in surprise.

"Sure, why not?"

He handed her a wine glass, stepping close to graze the side of her neck with a kiss. "I have other plans for tonight," he told her in a low voice. "We'll go for that walk in the morning."

Implying he would still be here then. Suddenly nervous, Ashli turned back toward the railing and sipped her wine. She studied the twinkling stars overhead for a long moment. When she spoke, her words were soft and serious. "I'm not drunk, you know. Not on wine. But I think I am drunk with happiness."

"I've heard that happiness can do that." Although he didn't sound convinced, neither did he sound cynical. Ashli took that as an encouraging sign.

"You've never been happy, have you, Lange?" she asked. Her back was still to him, and she knew it would be easier for him to be honest with her, with himself, if she weren't looking directly at him.

"There was always something missing," he admitted. He stepped closer to her, brushing against the back of her skirt, but flesh didn't touch.

"Even with Lauren?" she dared to whisper.

He tensed, but finally he answered. "Even with Lauren." A long moment of silence followed before he elaborated. "I'm not sure I even knew what it was, until I saw you with your family. Then I knew. It was that sense of being wanted, of belonging. It was having a home. Roots."

He abandoned his wine glass in favor of holding her. Her back still to him, he moved closer, sliding his hands low around her waist, just above the flare of her hips. There was a gap between them, until she reached back and sought out his cheek. Her tender touch spoke more than words ever could, as she drew his face down against her head in a tender act of care.

Swallowing hard, Lange pulled her close against him, pressing her into his hard, aching body, pulling her into his empty, aching heart. Turning his lips into the palm of her hand, he whispered unsteadily, "I'm happy tonight."

Ashli turned into his arms, knowing what it must have cost him to make such an honest admission. She took his handsome face into her hands and stared into his eyes, then reached up and initiated the kiss. He moaned as his mouth hungrily met hers.

The kiss went on, and on. They moved closer, straining against one another as the kiss deepened. They were moving into the other's soul, pressing their bodies and their hearts together beneath the glow of a lover's moon. Lange wedged his leg between her thighs, aching to become a part of this woman. He twisted his hips, grinding against her.

His all-out assault on her senses made her legs unsteady. The high-heeled shoes made it even worse. Her foot slipped, breaking their heated kiss.

"These shoes are going to kill me yet," she managed to laugh. She hardly noticed any pain associated with twisting her ankle; there were far more glorious feelings surging through her body right now, and they had her gasping for breath.

"Then let's get rid of them." Lange fell on one knee, where he proceeded to take her foot into his hand and sensually remove her shoe. She placed her hands onto the broad planes of his shoulders for balance. He skimmed his hand along her ankle, sliding long fingers slowly beneath the strap, easing the leather down with gentle finesse. If he made removing a shoe such a sensual delight, Ashli could only imagine the magic he created with a bra.

When he finished with one shoe, he started on the other. She was considerably shorter without the high heels but felt steadier on her feet. Until his hands started to move.

"N-not here," she finally managed to pant. She tugged on his hair to get his attention. "Not here."

Lange was on his feet, appalled at how his passion overruled his good judgement. He glanced around the veranda and the grounds beyond, making certain no one had witnessed their little show. Not only had he compromised her privacy by practically making love to her right there on the balcony, he had compromised her safety. What if her stalker was out there, watching? What would seeing them together do to an unsteady mind?

That was the problem with getting involved, he reminded himself.

But the real problem was that he had no intention of stopping. Not tonight.

"You get the wine, I'll bring the shoes," he said. He waited for her to go in, checked their surroundings outside once more, then followed her into the house, closed the shutters, and locked the doors.

"I'm sorry, Ashli," he said. "I shouldn't have—"

Ashli misread his apology. Slamming the wine glasses down so hard that wine sloshed over their sides, she didn't care that it soaked into her antique trunk. Eyes blazing, she glared up at Lange. "Are we back to that again? Are you going to stand there — after tonight, after everything we have been through these past few weeks — and try to tell me we can't get involved?"

He loved the look of passion blazing in her eyes. He loved that she was mad, that she was angry enough to fight for what she wanted. He loved that *he* was what she wanted. He loved . . .

Shaking that thought right out of his head, he stepped closer, trying to take her hand. Still angry, she shook out of his hold, stepping back. "No, Lange. I am sick and tired of your little games. One minute you want me, the next you don't. I'm not playing anymore."

"I'm not playing, either." He advanced toward her with a self-deprecating little laugh. "Come on, Ashli, we both know what a liar I am. No, we can't be involved." Pain flared in her eyes at his words. He moved close enough to brush his knuckles along the cheek, his voice softening. "But we are."

Her breath caught in her chest. "Then . . . why were you sorry?" she asked.

"Because I forgot where we were. You have a stalker, a Peeping Tom on that very balcony, and instead of protecting you, all I could think about was making love to you." He tucked a wayward curl behind her ear, his eyes fascinated by the strand of sunshine. With a sigh, he seemed to be thinking aloud, instead of speaking to her. Maybe her habits had rubbed off on him. "To be honest, it's all I ever think about," he murmured. "I've fought it so hard, trying to deny this attraction between us, but God, I can't even think straight around you." He frowned and shifted his eyes to hers. "Did I just say all that aloud?"

"You did," she said with a smile. "So . . . no more games?"

His large thumb traced the curve of her gorgeous smile, the one that had a way of warming him from the inside out. "No more games," he agreed.

"You admit that there's something between us?"

"You know how to kick a man when he's down, don't you?" he mumbled.

"You didn't answer my question. Do you want me, Lange?"

Her question was blunt and direct, but he could see the fear in her eyes. Despite asking such a daring question, he saw the doubt clouding her blue eyes, he heard the breathless hope in her voice. A week ago, he might have denied the truth, he might have lied. Again. Tonight, there was too much honesty in her gaze, too much emotion in her voice. Too much at stake. Her brave handling of the situation demanded that he man up and be just as brave.

"Yes, Ashli," he answered, but he didn't quite meet her eyes. He still studied the curve of her fascinating mouth. "Yes, I want you. I want you more than . . . more than I've ever wanted anyone or anything. It's not smart. It's not professional. It's not logical, the way I want you. It doesn't make a damn bit of sense. But it's there, and it's bigger than anything I've ever felt before." He finally lifted his gaze to hers, his expression almost pained. The admission hadn't been easy. "Are you satisfied now?"

She smiled, as much with her twinkling blue eyes as with her delicious mouth. "Yes." To his surprise, she pulled away. "Wait here," she instructed and left him standing in the living room as she disappeared up the stairs.

He gaped after her, wondering what had just happened. He poured his heart out to her, and she just took off? Had he finally gone too far? Maybe he had pushed her away one too many times. Maybe she wanted to get even. Maybe she wanted him to grovel.

No, not Ashli. She wasn't a tease, and she wasn't vindictive. He growled in frustration, running his hands through his hair. Wondering if he should go after her or wait it out, he tugged off his tuxedo jacket and tie, throwing them both on the couch. He picked up a wine glass and had just finished draining its contents when he heard her small cry of pain.

He took the stairs two at a time, racing to the top to check on her. He shouldn't have let her go up there alone. What if her stalker had been up there, waiting on her? What if . . .

What if his every fantasy was coming true?

He stepped into Ashli's room and saw the flicker of a dozen lit candles, and the woman of his dreams standing among them, in a pink nightgown spun of fluff and fantasy. She was covered from neck to toe in an opulent filmy material, just one shade darker than transparent. Even with ruffles, the high-necked robe did little to conceal the negligee, or the woman, beneath it. The gown itself was a vision of pink mist, a delicate fantasy of billowing clouds. Plunging deep and low before falling to her toes, the negligee hid more of her body in shadows than in actual fabric.

Lange made a strangling noise in the back of his throat, a deep guttural sound that was neither word nor cry. He crossed the room in three long strides, stopping just inches from her.

"I thought . . . I thought I heard you cry out," he said, trying to peel his eyes from her body long enough to check out the room, but failing miserably. Once again, he couldn't take his eyes off her.

"I burned myself," she said in her whispery soft voice, "lighting a candle." She held up a finger, slightly puffed and red at the tip.

Lange reached out and took her hand, pulling the injured flesh to his mouth for a gentle caress with his tongue. She gasped, not from pain, but from the sensation of his tongue on her skin. She wanted more of that, much more.

He tugged on her waist, pulling her up against his throbbing body. The thin material was little barrier to the warm woman beneath it. He nuzzled her ear, murmuring another sound that could have been an endearment, could have been a curse. When he nibbled his way down her neck, lacy ruffles teased his lips. He raised his head and pulled slightly away, just enough that his gaze could devour the length of her.

"Tonight, when I saw you in that red dress," he told her, his voice hoarse with emotion, "I thought no woman could ever look more tempting, more beautiful, more desirable. I thought I could never want you more than I did then." His eyes lingered on the deep plunge of her gown's neckline, so vaguely covered by the opaque robe. His voice dropped to a rough whisper. "I was wrong."

Three ribbons held the edges of her filmy robe together. Ashli reached up to untie the first one. Lange maneuvered the second, his hand unsteady as it freed the ribbons near her breast. The third and final ribbon offered the last chance of resistance, the last hint of restraint between them. They knew that once the ribbon was released, their relationship would never be the same. They would become lovers, their entire world changed by the simple act of untying a ribbon.

Ashli lifted blue eyes to his, staring deep into the inky depths of his soul. Air collected in his lungs when he saw her hesitate. She slowly wound the pink ribbons around her finger. Looking him straight in the eye, she tugged the last ribbon free. Lange's breath came out in a ragged release as he reached out and dispensed of the robe, pushing it from her shoulders.

He concentrated on the task of unveiling her sumptuous body. As his hands slid over the near-sheer fabric, he could see her flesh quiver beneath his touch, waiting.

"Ashli." He murmured her name with need, burying his face into the crook of her neck. "Good God, Ashli, how I want you."

"I want you, too," she confessed in a breathy whisper that turned his heart inside out.

They came together with a sigh, their lips and their hands curious and seeking.

"This is your last chance," Lange whispered. "If this doesn't feel right, stop me now."

"This feels very, very right." She stood on tiptoe to kiss him. "This feels perfect."

With a strangled sound of need and pleasure, Lange swept her into his arms and onto the bed. He buried his hands in her hair, fanning out the strands of white sunshine before working his way downward.

Lange took only a moment to slip on protection, then he poised himself above her. Still, he hesitated. "I can't make you promises, Ashli."

"Neither can I. I can't even promise tomorrow." When he started to protest, she touched her fingers to his lips. "But we have tonight, Lange," she whispered. "Give me tonight."

She arched her body beneath him, offering herself. It was a gift no mortal man could refuse. He pushed inside her, burying himself in velvet, losing himself to the wonders of her body. As they moved together in harmony, Lange felt the old, familiar emptiness inside him fill. The craving he had always known, the hunger for that elusive sense of belonging, ebbed.

He saw the wide-eyed wonder that filled her eyes and racked her body with amazement; he saw her eyes close to ride out a tidal wave of pleasure. His own body rushed after hers in a maelstrom of raging passion, and as Lange buried his very heart and soul deep within her, he had the most incredible sense of coming home.

Ashli, he realized. Ashli was his home.

Ashli was where he belonged.

CHAPTER EIGHTEEN

Sunlight danced through the bedroom blinds, coaxing Ashli into the brilliance of the day. She stretched lazily beneath the covers without opening her eyes. Her body was sore in the most curious places, but the sweet discomfort left her revitalized and full of life. And hope.

As memories of the previous night swept through her heart, she stretched her hand out to the other side of the bed. She wasn't surprised to find it empty, but it stung knowing Lange hadn't bothered with goodbye. She pulled the vacated pillow to her and took a deep breath. The spicy scent of his cologne was still trapped in its fibers.

Hugging the pillow close, she smiled. Last night had been the best night of her life. Professionally, she had achieved the height of local fame. Personally, she had broken through the hard shell of indifference Lange surrounded himself with. Physically, she had soared to heights she never knew existed.

Lange had given her a part of himself last night. Not just his body, although he shared that with her quite generously. Her blood warmed just with the memory. More than that, he had given her a piece of his soul, and, she dared believe, at least a small piece of his heart.

The tantalizing aroma of coffee wafted through the air and snagged her attention, just before she heard footsteps on the stairs. He hadn't left, after all.

"I knew coffee would do the trick," he said. "You've been dead to the world. The phone rang, I took a shower, I dropped a book. You never even stirred, until I made coffee."

Ashli sat up in bed, tucking the sheet around her naked breasts as she reached for the cup. She had no idea how the sight of her, naked and smiling, her hair mussed and her makeup either missing or smeared, made his heart do a summersault within his chest. She took several sips before she asked, "Who called?"

"Your mom."

"You answered?" she squeaked, mortified at the mere thought.

"No, Ashli, I'm not that careless. I heard the machine pick up."

"All right, good." She took another sip in relief.

He lifted a dark, sexy eyebrow. It matched the look he had going on; bare sexy chest, tight sexy tuxedo pants, shoeless sexy feet. "Regrets already?" There was a teasing tone in his voice, but she could see the uncertainty in his eyes.

"Not regret. Embarrassment. This is my mother we're talking about."

"You might want to call her. She said something about coming by."

"My mother's in town?" she cried. She groped for the phone on her bedside table, forgetting to keep the sheet tucked in.

Getting exactly the response he had hoped for, Lange enjoyed the view. As she dialed, he broke his gaze and turned toward the stairs. "I'll bring you breakfast," he offered.

"That's not nec— Hello, Mom?" She turned away from the view of his fine-looking backside, afraid her mother would hear the distraction in her voice.

By the time Lange returned, she was off the phone. He was still on the top step when she accused, "You tricked me!

You know good and well she said they weren't coming until this evening!"

"It got you up and moving, didn't it?" He carried a cookie sheet in lieu of a serving tray, but it was piled with food and two cups of coffee. As he set the tray down at the foot of the bed, he noted she had slipped into a shirt. His white tuxedo shirt, if he wasn't mistaken.

"That definitely looks better on you than on me," he murmured.

"I don't know about that. You turned quite a few heads last night." She surveyed the tray before her. "Hmm, let's see. Toast, strawberry preserves, fresh oranges, chicken puffs, chocolate cake, and coffee." She beamed up at him. "Perfect!"

Dazzled by the brilliance of her smile, Lange felt an odd catch in his chest. He handed her a full cup of coffee in exchange for her empty one, willing his hand to remain steady. "I raided your little yellow boxes," he admitted.

"The toast was an original touch."

"Didn't want you to think I was totally inept in the kitchen."

The easy bantering was a nice change of pace between them. What could have been an awkward morning turned fun and playful with their light flirtation and original menu.

"Oh, I almost forgot," Lange said, pulling something from his back pocket. He tossed the *Lifestyle* section of the Sunday morning paper toward her. She saw her own face smiling back at her, beaming with pride and excitement. There was a big headline, accompanied by a nice story about her and the Tea Party. She squealed in delight, scanning the story as she nibbled on a slice of toast.

"What a sweet thing to say," Ashli said as she finished the article. She read a few of her favorite lines aloud, clearly pleased with the paper's portrayal of her business. "I think I may have this framed and hung at the Tea Party, what do you think?"

"I think that's a very good idea."

They finished their meal in companionable silence, before Ashli finally looked at the clock and groaned. "I guess I should get up and take a shower."

He was oddly disappointed she had plans for the day. Odd, normally he was eager to leave the morning after. "What's on your agenda for today?" He strived for casual.

Ashli thought for a moment, then gave him another of her brilliant smiles. "Absolutely nothing. For the first time in weeks, I don't have a single thing planned for the day. Oh, except for dinner with my parents, later this evening." She hesitated before adding, "They wanted to know if you'd be joining us."

"I might be free this evening." He couldn't help the satisfied little smile hovering on his lips.

"Then you might be treated to dinner at Southern Pride around seven," she replied.

"I'm assuming I'd be over-dressed in a tux?"

"Maybe just a little bit."

"Then I'll have to ask for my shirt back." His dark eyes glittered.

"I said no to the tux."

"But I'll have to go home and change." He held out his hand, his gaze already roaming over her in anticipation of seeing her naked once again.

"Not so fast, mister. You did make one promise last night that I intend to hold you to."

He groaned, wondering what he might have promised in the throes of passion. With Ashli, there was no telling. He had lost all control last night.

"You promised me a walk in the gardens."

Relieved to know that was all she expected of him, he relaxed. "I did, didn't I? Hand over the shirt so you can take your shower, and we can go for our walk."

"Nice try." When Ashli stood, the shirt brushed the tops of her knees. She hurried to the bathroom, where she stripped just out of his line of vision and tossed the shirt out the door.

"I'll be ready in thirty," she called over her shoulder. "Twenty, if you promise another cup of coffee."

Twenty-five minutes and a cup of coffee later, Ashli and Lange stepped out of the apartment. He wore the tuxedo shirt now, sleeves rolled up and jacket nowhere in sight. To his delight, Ashli was dressed in denim capri pants, with a simple camisole top and a floral over-shirt.

It was a look he had never seen on her before, but one he fully appreciated. She looked fresh and fashionable and insanely sexy, even though there was nothing particularly revealing about her outfit.

"Our gardens are spectacular," Ashli said as they descended the staircase. "Mr. Parnell has a real green thumb." She glanced down and saw the door open to the elderly man's apartment. "It looks like he's coming out right now. He might be able to give us a guided tour. He's very knowledgeable about the various types of flowers and plants."

Lange didn't want to share her with anyone this morning, especially her over-protective landlord. He would have said as much, but it wasn't Mr. Parnell coming out of the apartment; it was a woman dressed in nurse's scrubs. A woman he recognized.

Ashli saw the woman, too, and hurried down the step to greet her in surprise. "Veronica! What are you doing here? Is Mr. Parnell all right? You don't usually come on Sunday morning. Is anything wrong?" In typical fashion, she continued to ask questions before receiving an answer to the first.

"Mr. Parnell called me this morning, terribly disoriented," the nurse answered, nonplussed by the bombard of questions. "I'm surprised he could even dial my number, although I think it may have been a lucky fluke. He kept talking about his wife, then thought I was his wife."

Ashli sighed. "Bless his heart. Is he all right now?"

"I've given him something to relax and calm down. He's sleeping now." As Lange reached the bottom step behind Ashli, the nurse shifted her gaze to him. Surprise clearly registered on her face. "Lange! What are you do—" Her question trailed off as she noted his formal attire, from the night before. Her back visibly stiffened as her eyes darted back and forth between him and Ashli.

"I'm sorry," Ashli murmured, ashamed to have forgotten her manners. "Lange Sterling, Veronica Ables." Then the other woman's words sank in. "But wait. You two know each other?"

Neither directly answered. "Good to see you, Veronica," Lange said to the nurse, but his tone didn't match his words.

She looked pointedly down at his clothes before returning a cool gaze to his eyes. "Yes, you, too." With a falsely sweet smile, she added, "My sister never mentioned you knew Ashli."

"There's no reason she would," Lange said. "I haven't spoken to your sister in a while." His relationship with Diane seemed like ages ago, even if the calendar measured it in weeks.

"I see," she said in a clipped tone. "Well, I have to go now."

Confused about what had just transpired, Ashli was still concerned about her neighbor. "Should I check on Mr. Parnell later?"

"That would be nice. If you're not too busy." This, with a sharp look thrown toward Lange.

"Of-of course not. I always have time for a friend."

"I'm sure you do. Goodbye, Ashli. Lange." With a smart toss of her head, the nurse flounced across the foyer and out the door.

After the door slammed shut, silence echoed. "What just happened here?" Ashli asked.

Lange caught the hand she waved through the air and tugged, dragging her toward the back door and the awaiting gardens.

"Lange, why was Veronica acting so strangely? And how do you know her, anyway? What was that about her sister?" He was still holding her hand, pulling her down the hallway. "Are you going to answer me or not?"

"Do I have a choice?" he muttered, knowing she would go on and on until he did. He opened one of the stained-glass doors with its intricate pattern of daisies and waited for her to go first.

"Don't think you're going to distract me with a sudden display of manners," she chided. "Although it is nice, thank you. Now, back to Veronica. How do you know her, and why was she so rude just now?"

"I don't know Veronica that well. I've met her a handful of times, through her sister. We . . . dated," he said, for lack of a better word.

Ashli was quiet for a long moment. So long, in fact, Lange grew nervous. She didn't say anything, just walked across the covered patio and into the sunshine. He trailed behind, blinded by the halo that glowed around her head. With the sunlight bouncing off her white-blonde tresses, she looked like an angel sent down from heaven.

Lange caught up with her and tried to take her arm. She shook it away, her blue eyes accusing. Her voice, normally soft and gentle, dripped with disdain. "You're in a relationship? You're involved with someone else, and you spent the night with me?"

"No! No, I'm not in a relationship."

"Then what was all that about her sister? Why was she so rude to you, unless she caught you cheating on her sister?"

"She may think I was cheating, but I'm not. I broke it off with her sister."

Ashli looked up at him and asked directly, "When?"

He couldn't hold her gaze. He knew what she would think of him. "After I kissed you for the first time," he told her.

"I'm the other woman now?" Ashli threw her hands up and stalked off, toward the gardens. Neither appreciated the bounty of nature now.

"You never even hinted," Ashli said, knowing he was right behind her. "I would never have gotten involved with you if I had known you were in a relationship."

"It wasn't a relationship," he defended himself. She whirled around, incredulous, but he stuck to his story. "It was more of an . . . arrangement. Neither of us wanted any strings, both of us needed an occasional date for social engagements. It was convenient."

"You were sleeping together." It wasn't a question.

When he made no reply, she took off walking again. He let her go at first, but a few paces with his long legs brought him to her side.

"No wonder you kept pushing me away. You tried to tell me we couldn't be involved, but I wouldn't listen, would I? You tried to distance yourself from me, tried to keep things professional, but I kept pecking away, trying to break through your shell. I should have just let well enough alone, but no, I had to push." In typical Ashli fashion, she was talking to herself, as much as to him.

He couldn't stand to hear the derision in her voice. He couldn't let her blame herself, when he was the one at fault. Catching her arm, he forced her to stop. He stepped in front of her and made her look at him. "She's not the reason I didn't want to get involved with you," he said. He slipped his hand into her hair, cupping the back of her head and forcing her face up toward his. "I was never romantically involved with her. Not on an emotional level. Our relationship was purely physical."

"If you're trying to make me feel better about last night, you have a very strange method."

"No, I'm trying to explain my involvement with her."

"You were friends with benefits. I get it. I just don't happen to like being the other woman."

"You were never the other woman, Ashli." Lange's words were low and husky, his eyes dark. "From the first moment I saw you, you were the only woman."

Ashli felt her heart melt. It oozed all the way down to her toes, making her all warm and tingly inside. With great discipline, she forced herself to remember their argument.

"It's true, Ashli," he insisted, seeing the indecision in her eyes. "I saw her exactly once after I met you. I broke it off with her that very night." Lange frowned, weighing his words before he spoke. His eyes were on his thumb, which trailed back and forth over the soft swell of her cheek. A raw admission raked from his too-tight chest. "I know it sounds cold; I know what you must think of me when I tell you this. But she was never a factor in my relationship with you, because she was never that important to me. I never let her in, Ashli. She knew I had lost a woman named Lauren, but

I never told her the whole story. I never told her about my grandmother. I never took her to my apartment." He slid his eyes to hers. They were naked with emotion and had a moist sheen Ashli had never seen in them before. "I had sex with her many times," he admitted. His voice dropped to a rough whisper. "But I never made love with her, like I did with you last night."

This time when Ashli melted, it was in his arms. Still cupping the back of her head, Lange held her face at just the right angle, so he could bring his mouth down on hers with slow and deliberate finesse. He brushed his mouth back and forth across hers, sliding his lips across hers. After a long moment, he ran the tip of his tongue over the lower rim of her bottom lip, back across the plump middle, then slid it along the seam of her mouth. Lost to the mastery of his kiss, Ashli let him gently tug her lips apart, until the tip of his tongue was just inside, tracing the sweet cavern. When his tongue finally touched hers, she gasped as if he were kissing her for the first time. He pulled her closer, his hand still buried in the glory of her hair, as he continued to kiss her long and slow, and with great reverence.

When he raised his head, he held her for another long moment, allowing their heart rates to slow, and their breathing to even out. At last he spoke, but his voice was slightly unsteady. "Let's see that garden now."

Ashli took his hand with a smile, her lips pink and full and still tingling from his kiss. "They're very lovely," she said, her thoughts still on their kiss. She hugged his arm to her side.

"Keep staring at me like that, and we'll never make it past the first rosebush," he threatened in a sinful, rich voice.

"Hmm. Maybe we'll get lost off one of the trails," she suggested.

"I'm warning you. Look at me like that for ten seconds longer, and we won't make it to the trail."

Ashli let her gaze linger on his mouth for a good five seconds, then laughed at his growl of desire. "Come on," she said, pulling him along. "I want you to see the goldfish pond."

They wandered past a wild profusion of color and wound their way along the brick-paved pathway until they reached the pond. With its irregular shape edged in limestone, the pond was cool and clear and bubbly. Small pumps kept the water moving, with small sprinkler fountains scattered throughout. The staggered depths added the illusion of tiny waterfalls. More water flowed down a layered pile of limestone and granite and offered the pleasant gurgle of a running brook. Amid the sparkling water, flowers and fauna and fish abounded.

"Very nice," Lange said with approval. "Very nice."

"I love the pond. Sometimes I come down here and read, or just sit and think." She nodded to the two benches placed on opposite sides of the pond. She frowned suddenly. "Or at least, I used to."

Since she was the one to bring up the subject, Lange expanded on it. "I wonder if this is where your goldfish came from."

She looked duly surprised. "I don't know, I never thought of that."

"Doesn't matter. Come on, let's see more of this garden wonderland."

"Don't jest. We're only getting started. I have no idea what all these flowers are, but Mr. Parnell can name them all. He has a huge vegetable garden back here, too, and all sorts of trees and plants. We'll go this way first."

"I'll follow you wherever you lead me." His words were light, but he knew they carried a heavy truth.

After an hour of wandering through the gardens, lingering more than once for a stolen kiss, they made their way back up the other side of the garden. As predicted, Lange was quite impressed with the extensive system and the profuse growth.

"I can't believe that old man takes care of all this by himself," Lange said with new appreciation for her neighbor. "This is a huge plot."

"I know. It's amazing when you think about it, given his age. But he's in good physical condition, and still strong as an ox. It's just his mind that seems to be failing him."

"Is this the carriage house?" Lange asked as they came in view of the old brick structure.

"Yep. Guess it used to hold all the carriages and wagons for the property. Now it's Mr. Parnell's storage shed."

"Awfully big shed," Lange said, eyeing the large building.

"And he's got it all full, too." Ashli laughed. "All sorts of worktables and potting tables and tools, lawn mowers and edgers and weed eaters, and that big machine where he mixes his fertilizer."

"I'd like to see what kind of mower he uses," Lange said, stepping up to try the door. Finding it locked, he stepped over to a window. "I bet he has a zero-turning-degree lawn mower. Wonder what brand," he murmured, trying to see past the chest freezer for a glimpse of the machinery. "Hmmm, can't see from here. Good Lord, what is that smell?" he asked, getting a whiff of the foul odor.

Ashli chuckled. "That," she said, "is the secret formula to these magnificent gardens. Mr. Parnell swears by the stuff. I have no idea what's in it, but it's his own concoction, and he's very secretive about it. He's won several different awards and contests for his flowers and vegetables, and he says he owes it all to his secret plant food and fertilizer."

"It stinks to high heaven," Lange complained, moving away from the window.

"You're telling me. But he's good to only spray it when no one is out and about. Sometimes the yard will smell after he first puts it out, but that dissipates with a bit of a breeze. See this back wall? This is where we play our movies. You should come next time."

"Maybe I will. I'm assuming it will be a Doris Day flick?"

"If Mr. Parnell has anything to say about it, it will be. I still can't believe I never knew he had a movie theater. He's always talking about the past. I wonder how that never came up."

"Maybe he forgot," Lange said.

"That's a terrible thing to say," she chided, but she was smiling as she bumped his arm with her shoulder. "You should be ashamed of yourself."

"I'm ashamed of myself for what I'm thinking right now," he told her.

"Which is?"

"I'm thinking of the things we could do beneath that rose bush. And over by those daisies over there." He pulled her against him. "And what I'd love to do to you under that mimosa tree," he breathed, nibbling on an ear.

"You're right. You should be ashamed," she murmured in agreement, without any real conviction. Then, with a wicked grin that flipped his heart on its side, she countered, "My bed is much more comfortable."

She heard his breathing quicken and loved the bright flicker that sparked his eyes. He leaned in to say, "Race you," low and slow. Then he took off with a head start.

"Hey, no fair!" she protested with a laugh.

When he came to a sudden stop, Ashli ran into him. "What in the world is the matter with you?" she laughed. "Letting me win? What are you looking at?" She followed his gaze to the corner of the mansion where her condo was.

Morning sun streamed over her balconies, offering no shade and easy visibility. Ashli gasped when she saw the red letters splashed across the French windows of her living room. The word "BITCH" glistened in the bright sunlight, the paint — or was it blood — still wet and beginning to drip.

Lange reached for her as she crumpled to the ground in despair.

CHAPTER NINETEEN

Detective Sullivan and his forensics team arrived within twenty minutes. While they set to work swabbing, printing, and taking photos, Ashli disappeared into her kitchen. She needed the distraction of keeping busy and the comfort she found in cooking. By the time the detective came back inside to question her in depth, the house smelled of cinnamon and yeast.

Ashli carried a tray into the living room, where the policeman and Lange were speaking in clipped, terse tones. She caught some of their words as she approached.

"Please, don't let us keep you from your event, Mr. Sterling." Detective Sullivan eyed Lange's formal attire with a downward tilt of his lips. "It's not necessary for you to be here while I question Ms. Wilson."

"Our event was last night." Lange goaded the other man. "And she prefers to be addressed as 'Miss'."

High levels of testosterone circled between the two men as they stared each other down. A sigh escaped Ashli's lips. She pushed through their ridiculous competition and set her tray on the coffee table.

"I fixed us a bite to eat." She stated the obvious as she motioned for the officer to take a seat.

"That wasn't necessary." The pleased expression on his handsome face didn't match the protest from his lips. "But it looks delicious."

Lange felt an unexpected pang of jealousy as he watched Ashli hand the other man a plate. She cooked for the detective, the same way she had cooked for him! What did she do, go around collecting lost hearts? He could clearly see the other man's heart, hanging right there on his sleeve, shining through that silly lovelorn expression in his eyes. She wasn't just handing the man a sandwich, she was handing him a piece of herself, a piece of her kindness. Resisting the urge to knock the plate from the other man's reach, Lange willed his jealousy under control.

"It's not much." Ashli shrugged. She presented crusty grilled sandwiches, made with thick slices of potato bread, two kinds of cheeses, slabs of honey-cured ham, and a tangy mustard sauce. Potato chips, pickle spears, and the last of the chicken puffs rounded out the meal, with fresh-from-the-oven coffee cake for dessert.

"It looks like a feast, ma'am. It's not often that a victim makes me a meal."

Ashli handed him his tea glass with a frown. "Is that how you see me, Detective Sullivan? As a victim?"

"I meant no disrespect, ma'am. But the fact is, someone is stalking you. That makes you a victim."

"No, that makes me the target. I refuse to be a victim."

God, she was brave, Lange thought, taking the glass she offered. His chest swelled with pride at her courageous attitude. Lifting the glass in salute, he wondered if he even had the right to feel that pride. It implied a definite involvement, a relationship. Catching her eye, he relaxed. The light in her blue eyes told him he had the right.

"That's a very good attitude to have, ma'am. I commend you for your bravery."

The officer's praise paled in comparison to the warm glow Ashli saw in Lange's eyes. Forcing her mind to stay focused, she pulled her gaze from those deliciously dark orbs.

"I'm not sure how brave I am. I simply refuse to allow this person to control my life."

"And there have been no other stalking events in the past week?"

"No, although I did remember a rhododendron bloom on my balcony the day Jasmine was . . . that morning. I had forgotten all about it until a couple of days ago."

"And you feel that is significant?" the detective asked with a perplexed frown, glancing at Lange for confirmation.

Lange shrugged. "It could be, when you consider the meaning of the flower is 'beware'."

"Has there been any more word on Jasmine?" Ashli broke in.

"No. Forensics was able to confirm that her foot had been frozen, making it even more difficult to establish a time of death."

"Death?" Her intake of breath was sharp.

"At this point, I'm afraid we must proceed under the assumption that your friend is, in fact, dead. There has been no sight of her, no hospital admissions for anyone with a severed foot, no contact made with any of her friends or family, no activity on her credit cards or cell phone. If not for the foot, we would consider her a missing person. But given the circumstances, we are now handling the investigation as a murder."

Until now, Lange had remained standing. It had been his feeble but very male approach to prove dominance over the situation. Now he sank onto the sofa beside Ashli, allowing her to lean into him for support. He no longer cared about making his claim obvious to the other man. He only cared about comforting her.

"Frozen?" she murmured, leaning into him. "Why would someone do that?"

"It's impossible to understand the mind of a murderer, Miss Wilson," Detective Sullivan told her. He didn't miss the ease in which she leaned into the private investigator, or the familiarity between them. Even before today, he had suspected there was more between them than a professional relationship. The rumpled tux and this intimate gesture confirmed his worse fears. Lange Sterling was one lucky man. "We have confirmed that your neighbor missed her flight to Milan and hasn't reported to her job in more than four weeks. That leaves a broad time frame to work within to establish a time of death and dismemberment."

"And there are still no clues? No traces of the rest of . . . the rest of her body?"

"I'm afraid not." He finished half of his sandwich and changed the subject. "Other than the flower on your balcony, has anything else happened in the past few days? Has anyone seemed angry at you, argued with you, anything out of the ordinary?"

"It's been such a crazy week," Ashli said with a sigh, straightening away from Lange, "but no, nothing."

"You sound hesitant."

She thought of Veronica and her odd behavior. Reluctant to reveal information about Lange's recent relationship with another woman, she brushed her concerns away. "Just tired. Like I said, it's been a crazy week."

"I saw this morning's paper. Congratulations."

Ashli's smile for the officer was wide and genuine. "Thank you."

Beside her, Lange stiffened. Maybe he did need to stake his claim, after all. The two of them were grinning at one another like he wasn't even there.

Before he was forced to make a fool of himself, the forensics team stepped through the French doors. "All done," one of them announced.

"I don't think I have any more questions at this time," Detective Sullivan said, setting down his empty plate. "Miss Wilson, you will keep me posted if anything else happens?"

"Of course." When she started to rise, Lange stilled her with a hand upon her knee. "You sit here and relax. I'll see the detective out." He picked up her untouched coffee and pressed it into her hand. "I can't believe I'm encouraging you to drink more coffee, but drink this."

She wrinkled her nose at his teasing but took the mug and wrapped her hands around its warmth. Suddenly extremely tired, she skipped the role of hostess and allowed Lange to see their guests out.

Their guests. Ashli berated herself for thinking in such terms. She acted like this was a social call, and that she and Lange were a couple. There was nothing social about being stalked. Detective Sullivan and his team were there on business, because someone hated her enough to write on her windows with bright-red paint. And despite spending last night in his arms, Lange was still the man hired to protect her. She couldn't be spinning daydreams from this nightmare.

Lange came back into the room and resumed his position beside her. Tucking her under the curve of his arm, he kissed the top of her head. "Maybe you should stay at my place for a few days."

Her heart took a funny leap at his words, but she knew they were spoken out of concern, not commitment. "I appreciate the offer, but like I told Detective Sullivan, I refuse to let this person control my life. I was thinking, though, maybe we should have my parents meet us at the restaurant." Her eyes drifted to the windows. The blinds were closed, but there was no forgetting the ugly message they hid.

"I'll get that cleaned up for you. But I think it's time you told your parents what's going on."

Ashli sighed. "I know. I haven't wanted to worry them, but I know they'll be hurt that I've kept this from them."

"What have you told them about Jasmine?"

"Nothing, actually. Somehow, they missed all the news coverage showing Daisy House in the background, and for once, the media didn't give the exact address. If they've heard the story, they haven't made the connection to me, and I haven't enlightened them."

"Come clean now."

"I will. But, still, can we meet them at the restaurant?"

"If that's what you want." He shrugged.

"I can't risk putting them in danger."

"Ashli," he growled, "if you're afraid of being in danger, there's no way I'm letting you stay here."

Ashli pulled away from his arm and perched on the edge of the cushion, shoving a plate of the untouched coffee cake into his hands. "It's not up to you. This is my decision. Now eat your dessert while I call my mom and tell her there's been a change in plans."

* * *

As predicted, her parents were upset with her for not telling them about her stalker before now, but mostly, they were worried.

"You are coming home with us," her mother declared.

"Mom, I can't do that. I have a business to run."

"Let Rachel take care of it. You're always saying how she's your right hand, and how she knows the business as well as you do. Now's the perfect time to prove your claim."

"I can't, Mom."

"And why not? You haven't had a vacation since you opened. You're way past due a break." Alice Wilson reached out to take her daughter's hand, squeezing it for emphasis. "I know this wouldn't be a vacation, but it could be. We could go to Vermont like we've always talked about doing."

"We talked about a fall trip, Mom, when the leaves are changing. And while I appreciate the sentiment, I can't just walk off and leave. I know Rachel could run things without me, probably so well that no one would know I was even gone, but it's not just that. There's some idiot out there stalking me, and I doubt my disappearing for a few days will change that. Delay it, perhaps, but not change it. I need to find out who this person is and stop them."

"And just how do you plan to do that?" her father demanded.

"I'm not sure yet." She glanced at Lange, hoping he could offer a solution. Taking a deep breath, she made another confession. "Lange is helping me more than you know. To be honest, he's a private investigator. I hired him to protect me and to find whoever is stalking me."

"Hired him?" her mother asked in confusion. "Then you two aren't . . . ?" She waved a hand between them, a disappointed frown marring her forehead.

"Protect?" Her father picked up on the hint of an imminent threat.

When Ashli hesitated, Lange surprised her by answering. He leaned slightly forward, staring across the table to look her father solemnly in the eyes. "Mr. Wilson, I take my job very seriously and pride myself on being a true professional. As a professional, I know to never become personally involved with my client. It can cloud judgment and distract attention to detail." His tone softened as he placed his hand on Ashli's and glanced at her with dark eyes. "As a man, I find your daughter particularly distracting." He refused to let himself get distracted now, forcing his eyes back to meet her father's. "But you have my word, sir. I will do whatever it takes to protect her. I'm going to find this man, and I'm going to make certain he doesn't harm your daughter, and that he never bothers her again. I swear, I will protect Ashli with my life."

He held Albert Wilson's steady gaze, resisting the urge to squirm beneath the older man's scrutiny. They were talking about more than just keeping her physically safe, although that was paramount at this moment. After a painfully long moment of taking the other's measure, Ashli's father gave a slight nod of the head. Lange released the breath he hadn't realized he held.

"All right, Lange," he said. "I will hold you to that promise. Now tell me how you intend to do that."

Ashli, too, breathed a sigh of relief as the tension eased between the two men. Lange's hand remained over hers as he discussed the case with her father. After a few private words with her mother, she joined the conversation. By the time the meal was over, and all the details of the case were revealed to her parents, Lange's arm had come to curl around her shoulders, and she was tucked up against his side, a fact not lost upon the couple across from them.

"You still refuse to come home for a few days?" her father asked as they made their way out to the parking lot.

"Dad, you understand why I can't."

"I do. I don't like it, but I do understand," Albert said. He stopped as they reached his car and put his hands on his daughter's shoulders, turning her toward him. "That's why I want you to do something for me. I want you to stay at Lange's apartment until this mess is taken care of."

Her eyes widened at her father's suggestion. Blushing in spite of herself, Ashli wondered if he would still be asking that if he knew about last night. "Dad, I can't do that, either. I refuse to let my stalker have this kind of control over me. If he drives me from my own home . . . No, I won't let him."

Albert sighed and pulled her in for a hug. "Looks like my little girl is all grown up now, and quite a determined and brave young woman. You just be careful."

"I will be, I promise." She hugged him back, then turned to do the same with her mother. After hearing a long list of instructions that included locking her door and calling at least twice a day to let them know she was all right, Ashli moved to Lange's side.

"One last thing," her father said, pausing as he slid behind the steering wheel. "If you won't stay with Lange, then let him stay with you."

"Dad!" Ashli cried in chagrin. "I can't believe you just said that!"

"I didn't specify sleeping arrangements, although we are all adults here. Right now, I'm more concerned about your safety, than your virtue."

"Don't worry, sir," Lange said, putting his arm around Ashli's waist. "I don't plan to let her out of my sight."

* * *

Back at Daisy House, Lange made Ashli wait in the hallway while he checked out her apartment. Once he cleared each room, he swept her inside and locked the door behind her.

"Lange, it's not necessary that you stay here tonight. You've checked out the entire place, and it's fine. I'm fine." She dropped her purse on the table as she passed through the entry.

"I'm staying." His tone was unyielding as he followed her into the living room.

"Honestly, I'm a big girl. I'm fine."

"Oh, I'm very aware of how fine you are," Lange said. He grabbed her arm to turn her around, sliding his lean, firm body up next to hers. His voice turned sultry. "And I know perfectly well that you are, indeed, a big girl." He dipped his head to whisper seductively in her ear. "A woman. A very fine, very beautiful, very sexy woman. That's why I'm staying."

She melted again. One touch of his body against hers, a few husky words from his silken tongue, and she was dissolving into a quivering mess of molten lava. "Lange." It could have been a protest, could have been a plea. It came out as a whimper.

"We have your father's permission," he reminded her, trailing his lips down the side of her neck. With nimble fingers, he unzipped her dress and pushed the fabric from her shoulders. His rough palms slid over the creamy perfection of her skin, leaving tiny goosebumps of pleasure. "What more could you want?" He nibbled on the graceful curve of her neck, as his hands trailed lower, his fingers tracing the lacy edge of her bra.

"You," she managed to say, her husky voice vibrating against his mouth. He pressed his tongue to her skin, loving how she purred against him. Her hands fell to his belt, and she fumbled with the buckle, eager to have him free. "I want you."

"Baby, you have me."

CHAPTER TWENTY

"I think this was a wonderful idea," Ashli told her friends a few days later, sinking into the booth at the Mexican food restaurant. "Shopping makes me hungry."

"Hey, scoot over," Rachel laughed, nudging Ashli as she slid in beside her. "Molly's taking up the whole booth with all her bags."

"What can I say? There was a sale. I believe in saving money," the other woman said with a smile of feigned innocence.

"I totally agree. Like I always tell Kevin, sometimes you must spend it, to save it." As the waitress appeared with warm chips and salsa, Rachel took the liberty of ordering for her friends. They had been talking about it all afternoon. "Frozen Grande Margaritas, please, with salt."

"I definitely worked up a thirst, carrying all these bags." Molly sighed, readjusting the shifting pile.

"What's your excuse?" Rachel turned to Ashli with a mischievous glint in her eyes. "There's not enough fabric in that little bag of yours to work up anything other than a man."

"Rachel, lower your voice!" Ashli wailed, her cheeks turning the same shade as the silky lingerie in question.

Her friends just laughed. "You never did tell us about that private celebration of yours Saturday night." Rachel bit into a chip, watching the blush spread on her friend's face.

"No, I don't believe I did," Ashli agreed.

"Come on, girl, you gotta dish," Molly insisted. "We're two old married women here. We need a little reminder of what it's like to be in a hot new romance."

"I'm not sure I would call it a romance," Ashli hedged. "I'm not sure what it is."

"But it's hot, isn't it?" Molly asked with a knowing gleam in her eye.

Ashli hesitated for a moment. She normally didn't talk about her private life, particularly with her employees. But Molly was becoming so much more, and Rachel had always been her best and dearest friend. Indulging in the sheer joy of merely having a relationship to talk about, Ashli gave in to the impulse and admitted with a raw, indulgent groan. "God, yes," she shuddered.

Molly squealed in delight, and even Rachel smiled, happy that her friend had finally found someone. She still had her doubts about Lange Sterling, knowing that men as deep and mysterious and as blatantly sexy as the private investigator seldom stayed around to pick up the pieces of the hearts they shattered. She only hoped Ashli could survive a relationship with him and get out with her heart in one piece.

Without giving away too many details, Ashli admitted Lange had stayed at her apartment the last three nights. Her friends didn't need to know that part of the reason he stayed was to protect her. Nor did they need to know how little sleep they had gotten, their insatiable need for one another greater than their need for slumber. And if she modeled her new little teddy for him tonight as she planned, that pattern wouldn't be changing anytime soon. Just thinking about it brought a blush of anticipation to her cheeks.

"Look at her, she's still blushing!" Molly teased. "After three straight nights, surely there's nothing left to embarrass you, girl."

"It's the alcohol." Ashli hid her flaming cheeks behind the salt-crusted rim of her oversized drink.

"Hmm. I'm just glad to see you finally getting a man. You could have your pick of just about any of them, but you never seemed too interested until you met Lange."

"See, exactly what I've been saying," Rachel interjected. "Men fall all over themselves around you, even though you hardly notice."

"Oh, please, that's not true," Ashli denied.

"It is! Do you know how many men stare at you daily at Ashli's Tea Party? And how many I saw drooling — actually drooling — over you Saturday night in that dress?"

"You're exaggerating." Ashli squirmed in modesty.

"Is she exaggerating how that man over there keeps staring at you?" Molly asked, nodding to a booth across the way.

"Oh, Lordy, that's Jason Madison."

"Who is Jason Madison?"

"One of my neighbors. He's a total womanizer. I've made it perfectly clear that I'm not interested in him, but he just can't seem to take a hint. Especially now that he's seen Lange stay overnight."

"I guess he thinks since you welcomed Lange, you would welcome him?" Rachel guessed.

"Exactly. Oh, good, here comes our food. Let's just ignore him and eat our dinner."

"Hey, isn't that the elderly couple from your condo?" Rachel nodded to the couple about to exit the restaurant.

"It sure is. And they have Mr. Parnell with them. I'm sorry I didn't see them earlier, or I would have spoken to them. Mmm, this looks delicious."

"It must be Daisy House day at Senor Montelongo's," Rachel quipped. She took a bite of an enchilada and purred. "Oh, this sauce is fabulous. You've got to try this. Here, Molly, you, too."

"Mmm, wonderful," Ashli agreed. "What's in that? Maybe we should try to come up with our own version for the Tea

Party. It would be wonderful in a casserole. Is that some sort of a smoky paprika I taste?"

As the women dissected the melded flavors in the dish, the topic of men fell by the wayside. By the time they finished their meal and their margaritas, they had full tummies, lightened spirits, and slightly buzzed brains. Molly had to leave for home, but Rachel stayed with Ashli as she made a final stop at the beauty care store.

They were meandering down an aisle, browsing for new fragrances, when Ashli got the familiar sensation of being watched. Any buzz left from the alcohol vanished as she sobered.

"Rachel," she whispered, "do me a favor. Look around and see if anyone is watching me."

"Why? Do you think your stalker is here? Is he watching you right now?"

"Yes, I think so. Don't make it obvious, but do you see anyone looking our way?"

Rachel scanned the store. "Not that I can tell. This is so freaky. Didn't it happen at this store once before? Maybe he works here." She peered toward the cash registers, but all the clerks were busy with customers. None of the customers paid them any attention.

"Let's just go. I'm not in the mood for shopping anymore." Ashli put the sample bottle back on the shelf with the other fragrances.

They made a corner and came face to face with her friend from Ashli's Tea Party.

"D-Diane!" Ashli stammered in surprise. She couldn't help but peer past her, searching for anyone who might be watching.

"Ashli, I've been meaning to stop by and congratulate you. You had a marvelous showing Saturday night," the red-haired lawyer said with a wide smile. Noticing Ashli's distraction, she glanced over her shoulder. "Are you looking for someone?"

"Oh, no, no." Ashli tried to laugh off her own foolishness. "I'm sorry, please forgive my rudeness. And thank you so much for that. I do appreciate you thinking of us." Ashli put her hand on the other woman's arm, hoping to convey her sincerity.

"A well-deserved honor," Diane assured her, encompassing Rachel in her smile. "Did you buy the dress?"

"Not *that* dress," Ashli said with a nervous laugh. She explained their conversation to Rachel. "Diane was the one to tell me about the little boutique where I bought my dress. She actually suggested another one, but it was a bit too . . . daring for my tastes."

"It wasn't *your* tastes we were trying to please. It was your Romeo's," Diane reminded her.

"Oh, he was plenty pleased with the dress she chose," Rachel assured her with a laugh. She was slightly hurt that Ashli had confided in the other woman about Lange and consulted her in choosing a dress. That was what best friends were for. "The way he looked at her had to be illegal in some states. It was downright sinful."

"Rachel!" Ashli threw her friend a look of chagrin, almost missing the pained expression that crossed the lawyer's face. Catching a glimpse of it, she felt sympathy for the other woman. "How about you? Any word from your ex?"

Diane brightened. "Actually, yes. He called yesterday. It seems the little distraction from work turned out to be just that: a distraction. Still, a home-cooked meal couldn't hurt, could it?"

"Absolutely not. I think it might just seal the deal." Ashli was truly pleased for her new friend, hoping Diane could be as happy with her boyfriend as she was with Lange.

"Are you free Saturday night?"

"Yes, I believe so. What did you have in mind?"

"Beats me, you're the genius in the kitchen! Just be at my place in time to cook and run. Will seven be enough time for you to work your magic?"

"Sure, I can be done by seven." It would still leave her plenty of time to cook at home for Lange, assuming he would still be there. The thought of him *not* being there was terrifying, and it had nothing to do with her safety.

"Great. Here's my address." Diane handed Ashli a business card with a handwritten address on the back. "And don't get too fancy, we want him to think I actually did the cooking."

"What are you two talking about?" Rachel asked in confusion.

"Didn't you know? Your innocent-looking friend here is secretly a devious little minx. I helped her get her man, now she's going to help me get mine back." With a smug smile, Diane waved her fingers in the air. "I've got to go. See you Saturday. Tootles."

Frowning, Rachel watched the redhead disappear. "Personally, I think your friend is a little strange. Did you see that gleam in her eyes? It was almost evil."

"She's just excited about the prospect of getting her boyfriend back. He dumped her for another lawyer, now apparently wants her back. She thinks if I fix a home-cooked meal that she supposedly made, she'll find her way back into his heart."

"Humph. Hope she's got more going for her than that. Apparently, she's either not too bright, or not too observant."

"Why do you say that?" Ashli asked. "She's a lawyer. She's both."

"Maybe so, but she had the wrong hair color in her basket. She picked up platinum blonde by mistake."

* * *

When Ashli arrived home, Lange was in the driveway waiting for her. He teased her about what she had in her little pink bag, recognizing the logo of a store known for its sexy lingerie.

"Do I at least get a private showing later?" he asked as they ascended the stairs.

"We'll see." Her words were noncommittal, but her smile was provocative.

"This is all you bought after an entire afternoon of shopping?"

"I mostly helped Molly replenish her wardrobe. That woman loves to shop." She laughed, remembering the pile of bags her friend had collected. "We also had a very long dinner with very large margaritas."

"That explains the glazed expression in your eyes."

Ashli handed him her keys to unlock the apartment, choosing to remain silent. Let him think she was still carrying an alcohol buzz. Better than letting him know the buzz she felt came solely from him, knowing he was there waiting for her. She was quickly becoming addicted to him. Having him in her home, in her bed, was a feeling she was getting all too comfortable with.

"Have you eaten?" she asked.

"No, but I can order a pizza or something."

"Nonsense. I'll fix you something. What would you like?" she asked, going into the kitchen.

"I'm not going to ask you to come home and fix me something to eat, when you went out for your own meal."

"You're not asking. I'm offering." She opened the refrigerator and surveyed its contents. "There's some of that meatloaf I made last night. Or I could make you an omelet, or a sandwich."

"Or you could go take a bath, and I could make my own supper."

"I thought I'd take another look at those files. I keep thinking I'll see something that will help find Jasmine."

He gave her a dubious look as he nudged her aside and took out the container holding the meatloaf. Ashli stood back and watched, thinking how incredibly sexy he looked in her kitchen. Of course, he looked sexy anywhere, doing anything.

While Lange heated his plate and sat down at the bar to eat, Ashli collected the old files and climbed onto the barstool beside him. A comfortable silence settled between them, making such mundane tasks as eating and reading individually seem more like a couple project.

It wasn't until Lange poured them a glass of Chardonnay that Ashli spoke. "I keep thinking there's some significance that four of the women had blonde hair and blue eyes."

"I would agree, if the other three weren't total opposites. It makes no sense."

"But three were ethnic, four were blondes. Not brunette, not redhead, not mousy brown. Blonde. All with blue eyes."

Lange swirled the wine in his goblet, watching the golden whirlpool and thinking how his own life was spinning out of control, and all because of a certain blue-eyed blonde. God, if he wasn't so weak, he would put an end to it right now. He didn't like not having control of his emotions, his thoughts. Hell, his very existence. She had taken over all of them. And for the life of him, he couldn't drum up the strength — not even the anger — to resist.

Disgusted with himself and his weakness for her, Lange tossed back the wine and welcomed the sting it delivered to the back of his throat. "Anything new happen today?"

"Actually, I think my stalker may have followed me to the mall."

Lange whirled around, angry with her for just now mentioning it, even angrier with himself for just now asking. "What are you talking about? And why are you just now telling me?"

"Because nothing actually happened. I just felt like I was being watched. But Rachel was with me, and neither one of us saw anyone. It was the first time I had been back to the store where he had gifted me the hair products, so maybe I was just jumpy."

"But you don't believe that, do you?"

She hesitated before admitting, "No."

He cursed beneath his breath. "I knew I should have followed you to the mall."

"Lange, you cannot follow me, every second of every day. You have other clients that need your attention. And Rachel and Molly never let me out of their sight, I can assure you. Rachel even followed me home."

"Still, I should have been there."

"I also ran into a friend of mine. She asked me to help her with a little cooking project on Saturday evening."

"Do I need to go with you?"

"No, I'm just going over to her apartment. I'll be home by seven."

"I should be in about the same time. I'm meeting that lawyer friend of mine for drinks, to see if there's a way we can force Mr. Parnell to allow security cameras on the house. I'm ready to catch this son of a bitch, once and for all."

"I agree completely." Ashli yawned and shut the file she had been reading. "Well, nothing new here that I can see. I think I may take that bath you suggested, after all."

Just like that, whatever resistance he had been working up toward her dissolved at the thought of her naked. He groaned, knowing he couldn't keep his mind on business, where it belonged, when his body kept sabotaging his best intentions.

"Maybe I should sleep on the sofa tonight," he announced.

Ashli frowned. She wondered if she had done something wrong, or if he was that angry at her for not telling him about the stalking incident when she first got home. Or maybe . . .

"It's not you, Ashli," he broke in on her thoughts.

"Then I don't understand. You would prefer to sleep on my sofa, rather than in my bed?"

He would rather sleep standing up, if it meant he could hold her in his arms. But this wasn't about what he wanted; it was about keeping her safe.

"I'm getting distracted, Ashli. I need to keep my head clear and in the game. This is too important for me not to stay focused."

"You don't want to sleep with me." She tried to keep the hurt out of her voice.

Lange lifted a dark eyebrow and looked down at her skeptically. "After the last three nights, I think you know the answer to that. Maybe I just need some actual sleep tonight."

"On that little sofa?"

He put his hands on her shoulders and dropped a kiss onto her forehead. "When I'm in your bed, the last thing

I'm thinking about is sleep. And the second last thing I'm thinking about is the case." He brushed another kiss along her cheek. "Go take your bath. I'll clean up down here."

Ashli indulged in a long, hot bath, soaking away the worries of the day and the pensive mood Lange had fallen into. Instead of the sheer teddy, she slipped on a comfortable pair of flannel pajama pants and a lacy but respectable camisole. Tucking her feet into her favorite pair of fuzzy slippers, she knew her outfit was far from sexy. If Lange wanted to sleep on the sofa, far be it from her to lure him upstairs with frilly lingerie.

She found him sitting in the wingback chair, nursing a second glass of wine as he stared out the opened blinds. The lights were off, eliminating a reflective glare from inside and allowing a clear view of the night sky. Although he had done his best to clean the painted message from the window, a few streak marks lingered on the glass as an ugly reminder.

"Lange?" she asked, making her way across the room in the darkness. "Are you all right?"

"Just having a glass of wine. Want some?" He pointed to the bottle that by now was practically empty. Maybe this was this third glass.

"No, thanks. I've already brushed my teeth," she murmured. She hung back for a moment before coming closer and touching his shoulder.

He flinched at the contact. A nerve worked along his clenched jaw. He stared straight ahead, refusing to look at her.

"Lange? Lange, honey, what's wrong?" It was the first time she had called him the endearment, but he suspected it had no romantic connotations. She was bringing little boys in from the rain again.

It took him a long while to answer. She waited patiently until he was ready to talk.

"Toby's been gone twelve years today." His voice was raw and rusty.

"He was the friend you lost?" she guessed.

Instead of answering, Lange caught her by the waist and pulled her across the arm of the chair and into his lap. He needed her warmth and softness when confronting the cold, sharp pain of the past.

"He was only nineteen." He spoke in a low voice full of pain. "We were going to conquer the world. Go to the police academy together, start our careers together, branch out as a private investigation team." There was a pregnant pause. "Never thought I'd be doing all this alone."

"Tell me about Toby."

He started slowly, but then the words flowed out of him. He told her story after story, some going back as far as elementary school. Some stories made her laugh, a few made her sad, but she listened to them all with only minimal comment. These were Lange's stories, Lange's memories. The fact he shared them with her was a huge comment on their relationship.

After the last story, Lange fell silent again. Finally, he spoke. "You know, this is the first time I've even said Toby's name aloud in probably ten years. Some friend I turned out to be."

"Sometimes memories are too painful to speak aloud." She stroked the back of his head, smoothing down the black ends of his hair.

"It doesn't seem right, just letting his memory die. But nobody I know now ever even knew him."

"You haven't kept in touch with anyone from your past?"

"Don't sound so shocked. There wasn't anyone to keep in touch with. I never had many friends, and no family other than my grandmother."

Ashli thought about her own life, so full and robust with friends and relatives. She had dozens of aunts and uncles and cousins, three grandparents who were still living, many close friends she could depend on in a crisis, casual friends by the score, and more acquaintances than she could ever count. She couldn't imagine her life without any of them. Her heart ached for Lange, knowing he didn't have that network of caring.

"Lange."

"Don't feel sorry for me!" he said, misinterpreting the softness in her voice. "I can't tolerate your pity."

"I don't pity you, Lange, but it does make my heart physically hurt, knowing you feel so alone," she whispered. She weighed her words before she spoke them. They were thickened with the tears she tried not to shed. "Lange, there's something I want you to know. If . . . if something should happen to me . . ."

"No!" The word tore from him.

"No, listen to me." She covered his mouth with her fingers. "Listen to me," she whispered. "If-if something should happen to me, I want you to know that you will always be welcomed by my family."

"Ashli, don't," he pleaded, his own voice thick. She felt his strong arms tremble as they held her.

"Please let me finish. This is important." She sniffed, keeping her eyes trained on the lips she still caressed with her fingers. "I want you to know you will always have a place to go. You'll always have a home with my family, Lange. They'll be your roots."

To her amazement, a tear rolled down his cheek and collected on her fingertip.

She snapped her gaze to his, stunned to see the depth of pain swimming in his dark eyes. He shuddered as he pulled her tight against him, his words torn from his heart with a ragged breath. "Don't talk like this, Ashli! Don't say such things. I can't lose you. I can't lose you, too."

Her hand was trapped between them as he held her too tightly. She wanted to hold him, she wanted to put her arms around him, but she was crushed to his trembling chest. She felt the sobs rack his body, and her own tears flowed hot and free, running down her cheeks and soaking into his shirt. She finally finagled her hand free, to slip both hands around his neck and press her face close against his. After another long moment, she managed to slide her lips over to his. Their kiss was long and sweet and desperate, flavored by their tears.

When Ashli pulled away at last, Lange lessened his grasp. She laid her head on his chest, and they settled into the chair, neither speaking. She sensed he would be embarrassed over his display of emotion, so she generously avoided eye contact. She drew lazy patterns over the damp wrinkles of his shirt, alternating smoothing out the fabric and patting the sacred area over his heart. They stayed that way for almost an hour, without words, until cramped muscles insisted they move.

She stood and reached out her hand.

"Let's get some sleep, Lange," she said, her blue eyes seeking his.

Without a word, he took her hand and followed her upstairs.

CHAPTER TWENTY-ONE

Late Saturday afternoon, Ashli packed a wicker basket with food to take to Diane's. She planned a simple meal of grilled chicken and penne pasta, tossed salad, a crusty loaf of bread, and thick, gooey chocolate brownies. It was a meal that could go from casual to sensual with a bottle of wine and the right music. She was certain her friend could provide both.

"I was about to get into the shower," Diane said as she opened the door. She was already in her robe and had her hair tied up in a turban. "The kitchen's through there. Make yourself at home. And do me proud," she called with a cheeky grin as she disappeared down the hall.

Laughing, Ashli found the small kitchen and set to work. Soon, she had the apartment filled with the delicious aroma of grilling chicken, Italian seasoning, and the sweet promise of chocolate.

She rummaged through Diane's cabinets and found everything she needed to create an intimate place setting for two. There was a round table in the corner of the living room, but with a white tablecloth, red candles in silver candlesticks, and a small ivy centerpiece, it became a romantic nook for lovers. Stepping back to survey her work, Ashli clapped her hands in delight. Hopefully, tonight would be everything her friend hoped for.

Back in the kitchen, Ashli tossed the pasta with the chicken and cherry tomatoes and set the heat on simmer. It was just after six thirty, and time she made her exit. The brownies were cooling on top of the stove, the salad was made, and the wine was ready to uncork. By pre-chilling the salad plates and pre-warming the breadbasket, there would be little room for error, even for the most inept cooks.

"This smells delicious!" Diane said as she came into the room.

"Thanks." Ashli worked with her back to her, adding the last dash of seasoning. "Just leave the pasta simmering, until the tomato skins burst. Stir it gently every so often, like this, to keep it from sticking. You can serve it directly on the plates, or I found this pretty serving bowl you might prefer. The bread—"

When she turned, she caught sight of Diane. Words died upon her lips as she stared at the other woman.

"What?" Diane asked with a laugh, pumping the ends of her very blonde, very bleached hair. "Don't you like it?"

"It-it's just so different," Ashli managed to say.

"Well, they say blondes have more fun, so I thought I'd give it a try. You certainly seem to be having a lot of fun these days."

Something about her words was a little too sharp, a little too bright. Ashli swallowed uncomfortably, belatedly noticing the red dress Diane wore. It was every bit as tight and daring as it appeared in the ad.

"You didn't take my advice and buy the dress, so I bought it for myself. You like?" She skimmed her hand down the ultra-tight fit, preening for effect.

"It's, ah, it's lovely. Look, I think I have everything done here, so I'm just going to get out of here, before your boyfriend arrives." Ashli's words were rushed. She hoped to escape as quickly as possible; the entire situation made her very uncomfortable.

"I can't imagine what's keeping him. He's usually very punctual." Cocking her head, Diane beamed. "Oh, listen, there's the doorbell now."

"I thought he wasn't coming until seven. How will I get out without him seeing me? You don't have a back door, do you?" Ashli felt trapped, and not just by the boyfriend. She had never seen her lawyer friend act this way before, and it was more than a little disconcerting.

"I guess we'll just have to come clean about our little trickery." She sounded unconcerned as she left the room. The tight skirt and killer stilettos made her exit more awkward than sweeping.

Ashli braced her arms on the cabinet, gulping in deep breaths to keep from panicking. Something wasn't right. Had Diane taken some sort of drug? Was she high? Or just crazy? Neither thought brought much comfort.

"Darling, you're here!" She heard Diane's voice, still too bright and too loud. Yes, Ashli decided, she was probably high. "I was so thrilled when you called and said you wanted to get back together." She heard the murmur of a man's voice, then Diane's again. "You like? I know you have a recent thing for blondes, so I thought 'what the hell'? Give the man what he likes. And I know what you like."

In the pause that followed, Ashli could only imagine what her last throaty comment had led to. Then Diane was laughing again. "Now, now, behave yourself, big boy. I take it you like the dress?" Another seductive laugh and a man's reply, too low to hear. "I know, I know, I've missed you, too. I'm glad you've gotten that little blonde bimbo out of your system and are ready for a real woman again."

This time, when Ashli heard the man's reply, her world fell out from beneath her feet, and the room began to spin. There was no denying the sound of Lange's voice, or the way he growled the other woman's name. She had heard that growl too often, sometimes in anger, but more often in desire. "Diane," he said now, and there was another gush of laughter from the living room.

"I guess one little kiss wouldn't hurt. Then there's someone I want you to meet," Diane said.

It was like watching a terrible accident, playing out before her eyes. She didn't want to see. She didn't have the strength to watch. Yet, she couldn't look away. Ashli stepped forward, compelled to witness the scene unfolding in the next room. She stepped through the doorway in time to see Diane capture Lange's head and pull his mouth down to hers. Tears blurred her eyes, making it impossible to see if he returned the kiss with her same gusto. When Diane pushed her body against his, Lange's hands came up to catch her hips. Suddenly sick to her stomach, Ashli wanted to turn away but found she was rooted to the spot.

"Diane!" Lange pushed the redhead turned platinum blonde away. She had rocked into him with such force he had to grab for her to keep his balance. "What the hell is wrong with you? What are you doing?"

"I'm giving you what you wanted . . . a blonde bimbo! What's wrong, aren't I good enough for you?" she spat.

"A blonde . . . what are you talking about? Why did you dye your hair? What—!" He stopped abruptly, seeing they weren't alone. "Ashli!" He paled when he saw the stricken expression on her face. "Ashli, what are you doing here?" This, in a shocked whisper.

"Surprised to see your little blonde bimbo here, in our love nest?" Diane sneered. She turned toward Ashli, her face distorted in ugly scorn. "That's right. This is our love nest. For two years, two frickin' years, we've been lovers in this very apartment. You wouldn't believe the things that gorgeous body of his has done to mine, right here in this very room!"

Ashli clutched the back of a chair. Her breathing came in pathetic spurts, depriving her lungs of its much-needed oxygen. Her skin grew clammy, her stomach churned. But her heart. Her heart was breaking into hundreds of little shards.

"Diane, that's enough!" Lange barked.

"Is it? Doesn't she deserve to know the truth? The truth about us, Lange? That we've been lovers for two years, that we were planning a future together, until she came along? Doesn't she deserve to know how you threw me aside to get into her pants, then how you laughed at her for thinking she could ever please you?"

The room spun wildly now, turning darker. Ashli could barely hear Diane's next word over the ringing in her ears.

"I'm willing to forgive your little tumble in the hay with her, Lange, since I know how pathetic it was. I know you want me back. I know what a man like you needs, what you want."

Diane thrust her red-clad body up against his, trying to grind her hips into his, but Lange shoved her away. He used more force than intended, inadvertently pushing her to the ground. His eyes were on Ashli and the way all the color had drained from her face.

"Ashli, don't listen to her; she's insane," Lange said. He tried to cross the room to reach her before she crumbled, but Diane clutched his leg. He shook her away angrily, until a sharp pain seared through his flesh.

"Damn it, Diane, what the—?" His bellow was more one of rage than of pain, even though it hurt like crazy. He glanced down, shocked to see blood. "What did you do?"

"I stabbed you, just like you stabbed me!" she yelled, brandishing the long blade that glistened with his blood. She tried to stab him again, but he jumped back, out of her reach.

"You are crazy!" he screamed at her. "Get up off the floor and give me the damn knife, you crazy woman!"

"Come and get it," she said. Not in the least intimidated by the thunderous scowl on his face as he slowly advanced toward her, Diane scrambled backwards, holding the knife between them.

Ashli watched the scene in horror, too shocked and too sick to act. Lange was bleeding, even though he seemed to ignore the wound across his lower thigh. Diane, her short, tight skirt hiked immodestly high, crawfished her way backwards, coming directly toward Ashli. Somewhere in her numbed brain, Ashli knew she should move, knew she should call for help or go to Lange or do *something*, but she was rooted to the spot, her legs and her mind immobile.

"Diane, you know you don't want to hurt me." Lange's voice was now deceptively calm and steady.

"But you hurt me! You stabbed me in the heart, as surely as if you had a knife!"

"I know I did. I'm sorry about that. Just give me the knife, and we'll talk about it."

"What's to talk about?" Still crawling backwards, she bumped into the leg of the coffee table with a curse but kept going. She stopped when she touched Ashli's leg. "You stabbed me in the heart, and she stabbed me in the back!"

Predicting Diane's next move, Lange yelled a warning. "Run, Ashli! Get out of here!"

Snapping out of her trance, Ashli leapt aside, just seconds before the long blade of the knife jabbed into the floor where her foot had been. In her haste to get away, Ashli stumbled over the arm of the chair and fell into its cushions.

"You were my friend!" Diane screamed in rage. "You stole him from me, and I want him back!"

"I-I didn't know," Ashli stammered. "I didn't know it was him." Her eyes flew to Lange's, as her shocked brain tried to make sense of it all. Lange and Diane, in a two-year love affair? Here in this apartment? Her stomach rolled again. Had he really laughed at her?

"Diane, put down the knife." Lange was steadily advancing toward them, his voice still calm and reassuring. "We can sit down and discuss this. I didn't realize you even knew Ashli. Tell me how you know her." He tried to distract her until he got close enough to take the knife.

"The restaurant, you idiot. Where do you think I bought that tomato basil soup you liked so well? The question is, how do *you* know her?"

"Business."

"Oh, that's right," she said with a sharp laugh. "Your new client, the one that sounded like Doris Day. I should have made the connection the day you told me about her."

Seeing an opportunity to escape, Ashli eased out of the chair and inched away from the woman with the knife. Lange caught the movement from the corner of his eye and quickly engaged Diane in more conversation.

"When did you realize Ashli was my client?"

Diane laughed harshly. "Stupid me, not until Veronica told me she saw you slinking out of her apartment, still wearing your clothes from the night before."

"Veronica!" Ashli gasped, forgetting she was trying to stealth away.

"Yes, Veronica, my sister. The nurse to the old man from your apartment building. Another fool with a thing for Doris Day. What is it with you men, anyway?" Diane waved the knife in irritation.

Lange tried a new tactic. His only concern was getting Ashli out of harm's way. With his best seductive grin, he shrugged and told Diane, "Sorry, I've got a thing for blondes . . . Did I tell you how much I like your hair? You look good as a blonde, Di." He glanced at Ashli for the briefest of seconds, praying she would recognize the lie for what it was. "Very hot."

"You think so?" For the first time, Diane seemed uncertain. She frowned, clearly wanting to believe him.

"Definitely." The word burned as it left his lips. His own stomach churning, Lange stepped closer. "And that dress." He glanced again at Ashli, seeing the stricken expression on her beautiful face. "I could never resist a blonde in red."

A sob broke from Ashli's throat, causing Diane to answer with a bitter laugh. "I should have dyed my hair weeks ago. Could have saved myself a lot of trouble. And a can of paint."

"That-that was you?" Ashli gasped. "You painted that on my window? But why?"

"Because you are nothing but a little lying, cheating, boyfriend-stealing, do-goody little blonde-haired bitch!" When Diane raised the knife to stab her, Lange grabbed for her hand. He missed but succeeded in knocking the knife off course. It slashed across his palm and flung blood into the air.

"Did you . . . did you do those other things?" Ashli whispered. Still in shock, she failed to notice how profusely Lange bled, or the fact she was in danger. "Have you been stalking me?"

"Stalking you? Why on earth would I stalk you?" Diane laughed. "You're nothing to me. I wouldn't waste my time on a pathetic little boring loser like you. Tell her, Lange. She's boring. Boring, boring, boring."

Ashli jerked her gaze to him, noticing his hand for the first time. "You're bleeding!" she gasped.

He had his hand wrapped in the tail of his shirt, but the blood soaked through. His jeans were sliced above the knee, where more blood freely flowed. Much more blood loss, and Lange knew he was in danger of passing out. He had to get Ashli out of the apartment and to safety before that happened.

"It's not too bad," he denied. "Diane's going to take me to the hospital and get it looked at, aren't you, Red?"

"Huh?" Confused at the affectionate tone in his voice and his use of the old nickname, Diane looked at him with dazed eyes.

"You always look out for me. Remember that time my appendix ruptured? You took me to the hospital. You took care of me, Red. But I guess I can't call you that anymore, can I?" He took advantage of her confusion and reached around to take the knife from her hands. "That's it, that's my girl," he cooed. "Just give me the knife, and it's going to be all right."

"But-but Ashli . . ." The hatred had seeped out of her voice, replaced now by the needling whine of a pouting child.

"Ashli's going home now. She's going to call her friend, Mr. Sullivan, and she's going to leave us here, just the two of us." He spoke to Diane, but his eyes were trained on Ashli. When Ashli started to protest, shaking her head, he ignored her. He pulled Diane to him with his one good arm, motioning behind her for Ashli to leave.

"But I hurt you!" Now the unstable woman began to cry.

Out of respect for their two-year relationship, Lange felt compelled to help the woman he had once been involved with. She was clearly mentally disturbed. Torn between his loyalty to Diane and his love for Ashli, Lange prayed that Ashli would understand.

"I know you didn't mean to, Di," he said, holding her as she cried. Over her head, he silently begged Ashli with his eyes, fully understanding for the first time that he was in love with her. It was Ashli he wanted to hold, Ashli he wanted to comfort. And it was Ashli he had to protect.

"You'll take care of me, right, Diane? You'll take me to the hospital and get me checked out."

"Just you and me?"

"Just you and me. Just the way it's always been."

"You left me before."

He heard the anger flash in her voice. He knew her moods could change in an instant, and she could become violent again. Lange kept his voice smooth and even, staring over her head into the bright-blue depths of Ashli's eyes as he promised, "I won't leave you now."

"What about Ashli?" Diane whined.

Ashli? He loved her more than life itself. He knew that now. He had always known it, on some level, but like a fool, he had fought it.

Aloud, he told both women, "Ashli's leaving. She's going to call her friend, Mr. Sullivan. He'll take care of her."

"Like you're going to take care of me?" Diane asked, snuggling against him.

"Like I'm going to take care of you." Unable to hold Ashli's bright gaze, Lange closed his eyes. For a moment, the blackness swooped in, threatening to send him to his knees. It could have been the loss of blood, or perhaps, the lost chance at love.

Either way, when he opened his eyes, Ashli was gone.

CHAPTER TWENTY-TWO

Ashli stumbled from Diane's apartment, her vision blurred with tears. She wasn't so distraught that she couldn't decipher the message hidden in Lange's words: call Detective Sullivan. Lange was bleeding and needed medical help. And Diane obviously needed a strait jacket.

With trembling fingers, she dialed the number the policemen had given her.

"Sullivan here."

"Detective Sullivan." Relief flooded through her when he answered on the first ring. "This is Ashli. I need your help."

"Is it your stalker? I can be there in five minutes."

"No! No, I'm not at home. I'm at . . ." She paused to look around the plush complex, trying to recall the exact address. "Castle Main Condominiums. Apartment thirty-four C. There's a woman. She has a knife. Lange was cut, and he's bleeding. I think he's taking her to the hospital, but I'm not sure. Just send someone, please."

"Wait a minute. Who's hurt, Sterling or the woman? Why is he taking her to the hospital if he's the one who was cut?" the detective asked, confused.

"Because she's crazy." The words rushed out, one upon another. "She asked me to come over to cook dinner and then she pulled a knife and then . . . just come. Please hurry."

"I'm dispatching a unit and an ambulance as we speak, and I'll be there in twelve minutes, tops. Stay where you are." She could hear the movement in his voice.

"No. No, I-I've got to get out of here!" She was already beginning to walk away, her pace getting faster and faster.

"This woman, is she your stalker?"

"No, but she's the one who wrote on my windows."

"And why is Sterling taking her to the hospital? What is his connection to all this?"

"She's his girlfriend."

* * *

She drove like a maniac to get home. She ran a red light and turned down a one-way street going the wrong direction, but she made it home in one piece. She managed to make it to Daisy House before unraveling, but not to her apartment. She made it no further than the garage.

She laid her head against the steering wheel and allowed the tears to come. They came in a torrent, racking her body with violent sobs. She was flooded with emotions, each one as powerful and ravishing as the next. Confusion. Shock. Hurt. Fear. Love. Betrayal.

The betrayal hurt most of all.

The tears subsided at last. Still, she sat there, too confused to even think. It grew dark outside, just like it had grown dark inside her heart. After another ten minutes of sitting inside her car like a zombie, Ashli pulled herself together. She dropped her cell phone and keys into her pocket, but somehow her purse seemed unimportant. She left it in the seat of her car as she stumbled out of the garage toward the back doors of the mansion.

Ashli's fingers were clumsy when she tried to enter her code. She could hear Mr. Parnell tinkering in the shed, and for a moment, thought she might have to call him for help. After three attempts, the doors unlocked, and she staggered inside. She wasn't aware of going up the stairs, but the next thing she knew, she was standing outside her door, where a package dangled from the doorknob.

There was no postage on the box and no return address, but Ashli was too distraught to notice. She unlocked her door, wondering for the hundredth time how Lange was. Had he driven himself to the hospital? Had he let that crazy woman drive him? Or did he wait for the ambulance? Why hadn't she stayed there and insisted on taking him, herself?

Because he sent her away, she reminded herself bitterly. He made it plain that he didn't want her there, didn't need her. He had chosen Diane.

But the look in his eyes! There had been so much sorrow, so much longing. He had been begging her for something, but for what? To understand? To play along? Or to give up? He had pushed her away, after all.

Diane said he had laughed at her. Diane said he wanted her back. Diane said . . .

Diane was crazy.

But he had chosen Diane.

Hadn't he?

"Ugh!" Ashli screamed at the voices in her head, thinking she might be going crazy, too. She ripped open the package in her hands, needing to tear something apart.

The contents fell to the floor with a thud, wrapped in black lace. She bent to retrieve a beautiful antique clock. The hands were set to twelve o'clock. Midday or midnight.

Her first reaction was one of fleeting pleasure. Someone sent her a present, a beautiful old timepiece that measured not only minutes, but also years.

Then it dawned on her. This was from her stalker.

Her second response was to fling the clock across the room. It crashed against the wall, knocking a porcelain figure down from a nearby shelf. Both broke to pieces on her hardwood floor.

"No!" Ashli cried. "No, no, no! I can't take this anymore! I *won't* take it! This ends now!"

She stormed out of her apartment, headed for the carriage house. Mr. Parnell may have seen someone. If his memory held long enough to recall the day's events, he might have the answers she needed. Of course, surveillance cameras would also yield answers. Tonight, she would insist he allow the cameras. She wouldn't take no for an answer.

"Mr. Parnell? Are you in here?" she called. She caught a whiff of an awful smell, this one more gut-wrenching than usual. She hoped her stomach wouldn't revolt.

"Doris? Is that you?"

She followed the sound of his voice, finding him at the contraption where he ground mulch and started the process for his prized fertilizer. His hands were covered in a dark substance, and the smell coming from the machine was enough to make her gag.

She was about to correct him when a smile split his wrinkled face. "Doris, it is you!" he crooned in pleasure. "But you're early. You're not supposed to be here until midnight."

"Mr. Parnell," she began, "it's me, Ashli." This wasn't good. In this condition, he would never be able to recall seeing anyone at her door. Not unless they had been there thirty years ago.

"Doris, what are talking about? Of course it's you. I'd know that beautiful face anywhere."

Ashli puffed out a weary sigh. She started to turn away, but something caught her eye. "Mr. Parnell, what's that over there in the corner?"

"Nothing. I don't see nothing," he answered quickly, without looking in the direction she pointed.

"It looks like a bracelet. See it shining over there? It looks like . . . this is Jasmine's ankle bracelet!" she said in surprise, reaching down to snag the silver chain from behind the mulcher.

"So? Found it in the yard."

"When? When did you find this, Mr. Parnell?"

"Don't know. Week or so ago, I reckon." He wiped his hands on his bib apron, streaking it with the red substance so dark, it was practically black.

"Did you tell the police about it?"

"Police?" He looked alarmed. "Why would I tell the police? Doris, you're acting awfully strange tonight."

"This might be important, Mr. Parnell. I think we should let Detective Sullivan know about this." She palmed the silver chain and started to leave, but he caught her arm, his grasp surprisingly strong.

"You leave that here, Doris. You got no right to be snooping around in here and taking things that aren't yours," he lectured her. "If you want a silver bracelet, I'll buy you one. I bought you all that other stuff."

"No, you don't understand. This belonged to Jasmine. Jasmine is missing, Mr. Parnell, and possibly dead. This could be a clue."

"Jasmine was making fun of you, Doris. She laughed at you. I had to teach her a lesson, Doris. That's why I did it."

"Did what?" Ashli's brow furrowed in total confusion. What on earth was he talking about now? She didn't have time for riddles, not tonight. Her head was pounding, and her nerves were raw. It had been a grueling day, and that smell was getting worse. It smelled like something rotten. Or dead. Her stomach rolled again. "I'm sorry, Mr. Parnell, but I need to get out of here." She tugged to free her arm, but he had a firm hold. "Really, Mr. Parnell, that smell is making me sick. I have to leave, right now."

"Oh, missy, why did you do it?" There was real sorrow in his voice as he tightened his grip. "I thought you were the one. But you're just like all the rest."

"You're . . . you're hurting me, Mr. Parnell," Ashli gasped. She knew it was silly, but she was getting frightened. He was such a nice old man, but his mind was playing tricks on him. Already once today, she had seen what a sick mind could do. She tried unsuccessfully to pry his fingers off her arm.

"Why did you do it? Cavorting with that television fellow!" He spat the words. "Then that private detective. I thought better of you, missy. I thought you were pure. But you're just like all the others." This time he did release her, with enough force she staggered backwards.

Ashli crashed against a black trash bag and knocked it to the ground. When some of its contents fell out, she threw her hands to her mouth in horror. "Ohmygod, ohmygod, ohmygod. Oh! My! God!" she screamed, recognizing the mutilated form of a human arm.

"Now look what you did!" the old man snarled. "Why'd you have to go snooping around? You should have met me in the garden, like I asked you to! Didn't you get the clues?"

Her eyes still riveted on the arm and pieces of things she dared not identify, Ashli had more pressing issues to worry about than an old man's ramblings. Still, she asked in a terrified whisper, "What-what clues?"

"The clues. The fish, the flowers, the clock."

"Those . . . those were from you?" Her eyes flew from the contents of the bag to the man who stood between her and the doorway.

"Of course they were from me, who else would they be from?" he grumbled.

"Clues?" She judged the distance to the door. If she could just make it around the mulching machine . . .

She took a tiny step to the right.

"Clues. Where can you find goldfish and roses and daisies and rhododendrons?"

"The-the garden?" she whispered. Why hadn't she thought of that before?

"Of course the garden! And what time was the clock set for?"

She swallowed hard and made a guess. "Midnight?"

"Why did you come down here early?" he roared. "I'm not ready for you yet!"

"I-I could come back," she offered.

"No, you've already ruined everything now. You've already seen the others."

"I didn't see anything, Mr. Parnell. Just-just this bracelet." She held up the thin chain. A shudder racked her body as she wondered if that was Jasmine's arm she had seen.

"You saw the bag. You saw the secret ingredient."

Ashli's eyes flew from the trash bag to the mulcher. Suddenly, it all made sense.

The bag, the awful smell, the dark stains on his clothes, Jasmine's missing body.

His prized fertilizer.

This time, her stomach did revolt. She vomited in the corner, right where the bracelet had been. When he turned on the machine and she heard the horrific sounds of grinding bone and human flesh, she feared she might faint. Reaching into her pocket for a tissue, her fingers touched her cell phone. She had forgotten she had it on her.

Pretending another dry heave that wasn't far from reality, Ashli leaned over and withdrew the phone, careful to keep it out of his sight. Lange's number was second on her recall list. She punched it without hesitation. The text screen popped up.

"What are you doing over there?" he asked. "Come over here where I can see you."

"I'm sick."

"Your stomach's empty. Come over here."

She saw teenagers do it all the time. They came into the restaurant and texted without even looking at their screen. Praying her fingers were somewhere near the right keys, she shot off the message *SOS* then slipped the phone back into her pocket.

She turned back around, wondering why she was surprised to see the wild, vacant look in his eyes. The man was obviously delusional. She had to keep him talking, keep him busy until Lange arrived.

If he arrived. What if they had taken his phone away from him at the emergency room? What if he never made it to the emergency room? What if Diane—

No, she had to stay positive. Lange would come. She had to believe that.

"I thought you would be different," he lamented. "I thought you would be worthy. I didn't want you to end up like the others." She could hear true regret in his voice.

"What . . . what others?" She had to ask. She didn't want to know. She couldn't bear to hear the answer. But she was compelled to ask.

"The others. The ones before you. Sarah, and Becky, and Marylou. They had such potential. But they weren't pure, either."

Sarah. Becky. Marylou. She had heard those names before, but where?

"They had the right looks, but not the heart and soul. Sarah was nothing but a slut, a dancer at one of them nightclubs."

If possible, Ashli felt even more ill. She recognized the names now. Sarah Millican, Becky Harper, and Marylou Peterson. Three of the four blondes that went missing thirty-some-odd years ago. The women with the severed feet.

"Ohmygod, ohmygod, ohmygod." This time, the words were whispered under her breath. The man standing before her, the man she had cared about as a grandfatherly figure, was a serial killer. He had killed seven women in the past, and now Jasmine, too.

"What-what-what about Pollyanna?"

"Couldn't sing," he said. He finished emptying the contents of the trash bag into the machine and wadded up the plastic. Seeing her perplexed expression, he was irritated that she didn't understand; he had to explain everything to her. Maybe she wasn't as smart as he had given her credit for. "Can't be the next Doris Day if you can't sing and dance and have a heart as big as the great outdoors! Gotta love dogs, too, and Becky didn't like dogs."

That explained the membership to the ASPCA. Funny how her brain could still function on some levels, even though she knew she was in shock. Her body trembled, as a terrible cold settled into her blood.

"And Marylou was older than she looked. What's the use in replacing an aging star with one just a few years younger? Gotta be young, and fresh, and still in your prime." He turned accusing eyes upon her, his voice turning solemn. "And pure. Can't be sleeping with men you aren't married to."

Crazy, random thoughts floated through Ashli's boggled mind. He had misinterpreted her relationship with Mitch. When she started going out with him, even though it was business, it set the old man off . . . From what she had read, dear little Doris had hardly been a virgin. She may have looked all wholesome and innocent, but her love life had been far from pure . . . Lange's eyes had been so sad tonight, so beseeching. He may have been holding Diane, but he had reached out to her with his eyes . . . The door. She had to get to the door, so she could get free.

"And-and the others?" She took another step away from him.

"Melanie didn't like Rock Hudson. Can't make another huge hit without your number one leading man."

Melanie? Who was Melanie?

Oh, God, there had been more than the seven!

"The last one, Spring, couldn't dance." He continued to ramble as he ran the machine a final time.

Spring. Few people named their daughters Spring in the middle of the last century. It was more of a modern trend. Hadn't there been a story about a college student named Spring who disappeared a few years ago? Spring Davidson, or Davenport, something with a "D."

With sickening fascination, Ashli watched the machine spit forth from two outlets. The dry ingredients — like bones — chipped off into neat little pieces and flew into a bin just waiting to catch the shards. The soft, wet ingredients, most of which she preferred not to think about, dripped from a spout and collected into a jug. The worst of the smell came from the wet ingredients. She would be sick again.

Propelling herself closer to the door, she heaved again, hoping he wouldn't suspect her deliberate placement. If she could get free of the machine, she could make a run for it. He might be stronger, but she was faster.

Mr. Parnell leaned down and retrieved a bottle from beneath the mulcher. With meticulous care, he cleaned the machine. The acrid smell of straight bleach burned her lungs and added to the lightheaded sensation.

As Ashli straightened, she took another step away. "What about Jasmine?" she asked.

"What about her? She was making fun of you, just like the others. Had to teach her a lesson." It was the same thing he had said earlier.

"Making fun of me? Or of Doris Day?"

He looked at her in the strangest way, as if he couldn't comprehend the difference. He was drifting in and out of coherent thought, at times knowing who she was, at times confusing her with his favorite movie star.

"Doris," he finally decided. "You heard her that day. Laughing all the way through the movie. Just like those others."

Which explained the women of ethnic background, the ones that didn't fit the pattern of blonde hair and blue eyes. In his sick mind, they must have insulted his idol.

But why leave the feet behind?

Again, she asked. Again, she wasn't sure she wanted to know. Her morbid curiosity, as Lange called it.

"You cut off one foot and left it behind. Why?" She was surprised at how calm her voice sounded, given she shook uncontrollably by now.

"Doris could have had a brilliant dancing career. Her leg was crushed when she was a child. Her foot kept her from dancing." He shrugged, as if the connection was obvious. As if the women deserved to suffer the same disappointment. As if losing their lives was equivalent to losing a career.

Detective Sullivan was right; it was impossible to understand the mind of a murderer.

Detective Sullivan. Maybe she could find a way to call him, too. She reached into her pocket and fiddled with the phone, but she couldn't tell what she was doing without at least glancing at the screen. Shouldn't Lange be here by now? She eased another step toward the door. She was almost to the edge of the horrid machine, almost to the edge of freedom.

"No need in trying to leave, missy," he said in a calm voice. "You know I can't let you do that."

She had to try. She dove for the small opening between the man and the machine, almost making it. He barely caught her, knocking her to the ground. She tumbled, but at least she fell forward, free of the machine and closer to the door. She tried scrambling to her feet, only to find he had her by the ankle.

"Let go of me!" she cried, kicking at him with both feet. She caught him in the jaw. He took the blow with a painful grunt and tightened his hold. "Let me go!"

"Can't do that, missy."

At least he was winded, Ashli thought with some satisfaction. He was strong, but maybe she could wear him down. All she had to do was outlast him.

She did a fancy maneuver with her feet. Forced to mimic her motions or lose the grip on her ankle, his breathing grew more labored. Unfortunately, so did hers. She paused for a moment to rest and to devise a new strategy.

"I'm a patient man, missy," he said, reading her mind.

"You must be, to carry out a thirty-something-year killing spree!" she retorted.

"Thirty years?" He looked surprised at her words. "It's not been thirty years." Doubt crept into his voice, making him sound vulnerable. "Has it?"

"What year do you think this is?"

"I know what year it is. It's 1986," he answered.

Just for a moment, Ashli felt pity for the man. He was clearly confused. *And clearly insane*, she reminded herself harshly. He didn't deserve her pity. She kicked with renewed vigor, twisting her body so she could reach the bottle of bleach he had replaced beneath the machine. She snagged it on the third try, kept her feet swinging to distract him as she unscrewed the cap, then stilled suddenly.

When he glanced up at her, curious as to why she abruptly stopped moving, Ashli splashed the bleach directly into his face. He clutched his eyes with both hands and let out a blood-curdling screech. Ashli scrambled to her feet and hit the door at a run, crashing into the warm body blocking the exit.

Ashli screamed, her fear-ravaged eyes not recognizing the man she slammed into. When hands reached for her, she blindly fought them off.

She had no way of knowing Lange was propped against the doorframe to keep himself upright. Weak from blood loss and pain medication, he slammed back against the door like a rag doll and made a desperate attempt to grab for her waist.

"Ashli! Ashli, it's me!"

"Lange?" She pulled her eyes into focus. "Lange, it is you! Oh, God, Lange, I was so scared!" She threw her arms around him, causing him to sway further.

"Are you all right?" he demanded. He was lightheaded again, but more from relief than blood loss.

"I-I think so. Ohmygod, Lange, it was Mr. Parnell. The whole time, it was Mr. Parnell."

"Is he hurt? Did your stalker get to him?"

"No, no. *He* is the stalker! Mr. Parnell killed all those women. He killed Jasmine."

"Whoa, whoa, slow down here. What are you talking about?" Maybe he had lost too much blood, after all. He couldn't make sense of her words.

"We have to call the police." Ashli pulled away, fumbling in her pocket for her cell phone. "I have to call Detective Sullivan." She glanced back over her shoulder. Mr. Parnell lay writhing on the cold stone floor, still holding his eyes and moaning.

"I already did. He's on his way."

"I don't understand. How did you know to call? Lange, are you all right? You're so pale. And you're still bleeding!" She looked down at his leg, which still seeped blood. "Why didn't they stitch you up? Didn't you go to the hospital?" In typical fashion, she pelted him with questions.

"They stitched my hand up first." He held up a thickly bandaged paw. "I got your text before they got to my leg.

Ripped the IV out and got here as soon as I could. I called Sullivan on the way."

"I was so afraid I wouldn't type the right letters." She slid her arms around his waist again and buried her face into his shirt.

"What's SOA?"

"It was supposed to be SOS. I couldn't let him see I had a phone."

"It was the old man?" Lange asked in amazement. He looked over her shoulder, making certain her landlord was still immobilized.

"Yes."

"You're shaking."

She leaned further into his warmth. "So cold," she admitted, teeth chattering.

"I hear the sirens. As soon as the ambulance gets here, you're going to the hospital. You need to be treated for shock."

"Not . . . not going without you. Your leg."

It became increasingly difficult for her to talk. She couldn't manage full sentences. She couldn't even manage a full thought. The only thing she knew for certain was that she was cold. Mind-numbing, bone-chilling, blood-stopping cold.

Just as the ambulance pulled into the driveway, Ashli passed out. Cold.

CHAPTER TWENTY-THREE

By the time Ashli and Lange were both treated and released from the hospital, and by the time they made preliminary statements to the police, the night had turned into a new day. An hour before sunrise, they crawled into bed at Lange's apartment and succumbed to exhaustion.

Four hours later, Lange waved a coffee mug beneath her nose, teasing her awake with the promise of caffeine.

"What time is it?" she muttered. Her hair was a disaster. The whites of her eyes were bloodshot, and her lids were puffy. Her skin was deathly pale, except for the dark circles beneath her eyes. Her cheeks were gaunt.

"God, you're beautiful." The words slipped out of his heart as he handed her the mug.

She didn't even laugh off his words. There was a haunted sadness in her eyes as she accepted his offering and gulped the hot liquid without a flinch. When she glanced around in search of a clock, he answered her earlier question. "Almost ten. Sullivan wants us down at the station before noon."

Ashli pressed the warm mug to her cheek. She was still so cold.

"Did yesterday happen, Lange?" she whispered. She hoped this was all a terrible nightmare.

He hated to see the fear in her eyes. The anguish. Cupping the back of her neck with his good hand, he traced the corner of her mouth with his thumb. "Yes, sweetheart, it happened."

She could hear the regret in his voice as he confirmed her worst fears. And if this was real, then he was injured. "How's your hand?"

"Sore."

"And your leg?" Her eyes fell to the bandage just below the hem of his plaid boxers.

"Sore."

She took a fortifying sip of caffeine. She didn't want to know, but, again, she had to ask. She and her morbid curiosity. "And Diane?"

He blew out a weary breath. "Undergoing psychiatric evaluation."

"Mr. Parnell?"

"He died on the way to the hospital. Cardiac arrest."

Ashli set her coffee mug aside and pulled her knees to her chest, curling into herself. Lange wrapped his arms around her shoulders, knees and all. She remained stiff at first, then eventually slid her knees down and allowed him to pull her close against his chest.

"Oh, Lange," she sobbed, and it was the sound of pure heartache. "He wanted to kill me. She wanted to hurt me. How could this happen? What did I . . . What did I do?"

"Nothing, sweetheart. You didn't do one thing to deserve any of this. They were both crazy. Certifiably insane. None of this is your fault." He pressed the words into the sunshine of her hair, pressed his warmth into her shivering body. She was so brave and strong; sometimes he forgot how fragile she was.

"It can't be real," she whimpered.

"It is."

"He killed Jasmine." This, rocking back and forth in grief.

"I know, sweetheart, I know."

"She stabbed you."

"I'm fine."

She stopped rocking and pulled away, just far enough to look up at him. "She tried to stab me. You stopped her. You got hurt, instead."

"I told you, Ashli," he whispered in a voice rough with emotion, as he pressed a kiss onto her forehead, "I would protect you with my life." His dark eyes were warm and glowing.

"But you chose her." Ashli's whisper, barely audible, was raw with pain.

Lange stared down at her for a long moment. Some of the warmth left his eyes. "Is that what you think?"

"You called her. You told her . . . You told me to leave."

"I had to get you out of there. I had to keep you safe."

Before she could formulate a reply, even a coherent thought to what he was saying, her cell phone rang. She would have ignored it, but Lange glanced at the number. "You need to take it. It's your mom."

"But . . ."

"We'll talk when we get back from the police station. Answer your phone. Your mom is worried about you."

When he pulled away from her, she knew it was more than just physically.

* * *

It was late afternoon when they returned to the loft. Ashli's parents met them at the police station and sat through the grueling questioning that took hours to complete. With their support, she made it through the day with minimal breakdowns. The police allowed them into Daisy House long enough to gather a few personal belongings, but the entire premises, particularly the gardens, were under strict police quarantine. The whole estate was covered with crime tape and reporters. Her parents begged her to go home with them, but in the end, Ashli stayed with Lange.

Back at the loft, an awkward silence settled between them. She was almost relieved when he announced he had to go out for a little while. She needed time alone to think, and the best way to do that was to get in the kitchen and cook. It was the best therapy she knew.

Ashli found the extra key to his apartment and ran a few errands of her own, making it back long before he returned. Fortified with a cup of coffee and a newly stocked refrigerator, she stepped into Lange's virgin kitchen.

The therapy session began.

CHAPTER TWENTY-FOUR

From the moment he stepped into his apartment, Lange was keenly aware of her presence. Signs of her were everywhere, assaulting his every sense.

He could hear her in the kitchen. She banged around pots and pans, rattling dishes and humming a song. After all that happened, she was humming. He shook his head in amazement.

He sniffed the air. The heady aroma of a home-cooked meal swirled around him, causing his stomach to rumble. He detected peppers and onions and cinnamon, and that unique sunshiny smell that was hers alone. Knowing she was in his kitchen, cooking him a meal, caused his heart to crumble.

He saw visual signs of her presence. A new rug peeked out from under his sleek black couch, some sort of long shag in deep, vibrant red. New throw pillows, some red, some dusty blue, added instant warmth to the cool leather. Looking through to the kitchen, he could see she had the table set for dinner. Damned if his table wasn't sporting a cheerful blue paisley cloth and an actual centerpiece.

Best of all, he could feel her. The cold, empty space of his apartment felt warmer, fuller. Homier.

Only half-teasing, he called out, "Honey, I'm home!"

Her laughter floated from the kitchen, drawing him to her. *As if that was something new.* He had been drawn to her from the very first moment he had seen her.

If he thought seeing her domestic beauty in her own kitchen had affected him, it was nothing compared to seeing her in his. The sight almost brought him to his knees. She had changed into the same yellow dress she had worn the first day he met her. The first day he had fallen for her. She was standing in the middle of his kitchen, whipping something in a bowl, and had a smile upon her face. If it was the last sight he ever saw, he could die a happy man.

"You've been busy," he said. It was a wry statement, spoken around a smile.

"A little. Go wash up, dinner's almost ready."

Awed by the transformation that had taken place — in his apartment, in her spirits — Lange did as told. He smiled at the new hand towel in the bathroom, deciding he liked the yellow and blue duck motif. It seemed he had been smiling since he stepped through the door.

When he returned, she had a half-dozen dishes on the table. Grilled pork chops, stuffed red bell peppers, sweetcorn, candied yams with marshmallows and pecans, fresh green snap beans, fried okra, and cornbread muffins filled every inch of the table. He could see dessert on the counter, some of her mouth-watering chocolate brownies with cashews.

"Lord, woman, did you think we were starving? You could feed the entire building with this spread."

Ashli shrugged. "I find cooking very therapeutic." She poured tea into his glass and took her seat across from him. "I needed a lot of therapy."

He filled his plate with samples of everything. "Did it work?"

"It definitely helped."

They ate for a while in silence, until he brought the subject back up. "You do realize you're not to blame for any of what happened, right?"

"Yes, I do realize that now. Mr. Parnell's obsession with Doris Day started long before I was even born. He was a very sick man."

"And his dementia made his mental illness even worse."

"I wonder if we'll ever know how many women he truly killed. He told me about at least two others, but I'm sure there were more."

"The police found a total of five chest freezers on the property. In time, after all the DNA testing is done, they may be able to identify more victims."

Ashli pushed the food around on her plate, finding the topic less than appetizing. "I still don't understand why he left the feet. He told me why he cut them off, his warped sense of reasoning, but not why he left some, and not others. Jasmine's was the only one since all those years ago."

"Sullivan and I talked about that. We think maybe it was his dementia kicking in. The foot is a signature. It's a killer's way of marking his work, taunting the police. For whatever reason, his killing activity seemed to slow down after the early eighties. Maybe it was the influence of his wife, maybe not. We'll probably never know. What kills he did make, he stopped leaving his signature, until Jasmine. We think maybe he was confused, living in the past again, thinking he was still making his mark as a serial killer."

"Yes, he thought it was 1986."

"He was one sick man."

"I almost feel sorry for him," she admitted.

"Ashli, he killed women. He mutilated their bodies and used them as fertilizer. He killed your friend, and he would have killed you. Don't waste your sympathy on his sorry soul."

"They said he repented in the end," Ashli murmured. "Asked for God's forgiveness. And for mine."

"Who told you that?" Lange asked with a frown.

"The medics from the ambulance. You were out of the room, talking with Sullivan. They told me he left me a message, said he was sorry, that he never wanted to hurt me."

"Ashli, don't do this to yourself. Don't make excuses for him. He's not worthy of your forgiveness."

"The forgiveness is for my sake, Lange, not his," she said. "I can't let bitterness control me."

"How can you possibly have sympathy for that man?"

Ashli put down her fork and looked him in the eyes. "The same way you have sympathy for Diane."

Lange squirmed uncomfortably in his chair. "That's different," he murmured.

"Not really. You had a relationship with her. I had a relationship with Mr. Parnell. Yours was physical, mine was emotional. They were both relationships, and both people were a part of our lives for a very long time. Even though they both turned out to be sick, mentally unstable, they . . . they weren't all bad, not always."

Lange pushed his plate away. "I always knew Diane had emotional issues. I thought she was bipolar. I never dreamed she could go so far off the deep end."

"I know what you mean. She had such a distinguished career. Who would have ever believed she would unravel so completely?"

Ashli carried her plate to the sink, even though it was still half full. She cut the brownies and dished out a portion for each of them. Like an old married couple familiar with the other's ways, Lange automatically made coffee. In tacit accord, they turned toward the living room as they continued their conversation.

"It's a shame, a brilliant career over, just like that. She was an excellent lawyer," Lange said.

"You know, I didn't understand at first," Ashli admitted.

"Understand what?"

"That you were just being a good friend." She took a seat on the sofa, curling her feet up beneath her. "I thought you were choosing her over me."

"How could you even think that?" The pain was evident in his dark eyes.

"I know. And I'm sorry. I'm sorry I doubted you. When she said all those things . . . when you first came in the door, and I couldn't see you, could only hear her side of the conversation, she made it sound as if . . . And when I looked, you were kissing her."

"Ashli, she threw herself at me. She was kissing me."

"I realized that, later. But she said you had called and wanted to see her, and that was . . . that was the same night you were going to sleep on the couch."

"But I ended up sleeping in your bed that night. We may not have made love, but we held each other all night long. We were connected."

Ashli settled in against his side. "Yes, it all became clear to me while I was cooking. That's when I realized most of what she said was lies, or at least just her twisted version of the truth. I also realized that as her friend, you couldn't just leave her. Not when she obviously needed help."

"Don't make me sound too noble," he grumbled. "Mostly I was just worried about you. All I could think about was getting you out of danger, and out of her reach."

"But you were the one who ended up getting hurt," she said, tracing the edge of the bandage where it bulged beneath his jeans.

"I'd do it all again — anything — to keep you safe." He set his mug on the coffee table and gave her a stern look. "You know, yesterday only proves the point I've been trying to make all along. I lost my objectivity because I got too close. I never saw the danger coming, and it was literally in your own backyard." He intertwined his fingers with hers and admitted in a low voice, "I don't know if I can ever forgive myself for not being there to protect you."

"But you were there! You came, even though you were injured. You literally jerked an IV out of your arm and rushed to my rescue."

"Some rescue. You'd already taken care of the situation, no help from me needed." Despite his rueful smile, his eyes held the unmistakable shine of pride. "Have I told you how proud I am of you? You handled yourself like a real pro yesterday. Both times."

Leaning her forehead against his, she drew an unsteady breath. "I'm not ashamed to admit how scared I actually was."

"Neither am I." He gently kissed her lips. "I was scared out of my mind."

"You haven't said anything about my little shopping spree. You don't mind, do you, that I bought a few things to warm the place up?" Ashli waved a hand toward the pillows and rug.

"I think I could get used to it." He pretended to scowl, but she could see the smile hovering just beneath the surface. Looking down at the hand he still held, he admitted, "I could also get used to having you here. For the first time since I've moved in, the place doesn't feel like a hotel room. I liked coming through the door, hearing you moving around, knowing you were cooking our supper, knowing I wouldn't be eating alone."

"You know," Ashli said, "our situation has changed. I no longer need a private investigator. A pessimist might say we no longer have a reason to be involved."

"But you're not a pessimist, are you?" he murmured, bringing his dark eyes up to her hopeful blue ones.

"No, I've always been an optimist. And an optimist would say there's no longer a reason why we *can't* be involved." She drew in a deep, steadying breath before taking a huge risk. "What about you, Lange? Are you a pessimist or an optimist?"

He was slow to answer. So slow, in fact, her heart sputtered and stopped at least three times before he spoke. It thumped in triple time when she heard his gravelly reply. "Before I met you, I was a pessimist. I would have come up with a hundred reasons why we couldn't get involved, case or no case. But then I met you, with your sunny smile and your cheerful ways. Your goodness." He swallowed hard, summoning the courage to continue. "I want to be an optimist, Ashli. I want to believe in the good things in life. I want to believe in us. Later, I want to think of a hundred reasons why we should be involved. But right now, all I can think about is one."

"And . . . and what is that?" She dared to breathe the words, afraid she might shatter this fragile spell he was spinning with his raw but eloquent prose.

"Because I love you, Ashli."

Sunshine had never been brighter. A radiant smile broke across her face, lighting her eyes to a shade of purest blue, warming her paled skin with an effervescent glow. "I love you, too, Lange," she whispered. "I love you, too."

Three little words. Three little words, and his life fell into place. When she threw her arms around his neck and kissed him, he knew he was holding his entire world in his arms.

After several kisses, and a few shared silly smiles, Lange tucked her against his side once more. "Did you figure that out during your therapy/cooking session?"

"Oh, no, I've known that for weeks now."

"Oh, you have, have you?"

She nodded vigorously, her blonde hair bouncing around her shoulders like dancing rays of sunshine. "Probably since . . . the first night you fell asleep on my couch and I covered you with a blanket," she decided.

"Bringing me in from the rain," he muttered, an old flash of irritation creeping into his voice.

"Huh?" She frowned.

"Nothing." He pushed the irritation away. Thank God she *had* rescued him. "I was just wondering what took you so long. After all, I fell in love with you when I woke up on my couch and saw you peering down at me with those big blue eyes."

"That was the first time you saw me!"

"Exactly." He dropped a kiss into her halo of gold. "This cooking therapy . . . Do you do this often?"

"Whenever I have a problem I need to work out. Or when I'm particularly depressed. And when I'm worried about something."

"What you're saying is, by the time I'm sixty, I'll be as big as a house?" His words were light, but Ashli caught the implied significance. "You know, I went on a little shopping spree of my own today."

"You did?" She just assumed he had gone to check on Diane.

"I remember you telling me about a little strip mall. Sparkle Station, you called it. Where there's all these jewelry stores lined up in a row. Turns out having all those stores together makes them very competitive." He tried to keep his tone casual.

Her heart sped up, thumping in triple time again. "I-I never knew you were a bargain hunter."

"I'm not. When I see something I want, I don't worry about the cost." His tone turned sensual, and a sexy light came into his dark eyes as his gaze fell to her lips. Damn, but her habits were rubbing off on him. He was about to get distracted by her tempting little mouth.

Forcing himself to focus, Lange cleared his throat and took the biggest risk of his life. Reaching into his shirt pocket, he hooked the ring onto his finger and presented it with a flourish.

Crafted in platinum, the half-carat solitaire sparkled almost as brilliantly as his eyes. Three smaller teardrop diamonds fanned out on one side, almost like petals. When fitted with the matching wedding band, a perfect flower would be formed. He had known the daisy design was for her, the moment he saw the ring.

"Ashli Wilson, will you marry me?" he whispered.

She simply nodded. For once in her life, she was speechless. Then she started crying, as she reached for the ring and him, all at the same time. With his one hand totally bandaged, Lange had trouble holding her hand steady enough to put the ring on her finger. Tears streaming down her face, she laughed at her own clumsy attempts to help. Finally, they had the ring secure on her left hand and sealed their promise with a salty kiss.

"I never thought I'd see the day when you were speechless," he teased.

"Me, neither," she managed to say. She squeezed his neck tightly, knowing there weren't enough words in her vocabulary to express how happy she was. "Give me time. I'll think of something to say."

"As long as you say yes, I don't care."

"Yes. Yes, yes, yes. A thousand times yes." She pulled back and took his handsome face into her hands. "A million times yes. Yes, I'll marry you. Yes, I'll share my life with you. Yes, I'll cook away our worries until you're as big as a house. Yes, I'll follow you to the moon and back if that's what you want. Yes, I'll grow old and gray with you. Yes, yes, yes."

Lange chuckled as she rambled the happy words. "That's more like it."

Jumping up unexpectedly, Ashli hopped off the couch. "Stay right here," she instructed. She disappeared for a moment, returning with a large gift-wrapped box.

"What is that?" he asked. She never ceased to surprise him.

"I bought one other thing today. A housewarming gift."

"This isn't a new house," he reminded her.

"No, but it's a new *home*." She emphasized the last word softly, handing him the box.

Lange tore away the wrappings. She was right; with her here, it was a home. He lifted the lid and, with her help because of his bandage, took out a large wooden art object. His first thought was that the creation had been carved by man, but closer inspection proved the intricate tendrils were a deliberate pattern of nature. Twisted and gnarled but somehow beautifully simplistic, the piece was preserved with a shiny lacquered finish.

"For my coffee table?" he guessed.

She knew he didn't understand. Tracing a finger along one of the spindly wooden threads, she explained, "They're roots, Lange. A foundation to build on. Something to keep you grounded." Blue eyes swimming in tears, she said softly, "I'm giving you roots, Lange."

Just when he thought he couldn't possibly love her more, she proved him wrong.

Lange gathered her into his arms, the best he could with a tree's life source between them. She was crying again, and he suspected his own eyes were dangerously moist.

"You'll never be alone again, Lange," she whispered. "I love you so much. I want to build my life with you. These are the roots for your home. Our home. Our future."

"You are my future." He pressed the insistent words into her mouth, his breath hot and moist and full of emotion. He cupped her face with his large palm. "You are my home." These, he pressed into her heart. "I'm finally home, Ashli." Another kiss, then another.

"Honey, I'm home," he murmured. "I'm home."

THE END

A NOTE FROM THE AUTHOR

Thank you for reading my book! If you enjoyed this story, please leave a word of encouragement for other readers on Amazon and the sites of your choice.

I love hearing from readers! Feel free to contact me at beckiwillis.ccp@gmail.com. You can also find me at www.facebook.com/beckiwillis.ccp and at www.beckiwillis.com

Thank you for allowing me to entertain you through the pages of my imagination. Happy reading!

THE JOFFE BOOKS STORY

We began in 2014 when Jasper agreed to publish his mum's much-rejected romance novel and it became a bestseller.

Since then we've grown into the largest independent publisher in the UK. We're extremely proud to publish some of the very best writers in the world, including Joy Ellis, Faith Martin, Caro Ramsay, Helen Forrester, Simon Brett and Robert Goddard. Everyone at Joffe Books loves reading and we never forget that it all begins with the magic of an author telling a story.

We are proud to publish talented first-time authors, as well as established writers whose books we love introducing to a new generation of readers.

We have been shortlisted for Independent Publisher of the Year at the British Book Awards three times, in 2020, 2021 and 2022, and for the Diversity and Inclusivity Award at the Independent Publishing Awards in 2022.

We built this company with your help, and we love to hear from you, so please email us about absolutely anything bookish at feedback@joffebooks.com

If you want to receive free books every Friday and hear about all our new releases, join our mailing list: www.joffebooks.com/contact

And when you tell your friends about us, just remember: it's pronounced Joffe as in coffee or toffee!

ALSO BY BECKI WILLIS

STANDALONES
THE WIDOW'S BABY
KEEP YOUR DOORS LOCKED
THE STALKER

Made in United States
Orlando, FL
10 March 2024

44603899R00157